HOSTILE TAKEOVER

VALE INVESTIGATION, BOOK ONE

CRISTELLE COMBY

Edition: 1

ISBN: 978-1981098309

Credits
Editor: Johnathon Haney
Cover artist: Miguel A. Ereza

1

WILE E. COYOTE

I was having a bad day.

The ugly thug facing me readied himself for the next swing. "What did you say, bastard?" His red-splattered knuckles were ready for the next round; my body wasn't.

"I'm haffin a fah fay," I managed to repeat through a mouthful of saliva and blood.

That made Julian Ragazzo, former welterweight boxing champ and top bodyguard to the city's prime Italian Mafia family, smile. His wet beard glistened with sweat beads around stained teeth. Glad one of us was happy.

I took stock of the damage Ragazzo had already done. Broken nose, check. Split lip, check. Swollen eye, check. Broken rib, double check, and the list went on and on. It could have been worse. The injuries, though painful, weren't enough to put me in the hospital. Sure, I'd hurt for a week or four, but I'd live to tell the tale outside of a body cast. I knew that, and Ragazzo did, too. This was a game we'd both played before ... not that I'd gotten any better at it.

I caught a reflection of myself in the glossy surface of a cabinet door. My messy mop of brown locks was matted with blood on one side, and the five o'clock shadow had a hard time concealing a fast-bruising chin. One eye was swollen shut and the other had a pale blue, haunted orb dancing amidst a sea of red veins. I was a mess, and not a hot one.

I closed my good eye and waited for the next blow. The bodyguard didn't disappoint. A second later, he delivered a power punch, and I saw stars. It didn't help that I was tied to a chair, and my already sore shoulders screamed in protest at the added strain. In a noise that only I could hear, my body cried out, 'How in all the hells was this part of the plan?' Fair question—it wasn't.

In truth, there may have been a few glitches here and there—like those two extra guards at the office building's back entrance, plus that wrong turn I took on the fourteenth floor. Yeah, okay ... the plan was just as screwed as I was.

Ragazzo followed up his haymaker with another kick in the guts. It would have ripped a scream out of me if I'd had any breath left for it. Instead, my lungs just took in short, choppy gasps I couldn't control.

"Well, well, well ... look what the cat dragged in," taunted an Italian-lilted voice.

I recognized the lazy drawl and opened my good eye to confirm my suspicions. Sure enough, Alonzo Vitorini, Cold City's resident wannabe kingpin, stood near the entrance in a dark-green pinstriped suit. Shit, looking at his ugly get-up hurt worse than any of Ragazzo's blows.

Vitorini sauntered into the room, smiling as he noticed my stare. "Like the suit?" he asked, doing a little pirouette to show off this walking insult to fashion.

I wasn't going to reply, but the second my eye caught sight of the finishing touch, a pair of black-and-white spectator shoes, my mouth kicked into gear on its own.

"Al Capone called," I wheezed out. "He wants his brogues back."

Vitorini laughed, the corners of his muddy-green eyes wrinkling. Not sure if he was laughing at the wisecrack or the fact that he was going to kill me for it in another minute or two.

Vito, as most of us on the street called him, was in his late forties and his family's only remaining heir. Upon his father's death, he'd inherited the business: gun running, money laundering, and illegal gambling, complete with a cover-up network of legit storefronts. He'd done what he could to keep the business afloat, but he wasn't his father. The Great Recession had hit everyone pretty hard, and things weren't like they were in his dear ol' dad's heyday. His father had built an empire, paid for in blood—an organization now turned to little more than a bitter aftertaste. More efficient predators than Vitorini had put him under new management, something he chafed at.

"Bellamy Vale," Vitorini said, forcing out a theatrical sigh. "I might have known."

I gave him my best Cheshire Cat smile and winced as it pulled at every sore spot on my face.

The mob boss chuckled before turning to his bodyguard. "Where's the girl?"

"Next office, with Giovanni," Ragazzo said, wiping his bloody knuckles with a handkerchief.

"Good." Vitorini brushed a thin hand through his greasy,

shoulder-length, dirty-blond hair. "Don't lose that one. She's worth two hundred thousand."

The girl was Marion Townsend. From what I'd seen of her, she was a thirteen-year-old kid with wavy brown locks, dark-brown eyes, and a shy smile. I had a picture of her in my army jacket's breast pocket to confirm it. Her mother's shaking fingers had crinkled one of its corners as she passed it to me—the person she felt was her only hope of finding her daughter.

Her husband had handed me a comfortable retainer and articulated an even bigger number if I brought his daughter home safely. While Mrs. Townsend was more expressive in her feelings of sadness, her husband showed more self-control, and that only made him more frightening. I feared the rage that would flow out of him if I did not complete the task that they had assigned me.

"Kidnapping kids, Vito?" I muttered through the blood in my mouth. I turned my head to the side and spat it out. "That's a new low, even for you."

"Business is business," he replied with a shrug of his epaulette-clad shoulders. "Money is money."

If my body wasn't so busy processing pain and firing nerves, I'd have rolled my eyes. Sure, Charlie Lucky had said the same things back in the day. But this little pissant wasn't fit to lick the founding father of the modern Mafia's much more tasteful shoes.

"I faced off ghouls who had higher moral values," I said.

"Been knocked on the head one too many time, huh, Vale?" Vitorini flashed a smile full of crooked, yellowed teeth.

"Now, don't take this the wrong way—" he opened the

side of his vest, revealing a white shoulder holster, and drew out a gun—"but it's time for you to die."

The pistol, a custom 1911 nickel-plated .45 Colt, was on a par with the rest of his outfit—stylized excess that leaped past the boundaries of form, function, and profanity alike. No wonder the Vitorini empire had deflated so quickly. Its leader was behind the rest of the world by at least four decades, caught somewhere between *The Godfather* and *The Untouchables*.

Vitorini took two steps closer, apparently so I could appreciate the gaudy silver-and-gold engravings on the pistol's barrel. Not that I wanted to get shot on top of everything else, but whatever happened to a good old-fashioned holdout pistol that you dumped after the *coup de grâce*?

My smile vanished, and I kept on working on loosening the ropes behind my back. I chanced a glance at Ragazzo to make sure he hadn't noticed. The beefy man was propped against a wall, taking long drags off a joint. He looked satisfied—as if getting out some of his aggression earlier had done him good.

Others might have been pissing themselves right now, but not me. "Private investigators always keep their cool," or so I'd read. Besides, the thought of getting killed by something as ridiculous as that gun was a good incentive to stay calm and focus on freeing my hands.

The rope wasn't coming free fast enough. For at least the twentieth time since I'd been hauled into this office, I cursed myself for taking this case. It was the type of job I usually refused. There were dozens of reasons why I should have said no from the start. For one, taking on mobsters wasn't a

PI's business; it was the police's responsibility. But damn if I didn't find one to make me say yes.

You're a big softie, man, I thought to myself. One broken-hearted mother comes to you with the picture of a smiling angel, and you come a-running, right into a trap. Some professional you are.

I felt the rope shift under my fingers. The next step was going to hurt, but there was no getting around it. I turned my hand sideways, pushing it as far as I could, and twisted my thumb. As the bone snapped out of the socket, I fought to not let the burning pain register on my face. That's right, keep talking, Vito.

Vitorini took another step. A cruel and devious smile crept across his face; strands of greasy blond hair fell into his deranged face as he pulled the trigger, savoring the moment of murder. Time slowed to a near standstill as my brain tried to order the details of my death: Bellamy Vale, died age 33, killed by baby mobster Alonzo Vitorini. He thought he was doing the right thing.

Was this it? I wondered. Was this my murder? Was today the day I would die? There was no fear in me as I looked down the pistol's barrel. I exhaled and waited, letting Vitorini's finger finish its long drag on the trigger.

I waited for the bang.

The pain.

The white light taking me beyond.

But it never came.

After all that build-up, all Vitorini, Ragazzo, and I got out of it was an annoying click. As a wise man once put it, "I might have known."

I took advantage of the confusion distracting my captors

to work my semi-broken hand free. I got through the rope, flipped it away, and lunged right at Vitorini. The Colt went flying into a corner, the bullet still jammed inside the barrel.

The would-be kingpin backpedaled under my weight until he hit a glass wall. He fell to the floor in a daze, momentarily out of commission. It gave me vital seconds to land a winning blow on Ragazzo. That human oak had been breast-fed on ring fights. I knew that if I let him get another punch in, I was toast. I kicked him low, catching him on the side of his knee. Something delicate cracked underneath my combat boot, making the man howl in pain. Off-balance, he tried to take a swing at me, but I sidestepped the blow. Bad footing is a bitch.

I reached for the phone on a nearby wooden desk and threw it at him. It went flying, the cord ripping right out of the wall socket. It caught Ragazzo on the side of the head. I'd sort of hoped that would be enough, but I should have known he'd stay on his feet. A boxer is trained to take that kind of punishment and keep swinging. A fine trickle of blood ran down the side of his face, and his gaze lost some of its focus.

I cursed and made a grab for the next item within reach. I hurled it at him with all the strength I had left. It hit him in the same place before exploding into glinting fragments. This time, the champ went down for the ten-count. Julian Ragazzo—zero. Orange World's Best Dad mug—one.

Bending in two to try and catch my breath, I turned to the place where I'd last seen Vitorini. Empty space stared back at me ... the damn coward had fled. His vanity-plated Colt was still there, lying at the foot of a potted plant. I reached down for it and yanked the slide back to clear the chamber. My ribs protested my movements, but I choked the pain down. There was no time for it. Thanks to me, Marion was now in grave danger. Her status had just gone from product of the year to major liability in the space of about five seconds.

I darted out of the office and veered left. I just managed to catch sight of the elevator's doors closing, a little girl's scream for help cut off in mid-yelp. Shit, definitely no time to lose. I ran forward and tried to make out the illuminated floor indicator with 50% visibility—thirteen.

A gun fired behind me. I ducked just in time. Plaster exploded inches over my head, covering me in fine white dust. I rolled to the left, got up on one knee and did a one-eighty. I fired two rounds from Vitorini's Colt and missed a bald man wearing gray fatigues by just a few hairs. He retreated for cover into the office he'd been hiding in.

I had maybe two seconds to do the same. In this barren corridor, I was a six-foot-tall sitting duck. I stayed in a low crouch, glanced at the elevator—ten—and used my shoulder to push the door in. Two more bullets narrowly missed me as I got in some executive's office. Once there, I checked the Colt's magazine—five rounds left in the clip plus the one in the chamber.

"The hells," I cursed. Vito was making his escape, with Marion in tow, while I was playing bullet tag with his boys. Once they got out of the building, I'd have a hard time tracking them down again ... and I doubted that Marion would be alive by the time I did.

I looked around for a solution, but this was just another office on a floor full of them. Two fully laden desks, high-backed leather office chairs on wheels, the latest gen in computers, one ugly potted plant in the back corner, inane corporate motivational posters urging their viewers to "be the best you can be" and "always aim for the top" ... wasn't there anything useful in here? Finally, I spotted what I needed. I grabbed the silver tray next to the coffee machine and reached for the nearest chair.

I rolled out of that room in style, letting the momentum carry me across the battlefield. I knelt on the chair, the tray sandwiched between me and the chair's back to act as makeshift Kevlar. Three nine mils came to a loud clanking end against the flat surface before I rolled to an abrupt stop against the corridor wall.

I jumped backward, kicking the chair towards my sparring partner. He kept firing at it while I fired at him. Two bullets nailed him: one at center mass and the other one a few inches below his left shoulder.

Now that my assailant was ancient history, I took a deep breath and got back on my feet. I did a quick check of the elevator indicator; it was stuck on three. With adrenaline taking the edge off my pain, I made a run for the stainless-steel doors that would lead me to the stairs.

As I ran down, I tried to recall the building's layout. It was a fourteen-floor, thin, rectangular building, maybe twenty feet wide and three times that in length. The exterior was comprised of beige stones and endless rows of windows, all except the front, which was a solid sheet of glass. SeaVenture, the luxury liner company started up by Vito's father just a few years before he croaked, owned the entire fourteenth floor. I had no idea who occupied the other floors ... companies who couldn't afford the top floor somewhere else?

With four shots left in the Colt's mag and the nagging

feeling that I was throwing myself into yet another trap, I pushed open the door to the third floor. A quiet, empty corridor awaited me on the other side. I breathed a sigh of relief as I advanced, my finger hovering over the Colt's trigger just in case. I rounded a corner, found nothing.

A whirr in the distance caught my attention. I picked up my pace as I retraced my steps. It was the elevator, going down again—two, one, ground floor.

"Shit!" I spat. That bastard in pompous shoes was getting away. I rushed back to the stairs. I had to get to him before—

Wait. I froze in my tracks, my hand resting on the staircase door handle. Something didn't add up ... the third floor, why had they stopped on the third floor? The elevator had been here for ... what, two, three minutes? Why?

I looked around the place some more. All I found were cubicles and private offices. One of them had another cheerful poster on the wall beside the entrance. It said in big, bold letters, "With Us, You Can" over a picture of an open can of white paint with a brush dipped inside.

Only one thing could have made that two-bit Mafia heir stop at this level ... he wanted to throw me off his trail. Marion had to be around here somewhere. I turned my back on the staircase and elevator and entered the lobby beyond the paint poster.

Much as I wanted to plug him with his own gun, Vito could get away for all I cared. He wasn't the mission. Marion was. I'd already promised her parents that I'd get her back, a promise I was going to keep or die trying. The pain of having to survive your own child's death is unspeakable. I'd do my damnedest to make sure the Townsends never found that out firsthand.

I moved forward, past a row of identical desks laden with identical fittings and stacks of paper. A sound disturbed the silence in the distance, a muffled scream ... Marion.

I quickened my pace, ran down another row of desks, turned a corner, and cruised through a conference room. There were three private offices on the far side with identical wooden doors. The last one on the right was ajar.

I made a run for it, kicked the door wide open, and fired the moment I had a lock on my target—no time for second-guessing.

"Aim and shoot, son. Just aim and shoot," my Navy Chief at Great Lakes used to say in that thick Southern drawl of his. It was a lesson I'd retained, the kind of behavior that had saved countless soldiers' lives, including my own. On the battlefield, there wasn't room for anything else but your training.

The floor-to-ceiling window behind the goon in front of me fractured as my bullet hit him right between the eyes. Gray matter and blood had just enough time to splatter on the glass before it all turned to splinters. There was no time to celebrate, though. I scanned the room for more thugs. My eyes found Marion in an instant. She was kneeling at the foot of a desk, fear plaguing her face while tears spilled from her eyes.

Weapon at the ready, I continued the sweep as I made my way over to my clients' daughter. A flurry of movement on the right got my attention. I threw myself behind a five-foot steel cabinet just as the first bullets flew my way. I returned fire, wasting two more precious bullets on a blurry shape I hadn't had time to identify, much less get a bead on.

The girl screamed. I glanced over at her to see if she was hurt—she wasn't. She'd recoiled as far back as she could, curled up into a tight ball of fear in the room's back left corner. She looked scared but unharmed. As I took it all in, I realized she was within striking distance of the door. Two or three long strides and she could be out of here. On the other hand, my jumping behind that filing cabinet had taken me further inside the room. I was almost equal distance between the entrance door and the large hole where a window used to be opposite it.

Vito's man, whom I now saw was some short, ginger-haired teen punk, had retreated further into the room. He was sandwiched between the gaping hole I'd made and a tall promotional display consisting of rows and rows of paint cans. My bullets had hit two of them; red and pink paint pooled on the gray-carpeted floor. I could make out the man's reflection in the ex-window's shiny frame, reloading his gun. Lucky bastard ... he had a spare clip while I was down to my last bullet, and my options were thinning as fast as the sun was setting.

I turned to Marion. She was a frightened ball of crumpled clothes and wild dark hair. I could barely make out her face.

"Marion," I hissed at her, "can you hear me?"

I didn't get a response, but I kept talking. "You're going to be all right, Marion. Your parents sent me to get you."

That got a sliver of recognition from the girl, making her uncurl an inch or two.

Two more bullets crashed into the metal filing cabinet.

"You and that girl ain't getting out of here alive, Pops!" Ginger shouted.

"Don't listen to him, Marion; listen to me!" I urged. "Look at me, Marion. It's going to be okay—I promise."

Three more bullets clanged against my shield cabinet to argue otherwise. But I saw a shy pair of brown eyes turned upwards and got my first real look at Marion Townsend. Although she was a mess, she was definitely the girl from the picture. The thin eyebrows came from her mother and the round cheeks from her father.

"Run," I mouthed to her. "Run!"

She shook her head.

"Go on!" I kept mouthing. "Run!"

She shook her head again.

Of course, it wouldn't be that easy. This kid didn't know me from Adam, and on top of all that, I looked like I'd just lost a fight with Rocky. I caught her gaze and willed her to believe me.

"Please, Marion!" I whispered. "It's time to be brave. Just get to your feet, and you'll be home in no time."

Her lips trembled, but she nodded and uncurled her legs. She was wearing blue jeans and a Bugs Bunny sweater. I smiled at that — I was a fan too. Marion was short and thin, and I hoped she'd move fast. Two or three quick strides in the right direction, and she'd be safe.

I gave her a nod and turned my head away from her. Ginger was hiding behind his paint display, probably lining up his next shot. With the Colt held in my right hand, I counted down from five with my left. When I ran out of fingers, I pushed my fist in the direction of the door. Marion bolted for the exit, and I ran forward to place myself in the line of fire. Vitorini's man missed the girl, but he didn't miss me.

A bullet ripped through my left arm, and a haze of red clouded my vision. I careened towards Ginger, dodging a couple more shots on the way. My vision blurred as I felt my body giving up on me. I forced myself to keep moving, to keep running. When I got close enough to make out my target through the haze, I aimed, shot ... and kept running.

I couldn't stop. My feet weren't responding anymore, and the momentum carried me forward, right through that mess I'd made of the window. I had just enough time to hear the crunch of the glass beneath my boots before I fell.

A misspent childhood watching *The Bugs Bunny Show* every Saturday hit me, and I chuckled as I said to no one but the gods and me, "Eh, look at me, I'm Wile E. Coyote!" Then it all went black.

———

Death smelled surprisingly nice. Every part of me hurt, and I was uncomfortable as hell, but at least death smelled sweet.

I rolled over and forced my functioning eye open. It was now dark and—I blinked, once, twice—what I was seeing looked an awful lot like the building I'd just made a graceless exit from. Why, it even had the same gaping broken window on the third floor.

A silhouette came into this confusing picture. It took me a moment to focus on the man towering over me, but I knew that face—forties, short brown hair, bushy eyebrows supporting a mile-long and all-too-familiar scowl.

I don't know how, but I managed to find enough strength

to giggle at the sight. In retrospect, it might have been the concussion talking, but at that moment, I found it hilarious to have drawn the short straw yet again.

"There's no way a guy like me could get the winning ticket and just die, is there?" I croaked.

"Shut your mouth, Vale," Detective Lieutenant Jeremy Morgan said, pulling out a pair of bracelets. "You're under arrest."

2

EVERY MAN'S DREAMS

Against the odds, I'd done it. I'd saved Marion Townsend. She would sleep in her bed tonight —safe and sound.

And I'd survived to tell the tale. Sure, I wouldn't be able to squeeze my own OJ for the next month, but the doc in ER had assured me that I'd live to drink it. They'd reset my ribs and thumb, sutured my arm, and bandaged everything else. Too bad that wasn't the end of my problems.

"Name?" a young female police officer asked at the intake desk. Her tone suggested that she'd been doing this all night, and she couldn't wait for her shift to end.

I bit down on a nasty retort and decided it would be over faster if I complied. Damn, if this wasn't a farce. I was tired, most of my body felt like a punching bag, and I couldn't wait to go home and sleep off the day, which had yet to dawn. "Bellamy Vale."

She typed it down and kept asking questions without looking up. "Profession?"

"Private investigator."

"Date of birth?"

"February second, nineteen eighty-five."

We kept playing twenty questions, with me answering like an automated teller, until she asked, "Charges?"

I perked up at that one. Try as I might, I couldn't imagine what Cold City's finest was arresting me for. "Rescuing an innocent child." I grinned, arching my right brow high on my forehead. "Now that's a serious offense."

Detective Lieutenant Morgan, who'd been standing one step behind me and breathing down my neck the entire time, pushed me to the side to say, "Damaging public property."

I turned to him. "Wait, what? What public property?"

"Gardenias," Morgan continued, still addressing the clerk. "A whole lot of 'em."

That didn't compute somehow. "What?"

Morgan turned to me with a smug smile that made me itch to punch him. "Gardenias," he repeated as if speaking to a child—a slow one. "The shrubs you landed on and destroyed."

I couldn't remember doing that, but then I didn't remember much of the trip to the ER either. But something had smelled nice when I woke up, I remembered. "I landed on some flowers?"

Morgan remained tight-lipped and looked at me as if I was a moron. That was pretty much the default setting for his face. I responded with my trademark Cheshire Cat smile, which had got a lot of ladies into my bed and pissed off alleged tough guys like Morgan no end.

The young woman kept typing, not caring one bit for our

antics. A minute or so later, she handed me a sheet of paper with the city's crest emblazoned at the top.

"You've got to be kidding me," I said, seeing the fine on it. "Three hundred bucks? For some damn flowers? The hell's wrong with you?"

The woman's eyes shot up to me at that—they were green and would have cut me in half if they'd been lasers. "Do you want to add 'Verbal assault on a police officer' to the list?"

I shut my mouth and turned my own murderous gaze on Morgan. The smug bastard kept smiling.

Detective Lieutenant Morgan and I had never gotten along. I had to admit that he was a good cop who worked homicides more thoroughly than most guys who'd got to his rank. But he seemed to have a real problem with private investigators. Our paths had first crossed when I'd been hired to look into some local jewelry thefts. On day three, one of my suspects turned up dead, and Morgan figured he'd found the triggerman when he ran into me. Everything between us had been going downhill ever since. I wasn't sure if he disliked every PI as much as me or if I got special treatment. But he hated my ass, and I wasn't too fond of him either.

I yanked the money out of my wallet, tossed it on the desk, turned on my heel, and started for the door.

"Where do you think you're going?" Morgan demanded, his basso voice reverberating against the precinct's tiled floor.

"Home," I said, my voice making a less impressive performance through exhaustion.

I could hear him right on my heels but didn't turn back or slow down. Christ, I just wanted this day to be over already. He reached for my arm, undoing some of the doc's handiwork in the process, so he could force me to face him.

My patience was wearing thin. I was maybe two more bad insults away from lashing out at him, badge or no badge. In the shape I was in, I'd probably lose, but I'd passed the point of caring somewhere between the ER and the precinct.

"What now, Morgan?" I growled, not bothering to hide my disgust. "You're gonna fine me again?"

"You best stay out of my sight, Vale," he growled back. It looked like he was making his own efforts to keep the anger at bay, but he didn't bother keeping the scorn out of his eyes. "There's something not right with you," he went on. "I can feel it. Next time you interfere in police business, mark my words"—he stepped closer to my face, so close I could feel his breath on my skin as he breathed, just above a whisper, through clenched teeth and tensed lips—"you're going down." His unblinking eyes stayed locked with mine for a few extra moments.

I should have nodded and walked out. I should have kept my mouth shut. But then again, as my boiling blood was telling me just then, he should have known better than to keep poking the hornet's nest with a sharp stick.

"That girl would be dead by now if it wasn't for me," I said, tone scathing. "I'm the one who saved her, me! And where were you, Detective ... handing out parking tickets?"

Morgan took a step forward, eyes darkening as he uncurled one of his fisted hands to point an accusatory finger at me. "Based on that scene you left for us to clean up, you could just as easily have got her killed, you moron. You need to learn your place in the food chain, Vale. This case was police business, not some glorified crusade for a two-bit hustler like you who's read too many Spillane novels."

"Jealous much?"

It hurt to smile at him, but boy, was it worth it to see him turn red with anger. I had no doubt that if we hadn't been in the middle of the precinct, Morgan would have done to me what my bullet had done to that window. With one last smile, I turned my back on him and walked out of the building.

A chilly night greeted me outside. I shivered at the autumn cold. The pain meds had started to wear off, and a killer headache settled in. I hailed a cab and fell asleep on the way home.

By the time I was paying off the driver, thirst was overwhelming me. I longed for some cool water and then maybe something stronger. A stiff drink to take the place of the meds.

I found a carton of milk in the fridge door and swallowed a glass down in one go. The thirst for something more was still there, and it was almost enough to make me reach for the whiskey bottle that sat on my kitchen counter. It was a twenty-five-year-old Bowmore that ranked as one of the best on the planet.

"No," I told myself as my hand froze in mid-air, and I closed my eyes. "Not tonight."

I ran my fingers through my hair while I let that particular bottle continue to gather dust on the counter. Some mistakes are not to be repeated, and I poured myself another glass of milk instead. I took it with me to the living room.

I owned a small flat in the building. It came with a tiny kitchen, a modest living room that benefited from a balcony, one bedroom, and a bathroom with a working shower, toilet, and sink. The wardrobe in the bedroom was just big enough for my clothes, spare bed sheets, shoes, and the cookbooks my mother kept offering and that I never read. The bookcase in the living room was just large enough for my mismatched collection of paperbacks and encyclopedias. It stood behind a comfortable sofa and opposite an LCD television. It wasn't much for a guy my age, as my mother liked to remind me when she was asking me why I didn't remarry, but it was mine, and it was home.

I flipped the TV on and landed on HDL, the Headliner news channel. The late news was on, and I turned my absentminded gaze to the screen. A guy was in the middle of a piece on a veggie restaurant that I'd never visit. I downed the last of the milk and crossed the living room to open the balcony doors, then stepped out to enjoy the real reason I'd put my late wife's life insurance payout towards this place.

The fresh seaside smell hit me full in the face, and I reveled in it. It was too dark to see the ocean, but I knew it was there. It lay in the gap between the hotels that had sprouted on the shoreline like mushrooms in damp shade. My balcony had one spot that offered an unobstructed view of the ocean to where it met the sky on the far horizon. I'd installed a plastic chair there and, for just a second, thought about plopping down in it for a few minutes.

"And now we join Candice Kennedy, live from Anglia Street, where a man was found dead earlier tonight," the news anchor said in the background.

The hell with it ... I'd fall asleep if I decided to sit down out here. I turned back to the news to focus on something other than my exhaustion.

"Yes, Jim, that's true," Kennedy's voice agreed in a soft Texan accent. "Ethan Nicholls, sixty-two, was found dead tonight in front of the Cinema Leone. Nicholls was well-known and loved in the neighborhood. He was a pillar of the community and the owner of the charming old cinema here on Anglia Street, where you can hear the flicker of the projector and watch a black-and-white film every Saturday."

I returned inside and glanced at the screen. The young blonde dressed in a dark-blue trench coat and standing in the night street had to be Kennedy. A bright light was on her, separating her short frame from the surrounding darkness. Around her, the night was punctuated by the red-and-blue flashes of the police cruisers' gumball lights.

"An official statement has yet to be issued, but we can already report that Mr. Nicholls was found dead in the street right outside his cinema," Kennedy continued, the camera panning to the right to show the sidewalk where it happened. Patrol cars hid the view, but there was an unmistakable impression that something bad had happened.

"According to several witnesses, Mr. Nicholls' death, which has been attributed to a wild animal, was gruesome." Despite the circumstances, pride showed on the blonde's face as she reported her next find. "A source close to the investigation told me earlier that several teams have been dispatched in the neighborhood to look for a wolf. Zoo officials have yet to comm—"

I flicked the TV off and moved to the shower. Something about that report annoyed me as the water washed the blood and pain of the last few hours from my skin. A lone wolf in the streets of this city? What next ... alligators in the sewers?

I'd just got out of the shower when *she* showed up. Same

entrance as usual. One second she wasn't there; the next, she sprawled languidly on my bed. That always gave me the creeps. And how in all the hells could she always have such perfect timing? But I knew better than to question how she appeared from nowhere, disappeared without a trace, or knew the things she knew.

We were old acquaintances, and she had seen into my soul and beyond. I had no problem with her seeing my nakedness. And even if I did, I was too worn down to care anyway. I flicked the bedside table lamp on, walked past her, ass-naked, and reached for a shirt and a pair of sweatpants. Someone else may have tried to educate her on social behavior, but I'd long ago given up on the hope that she would ever come to grips with a concept as trifling as privacy.

"I wasn't expecting to see you tonight," I said as I shrugged the clothes on. My sore shoulder protested, and I winced.

"Why would you?" she replied with a slight accent that was impossible to place.

I glanced at her for clues. Her hair was loose and dark brown again. She had a little makeup on and looked to be anywhere between twenty-five and forty. Her feet were bare, and she wore a long and oh-so-thin black dress.

I recognized the look. It was the one I'd dubbed "the Mediterranean", and I knew what it meant. She sat up, and her gaze darkened to a coal shade as she took a good, long look at me.

"I'm not in the mood," I said as I finished pulling down my shirt. I tried hard not to notice the movements her dress made against her feminine curves. But I was a man, and no straight man in his right mind could resist giving the attention demanded by that oh-so-perfect cleavage.

"You do not get to choose, *mon Bel-Ami*," she said.

Hearing her use my name like that did things to me that no human being could have ignored.

"Or have you forgotten how this works?" she added.

"I haven't, but no amount of French-silver-tonguing will make me like it," I retorted. It was a weak protest, and we both knew it.

She laughed, a deep, throaty, sultry sound that did things to me—I wish it didn't. Then she moved again, seeming to undulate as she rose to her feet. In two steps, she was in front of me, ripe for the taking, temptation personified. She was beautiful, every man's dream, and she knew it.

"What do you want?" I asked, throat dry.

"A man died tonight," she murmured. "I want you to investigate."

The change of topic helped me get my mind off ... other things. "For God's sake, why? Certainly, *you* would know what happened."

She remained stock still. It was as if I hadn't said anything, and maybe I hadn't as far as she was concerned. She sure tended to hear only what interested her.

I glanced at the clock and saw that it was just past three a.m. "Look," I told her, "I've had a lousy day that doesn't seem to want to end. I'm more banged up than a crash test dummy right now. So why don't you and I make an appointment for next Thursday, when I'll—"

That would be the part she heard clearly. She was on me in a second, swift as a viper. Her cold fingers laced themselves around my throat, pushing me backward until my back hit the wall. The pain of the injuries, which I kept finding new ways to aggravate, registered this time. Must have had something to do with how I felt my feet lift off the ground as she kept me there, pinned like an insect.

"You signed a contract with me, Bellamy Vale," she hissed. "Your life for a favor. It was granted to you; thus, I get your life."

Her gaze bore into me, and her vice-like grip did not relax. I tried to struggle, but she was as immobile as a statue.

"You are mine," she said. The sexy accent was long gone, replaced by something darker and deadlier. "I see the tapestry of life, and I hold your string in one hand and the scissors in the other."

I'd have swallowed if I could. Instead, I started to suffocate, spots clouding my vision as my heartbeat took up a staccato rhythm. In spite of all that, her arm remained rigid.

"I will cut it when it pleases me," she continued. "Until then, you are mine, and you *will* do as I command."

Blood thumped in my ears, and I could feel my heart slowing down. I nodded; it was all I could do.

"The man's name was Ethan Nicholls," she informed me.

Nicholls ... I'd heard that name before, hadn't I? Where, though? The world was starting to look very hazy, and a lot of things weren't making sense anymore. Pressure was building behind my eyes, and it felt as if they were going to pop. One thing couldn't be denied, though. My heart had stopped beating.

I should have died then and there, but I didn't. She had my life in her hands, literally. And she couldn't have found a better way to spell it out for me.

"He was but the first of many, and you will put an end to these killings," she said. "It is my command."

Darkness spread in her eyes until it consumed all of the white. "Disobey me, Bellamy Vale, and I will let death take you next time."

She let go of me, and I fell to the floor like a rag doll. My heart started pumping blood again, and pain ripped through my chest. I coughed as I struggled to remember how to breathe.

She was gone by the time I looked up. I got back to my feet on shaking legs. She'd meant every word of what she'd said. One day, she would be the death of me, just as she'd promised a long time ago. Until then, however, she wouldn't let anyone else have me ... that was the contract. Death would keep looking the other way, what with guns jamming, three-story falls being broken by beds of pretty flowers, and my heart beating no matter what happened. But one day ... or one night ...

I crashed onto my bed, too cold to stop shivering, too tired to pull up the covers. Yeah, Death Incarnate really was every man's dream. They call 'em *femme fatales* for a reason.

3

SOMETHING ROTTEN

A t first light, I headed out to the Cinema Leone. By the time I woke up, my brain had connected the dots between the news report I'd caught last night and what my boss of a dubious nature wanted me to do about it. I was battered, aching all over, and feeling every bit like I'd fallen from a three-story building just the day before. Don't get me wrong. The doc had done a good job patching me up. Nothing was bleeding anymore, and the swelling in my bad eye had gone down enough for me to open it, even if it was an ugly shade of purple. Just the same, I looked like a victim from a Freddy Krueger movie and felt just about as lively. I wanted to get this job over with, so I could sleep for the next month.

With my car still parked next to the SeaVenture building (assuming Morgan hadn't done something pissy like have it towed while I was being processed), I walked down to the crime scene, working out the kinks as I went.

A cold wind was coming in from the ocean and up the

streets, chilling my skin wherever that icy gust could touch it. Summer was over, making way for what local meteorologists and residents alike called "not-summer." Not-summer was an uneven mix of icy winds, rain, fog, and the rare hailstorm, that lasted three to four months. It was a major letdown after the rest of the year when summer ruled with a perfect combination of sun, cool breeze, and the occasional gray cloud. Whoever had named this burg Cold City had a sick sense of humor, but most of us had all long since stopped wondering about it.

I fell in love with Cold City the first time I ever laid eyes on it. Back then, I was in the Navy, serving on the Arleigh Burke-class guided missile destroyer USS *Ramage*. After an eight-month deployment into the US Navy 6th Fleet, we were finally heading back for Norfolk, but technical issues forced us to port in Cold City Bay instead.

We'd docked in the morning, and I got a first view of the city I'll never forget. The arc of scrapers glistening in the rising sun and the shining beams over the long golden sandy beach left an impression on my mind that forty-eight hours of leave and a lot of booze couldn't erase.

Cold City had been constructed in a bay area, sandwiched between the ocean and a range of tree-covered mountains at its back. It was first colonized in the eighteenth century when it was little better than a fishing village. The town fathers had concentrated on the port first, building docks along the shore before developing backward from there. By the mid-nineteenth century, they'd stopped referring to it as a village or even a town and had started calling it a city. Half a dozen villages sprang up around it, nestled near the foot of the mountains. By the end of the twentieth century, all of the villages were long gone, swallowed up by a city which had reached the limits of its growth.

It took a little while, but people came to grips with the idea that Cold City was never going to get any bigger than it was. The mountains were too steep for anything more solid than raccoon nests and hunting cabins. There were talks, once or twice, of blowing up the mountain or carving deep sections into its base, but that had always seemed too complicated and expensive, especially after the Great Recession sank its teeth into the city economy in '08. But entrepreneurs don't give up easily, and they found other ways to keep the pipe dream of expansion alive. All they wound up accomplishing, however, was the constant remodeling of what was already there, destroying the old buildings to make room for the new, which would get destroyed themselves in a few years if the pattern held. As the local saying goes, "Nothing changes like Cold City."

The sky was looking ominously gray when I turned into Anglia Street. I'm no weather expert, but it seemed to me like the clouds were minutes away from pelting rain. The street was empty, save for a car or two driving by. The cops had all gone, and so had the journalists.

I walked up the street until I found the Cinema Leone. Now that I was here, yet more history—this time, my own— hit me smack between the eyes. I remembered coming to this place once with my wife, Marissa, around the time we started dating. It had been for a Boris Karloff marathon, seeing him in everything from *Frankenstein* to *Bedlam* and *Targets*. The sweetness of that memory hurt with surprising strength ... damn if I wasn't in a nostalgic mood this morning.

I guess almost getting killed twice in one night will do that to a guy.

It'd been five years since that film fest, but the place hadn't changed one iota. The old white billboard was the same. The entrance arcade had that red-gone-brown carpet that looked like it'd been laid in the fifties. The building's façade still hadn't had that paint job it so badly needed.

The large bloodstains on the carpet were new, though. So was the line of yellow tape barring the entrance. Now I'm no more psychic than I am a weatherman, but I had a pretty good idea what would become of this place. Someone would rip the tape away at some point and, when no one came to reinstall it, people would start to forget what had happened and move on. Then, as the circle of life moved on, the entire building would be demolished by the end of the year to make room for some condos nobody in this town could afford, even if they worked 120 hours a week.

That "someone" who'd remove the tape and initiate this town's collective coping mechanism could be a junkie looking for something to steal or a hobo looking for a warm, safe place to spend the night—or it could be a brown-haired, six-foot PI in need of answers to questions nobody was asking. Behold the unpredictability of life.

I ripped the yellow tape away and entered the arcade. My nose was assaulted by a mixture of bleach and cleaning products. The cleaning team must have worked through the night. It wouldn't do for the neighbors to wake up to someone lying dead on their sidewalk. No amount of bleach was going to get rid of those bloodstains, though. And it was going to take a lot more than soap to repair the cuts in the carpet and the claw marks on the concrete walls.

My stomach churned at the sight. Either that or it was protesting against all the painkillers I'd popped down. I heaved a sigh, knowing the next step was going to make that feel like a paper cut in comparison. Closing my eyes, I forced my breathing to slow down and emptied my mind of everything superficial. I counted down from five to one, opened my eyes, and looked at the scene in front of me again.

The world had narrowed down, dimmed to a tunnel of sharp, laser-like focus, allowing me to make out the individual fibers of carpet even. The smells had multiplied into a rich palette of chemical compounds that I could separate and identify. Knowing I couldn't keep my concentration up like this for too long, I hastened to get to work, taking in all the tiniest details of the crime scene.

From the intensity of the claw marks and the pattern left by the blood splatter, I could map out the attack to the point of being able to discern the moves of the victim from those of the beast. Whatever it was that had made the attack, it had a cruel streak that would have done credit to Jack the Ripper. It had trapped the victim in a corner, pushed him further and further inside as it kept moving forward, claws digging into the carpet like some low-rent *Hellraiser* knock-off, ready to strike when the fear hit fever pitch.

Sweat and fear permeated the air around the place where the old man had stood, trembling and facing a voracious, tall monster. In one giant leap, the beast was on him, claws fully extended and shredding flesh into beef strips.

I recoiled at the thought then shook myself out of it. Despite the cold air, I'd broken into an even colder sweat. The world was spinning around me. I walked back to the street, desperate to get fresh air that didn't reek of death. I was shaking as I fought to suppress the dry heaving of my stomach. There would be no need to revisit the scene. Everything I'd seen of that massacre was deeply etched into my mind.

Being Lady McDeath's errand boy brought with it a useful bag of tricks. There were a few interesting tools in there, but the one I'd just turned on was the one I least liked to use. It didn't have a name attached to it—none of them did as far as she would tell me—so I'd dubbed it "the sixth sense." Using it was like an out-of-body experience to the most twisted hell. It left me feeling like I'd just come down from the worst acid trip of my life, combined with a hangover and the mother of all colds. I wasn't sure how it was even possible. She had never bothered explaining it to me, and I couldn't exactly Google it. Yet I knew, on a gut level, that it had its limits. Whatever it was, it wasn't something a mere human like me should have had access to. Then again, tapping into resources that weren't mine to use was all part of the gig with her.

I leaned against the nearest wall and fought to get my breathing back under control without passing out in the process. It wasn't just the sensory overload. I could feel the mark, *her* mark, on my shoulder, burning under my skin. On the outside, it looked like a tattoo—black ink that depicted a semi-circle above a plus sign, and a smaller full circle above it. It had appeared on my skin of its own volition when I signed my compact with her. And somehow, it bound us together.

I glanced back at the crime scene with my plain mortal eyes and swallowed hard. Contrary to the report I had caught last night, this was not the work of a hungry lone wolf. Whatever creature did this, it had chosen Nicholls as its prey. The way it had hunted him down, backed him into a corner, and torn him apart when his fear reached its peak spoke of a viciousness that couldn't be attributed to an animal just wanting to feed.

This was a murder of a different kind.

Rain fell from the clouds; the cool drops helped me come back to myself. I dragged my sore limbs to the nearest coffee shop and slumped into a booth. With a warm mug of tea in my hand, I went over what I'd figured out so far.

What possible motive could anyone have had to end Nicholls' life like that? The whole thing stank worse than a month-old corpse. Hells, I thought. It was always like this when Lady McDeath was involved.

"I should have known better," I muttered into my cup. After draining it, I added, "I did know better."

Yet here I was, dragging my sorry carcass through the not-summer streets, chilled to the bone and weary beyond words, looking for answers that appeared nowhere to be found. I stared into my empty mug, feeling as hollow as it was. I needed rest and food and that month's worth of sleep I mentioned before. Hells, I'd have settled for a week.

The empty mug stared back, and I swear the bottom looked as black as her eyes had last night. Shit, just thinking about that made my throat hurt again. I rubbed at the sore flesh underneath my dark-green jacket collar.

The waitress refilled my cup and brought me a new tea bag, and I re-examined the facts as I knew them. None of what I'd seen this morning lined up with the popular wolf theory. Besides, Lady McDeath was involved, so that was one more reason to believe something much nastier was roaming the streets of Cold City. But what could it be? And better yet, how could I find it? Bonus question—who would be stupid enough to want to hunt down such a creature?

A mother with her little girl walked by the coffee house window. The kid caught my attention. Her mom was hurrying, probably desperate to get out of this foul weather. But the little one looked like she was enjoying herself. She was about eight, with curly blonde hair and baby-blue eyes. She wore red wellies, a red raincoat, and she held in her tiny hands an equally red plastic umbrella. She was adorable, jumping up and down in the puddles. She made me think of a happier version of Marion Townsend.

I watched her go until she and her mom had disappeared around the street corner. They were a good reminder that this city was filled with people who had no idea what kind of otherworldly creatures might be around one of those corners. If there was a monster hiding in the shadows, it had to be found and dealt with before it had time to go after sweet, innocent children who giggle when it rains. I guessed Lady McDeath had worked that out long ago and had then set about finding someone stupid enough for the job ... only I had no idea what I was up against this time. I needed help. I couldn't fight something I couldn't find.

Desperate for a better option, I reached for my smartphone and pulled up the Conclave number. It wasn't a good idea to call them, but it was all I had right now. I dialed the fourteen-digit number. No one answered, but a beep told me I'd ended up on a voicemail.

"Hi, this is Bellamy Vale. I'm a PI in Cold City, USA," I said into the phone. I wasn't sure how much to explain, so I kept to the facts. "Look, there was an attack last night, fatal, and I have reasons to believe that whatever's responsible might be coming from the other side of the border." I paused, wondering what else to say. "Er, could you send someone here to investigate? Or at least tell me if there's been a breach? I don't know what—"

Another beep cut me off in mid-sentence, letting me know my time was up. I dropped the phone and took another sip of tea.

Our world, the Mortal Realm, isn't the only one. There's another just across an invisible border that even I don't understand: Alterum Mundum. Yeah, that's Latin for "other world." Don't sue me—I didn't come up with the name. No one knows how big Alterum Mundum is. Rumor has it that it could be infinite. What it does contain in the mapped regions is all the afterlives known to mankind: Heaven, Hell, Olympus, Elysium, Tartarus, Gehenna, Amenti, Sheol ... you name it. If someone wrote a book about it, you'd find it there.

Sounds crazy? Yeah, I know—I thought so too when I first heard about it. Except I'd just been brought back from the dead, so that put things in perspective real quick.

Now, I've never been to Alterum Mundum but, like anyone in the loop on this place, I've heard the stories, and they're not pretty. I've felt its presence a few times, and trust me when I tell you the mere aura of that place was enough to make me take a few steps back.

The two realms are separated, but they do touch in certain spots. Usually, these are places that have something in common with each other, a strong resonance of complementary energies. The Vatican, for instance, is supposed to have one or two gateways to Heaven. Places like the

Parthenon are connected with Olympus. Come at the right time of year, and Stonehenge will give you a ticket straight to Arcadia. And from what I've heard, Daemons who manage to make it through to this world always seem to claim good old Las Vegas as their first port of call.

So, yeah, travel between the two realms is a possibility, though it is technically forbidden. Of course, every rule has its exceptions—how else do you think I became Death's errand boy?—but for a trip to be licensed, it has to be approved by both sides. Though the other side breaks that rule as often as people over here break traffic laws, our side hasn't said yes to a major expedition in over two hundred years.

That's where the Conclave comes in. It's the body responsible for the safekeeping of the border on our side. I've never met any of them, but from the whispers I have heard, they're not a fun bunch. I had no idea then how they handled breaches, but if they were as good at cleaning up as they were at keeping secrets ... well, it looked like the next couple of days were going to be interesting. Only ...

I checked the clock on my phone. It'd been fifteen minutes since I'd made the call. They didn't seem to be in a hurry to call me back. I mean, this was kinda urgent, and what, they were just going to give me the cold shoulder?

I dialed them up again and waited for the beep. "Okay, guys, you and I don't know each other," I began, feeling my patience growing thin, "but you may know the lady I work for ... Lady McDeath? Pretty brunette—or stunning blonde when she feels like it—smoking body, low patience, tough as nails, zero sense of humor? Well, I work for her, and she asked me to look into this mess. I did, and trust me when I tell you something is rotten in the state of Denmark. What happened here wasn't—"

The damn beep cut me off again, making me curse. The couple in the next booth turned to look at me, and I shrugged apologetically. "Bad day on the stock market."

My phone chirped with a text message an instant later: "Border status: safe. No recent fluctuation detected. Thank you for your concern. Please do not call again."

I stared at the screen in dismay. Hells ... the authorities on that side of the great divide were every bit as useless as a stuffed, dead guard-dog. I know, shocker. I'd once heard a friend who was more in the know than me describe the Conclave as "a bunch of old jerks who couldn't find their own backsides in a windstorm even if they were looking for it with both hands." At the time, I'd thought Zian was exaggerating, but now I wasn't so sure.

"Thanks for nothing," I muttered, leaving some cash on the table for the tea, plus a tip for the waitress. I winced when I realized that was the last of my cash. The payment for the Townsend job couldn't get here soon enough.

On my way out, I dialed up an old friend in the hope that the mortal authorities would maybe prove a little less useless.

"Sergeant Ramirez," a young, feminine voice with a Latino accent answered.

Those two words alone were enough to make me smile. I always thought her voice was the sexiest thing about her. She had been born in the Dominican Republic, but her father had brought her and her mom back home to Cold City when she was about ten. Even though some twenty years had passed since then, she still had that accent.

"Hi, Mel, it's me," I said.

"What do you want, Bell?" she asked, on guard. "You promised you wouldn't call."

I zipped my thick cotton jacket, pulled the collar up and headed out in the rain. Okay, so it was too early to talk to her like a normal human being as opposed to like an ex. It wasn't that big a surprise, seeing as we were in the "off" period of our "off and on" relationship. We'd done this dance before. Twice.

"It's not like that, Melanie," I said, trying to keep all emotion out of my voice. If she wanted us to go back to being professionals, I could do that. "I need your help. You know, for work."

"I can't," she said. "Morgan would have my badge in a heartbeat if he heard a whisper about me giving you any help."

The lovely Melanie Ramirez was a CCPD Sergeant working Homicide in Morgan's division. I had no idea where she found the strength to put up with him. I'd once asked her about it, and all she'd said was, "I put up with you, don't I?" I didn't have any snappy comebacks for that one.

"Please, Mel, I'm working a case," I said in a patient tone. "I just need to know if you've heard something. It's the—"

"Whatever it is, I don't want to know," she snapped, cutting me off. "Morgan was pretty specific about that at roll call this morning. You're off-limits."

Well, that was new. "What? And you're just going to go with it? It's your life, Mel. He doesn't get to decide who you see."

"Professionally off-limits," she corrected in a tone that made it clear she was losing what little patience she had left.

After a world-weary sigh I knew too well, she added, "Look, Bell ... I don't know what you did, but Morgan's royally pissed this time. He ordered *all* of us"—she accentuated that part—"to stay away from you."

"Sunnofa..." I breathed. And I had thought my day couldn't get any worse. "Please, Mel. I'm working on a case: Ethan Nicholls—the guy who was killed last night. I don't give a damn what Morgan says. His family has a right to know what happened to him."

Come to think of it, did he have a family? I wondered.

"Oh, don't you dare, Bellamy Vale!" she said, turning up the anger in her voice. "Don't play the sympathy card with me just so you can get a little inside info. I get on Morgan's bad side, he'll make my life a living hell, and you know it."

"Please, Mel," I pleaded. It was as pathetic as it sounds, but I was out of cards to play.

I heard someone call out her name over the line. "Just a minute," she hollered back. She probably had to turn her head away from the phone because her voice was distant for a moment. "I've got to go, Bell. Nice talking to you."

I doubted the sincerity of that last part, but I rushed to stop her from hanging up. "Wait, Mel ... you have to give me something. Please, I'll make it up to you ... I promise."

"Fine," she said, knowing it was the only way to keep me from calling her back. "Come to the corner of Main and Seventh. You're going to want to see this."

A beep told me that the phone call was over ... but my day was just getting started.

4

AIN'T NO REST FOR THE WICKED

The corner Sergeant Ramirez had given me was just two blocks away, but I was drenched by the time I got there. To my surprise, she had directed me to a crime scene. Patrole cars were parked near the curb, cops in and out of uniform swarming all over the place.

As you might expect, the street corner was off-limits, yellow tape barring the way. The blockage was forcing the crowd of bystanders to stay at a reasonable distance from whatever had happened. Curious neighbors, sheltering under multicolored umbrellas, stood several deep in the street. Two officers in uniform had been dispatched to regulate traffic and make sure none of these yahoos got run over while they gawked.

I moved in closer and tried to squeeze through without being poked in the eye by an umbrella. Peering over an old woman's gray hair, I caught sight of bloodstains. No doubt about it, somebody had died here. It was impossible to lose that much blood and survive.

I pushed past the old lady and walked further down the line of onlookers until I was squeezed between a teen in a baseball cap and the wall of a Chinese restaurant. I watched as the medical examiner zipped up a body bag at the foot of an office building.

There was another pool of blood near the victim's bagged corpse, twice the size of the one I'd seen on the way in. As near as I could tell, the victim had been killed by the building's entrance, where the protruding rooftop had protected the scene from the elements. There were nameplates beside the front door, but I was too far away to make them out. On the other hand, the claw marks on the stone were clearly visible, even from where I was standing. Ditto the pieces of flesh that had been torn out of the victim's body and that now littered the street like so much lint on a carpet. The whole scene left me with a deep sense of déjà vu.

"You done here?" I heard a man call out to the ME. The basso voice was familiar. I ducked behind the teen standing next to me. Peering around his shoulder, I caught sight of Detective Lieutenant Morgan coming out of the building, notepad in hand. He was wearing the same clothes I'd seen him in last night, and he looked as tired as I felt myself. He was clearly in one of his characteristic bad moods.

The ME nodded back to him, and Morgan gestured for two guys in uniform to come and take the corpse away. They hefted it up on a stretcher and wheeled it off. Ramirez came out of the building and stopped where Morgan was standing, right at the edge of the area sheltered from the rain. She'd tied her long brown hair up in a ponytail and wore a black raincoat over a beige blouse and jeans.

"I'm going back to the station, Sergeant," Morgan told

Ramirez. "Stay here and monitor the scene until the cleaning team arrives."

Ramirez nodded, and Morgan turned on his heel to head back to his car. He'd gotten two steps when he froze, frowned, and cursed. I followed his gaze and saw why: two news vans had just arrived. I smiled a little, knowing there was one thing Morgan hated even more than me —journalists.

"Well, this ought to be good," I muttered as I watched the first van's door fly open. A young woman with wavy blonde hair stormed out, umbrella in one hand, smartphone in the other. She zeroed in on Morgan like a shark in a swimming pool.

"Detective Lieutenant Morgan, care to comment?" she asked, and I recognized the Texan accent. It was Candice Kennedy, the Headliner correspondent from last night's news.

"No comment," Morgan bit back, with all the grumpiness he could muster.

While my nemesis was distracted, I transferred my focus back to the crime scene. The ME was gone, as were the guys who'd picked up what was left of the victim. One junior officer was keeping an eye on the massed civilians, but he was standing at the other end of the street. Ramirez was by the building's entrance, busy on her phone. Good a chance as any.

I ducked beneath the yellow line. I was going to hate myself for it later, but I needed to take a closer look at the crime scene like I had at the last one. I jogged up the building's front steps. Ramirez looked up as she saw me approaching, and I could tell she was unhappy. She was about to say something, but I shushed her with a finger to my lips.

"Just give me one minute, Mel," I whispered. "I won't touch anything, I promise."

I didn't give her time to answer and took two more steps further up, stopping a foot from the first bloodstains. I crouched down.

"If Morgan sees you, you're a dead man," Ramirez told me, anxious eyes on her distracted boss. "And so am I."

"You're going for a sex change? That's a shame."

Ramirez gave me a well-deserved kick in the ass that only looked like it didn't hurt. "Would you just hurry up?"

"Who's the vic?" I asked, using the pain of the kick to focus on what I needed to do.

"Municipal worker, name of William Mallory ... why do you care about this?"

"Same as you, Mel," I said, bracing myself for what I'd have to do next. "Just doing my job."

She crossed her arms over her chest. "Who hired you?"

"Can't say," I responded, with an apologetic shrug. "Client confidentiality."

Her brows knitted, a clear sign she didn't like my answer. "Just get the hell out of here already."

"Can't, Mel," I repeated as I started to scan the scene. "I'll be a minute. I have to do this."

"Whatever," she said, throwing her hands up in the air.

I knew the gesture all too well. It meant she was exasperated to the point of giving up the fight. She'd said the same thing when she left my flat three weeks ago when we were calling it quits yet again. That had been on the heels of a lengthy argument about my commitment issues, my roving eye, and my—and I quote—"damn job that takes all of the air out of the room. Seriously Bell, that's not all there is to life." I didn't disagree with that last part, by the way, but how can you explain to your girlfriend my kind of situation in a way that didn't land you in a straitjacket?

"Remember those strange bruises I had on my back last week? I went up against a Golem, but no worries, it's been dealt with, and the city will sleep safely tonight." Yeah, that would go smoothly. At best, she would cut me out of her life; at worst, she'd have me committed.

Right now, she had turned her back on me and was walking away with tension in her shoulders. The uniformed cop at the other end of the scene had noticed the two of us talking, and she headed his way. I felt sorry for the guy. If I knew my dear Sergeant Ramirez like I thought I did, he was about to get orders to keep his mouth shut, backed up with the threat that grievous bodily harm was not the worst thing that could happen to him.

I moved closer to the crime scene, taking shelter from the rain. I felt dizzy just looking at it. I'd known from the start that a mere casual look wouldn't cut it. To get my kind of answers, I'd have to chance a deeper look. I could feel my body tense up in anticipation. In my battered state, I had pushed my limits hard enough this morning already. I had no idea if there was enough energy left in me for round two.

I passed a tired hand down my face and felt the stubble I hadn't had the strength to shave grate against my fingertips. "Ain't no rest for the wicked," I murmured as I gathered my strength to activate "the sixth sense" one more time.

I focused on what was left of the carnage, and the blood assaulted my senses like a sledgehammer to the face. It was barely congealed and bright carmine under the pale morning light. Even from a foot away, I could taste the iron particles on my tongue. Something churned inside of me at the mental impressions overwhelming me ... I sensed something old and bestial with a thirst for death.

Tremors ran through me, and both of my hands started shaking. I willed my fists closed and felt the smell of my own blood in the air as my fingernails pierced the skin of my palms. It smelled delicious, and I thirsted for more, like Dracula after a dry spell. I forced myself to focus, to get past this newfound morbid obsession with the macabre. Let me tell you, it took a real effort of will to get there. That was the biggest problem with using "the sixth sense"; the fresher the kill, the more intense the experience was.

I squatted down and took in the many splatters of blood, picturing the way the droplets had flowed in the air before hitting the pavement. I could see it happening, see the blurry shape of the victim and the red spray of blood suspended in the air as limbs got torn apart. The brutality of the crime was a dead match for what I'd seen at the Cinema Leone. The claw marks were the same size, the tactic used to corner the prey identical. Ditto the terror I felt from the vic in his last moments on this planet.

I could feel a raw, primal instinct at work, but there was more to it. The sheer brutality of the attack wasn't enough to overshadow the human intelligence that lay behind it. This attack had been planned and efficiently executed. This was obvious in the patterns. No time wasted, no chances left to the poor guy. Whoever he'd been in life, he'd been a dead man the minute the creature had shown up on this street. He just hadn't known it until the last minute.

I was about to back away when something got my attention—a faint shimmer in the rainwater that was making its way to the nearest sewer drain. It was faint, almost dissolved already, but not quite. I got up and moved closer.

To the onlookers, I must have looked pretty silly. Try to imagine a tall, thirty-something guy drenched to the bone and crouched down by a storm drain, captivated by the sight of water coursing down the pavement to the sewer. I can't imagine what they thought of me when I dipped my fingers in the running water and brought the drops in my hand up for closer inspection. If they could have seen what I saw, but then again ...

Here's the thing—otherworldly creatures often leave traces in our realm if you know what to look for. Now, I'm not talking about discarded bloody body parts or dazed mortals that wake up in the morning certain they've just spent the night with a siren. No, I'm talking about something much more subtle ... Glitter.

Have you ever wondered how strange-looking creatures like this thing I was tracking can drift through crowds undetected? Certainly, you'd think that a centaur or a dragon walking around Center Square at rush hour would turn a few heads, even in Cold City. Well, think again, because here comes Glitter, a rare and costly powder-like substance they make in Alterum Mundum. Cover yourself in it, and everyone around you will think you look like you belong.

I wasn't sure how it worked exactly. Maybe it reshaped the creature it covered, or maybe it changed the perception of onlookers. The only thing I did know was that it worked. Vanilla mortals were one hundred percent oblivious to what might be going on around them when Glitter was around.

With people from the other side of the border, it varied. Powerful god-like beings and actual gods could see right through Glitter like it was a light fog. Lesser beings like yours truly could only perceive the trickery when they were on the lookout for it. I'd once run into a six-foot-four quarterback who shimmered and glittered worse than one of those *Twilight* vampires. Once I'd knocked him off, he turned out to be a troll.

I was lucky to have arrived at the crime scene so quickly. It took a willful effort from the person who wore the Glitter to activate it and, rain or no rain, left alone that powdery stuff would have dissolved into nothingness in a few hours.

My fingers glistened in the pale morning sun, holding the proof that I'd been looking for. It was the undeniable neon sign that screamed: "not of this world." I shut off the sixth sense and stumbled away from the scene with a stagger that would have done credit to a drunk.

Ramirez was still busy threatening the uniformed cop, so I slipped away unnoticed and made my way through the crowd of men, women, and umbrellas, shivering from the cold and sweating from the exertion. My mind was on fire with the images I'd just taken in, to the point where my vision had turned as red as blood.

It was one thing to look intently at a missing kid's bedroom like I'd done for Marion. It was quite another to look upon a blood-splattered crime scene in such detail. The imprint left by that carnage would stay etched in my skull for a long time to come. I could feel my body protesting already, my insides churning and coiling from the strain I'd put them through. I'd have thrown up there and then if I'd had the energy.

It's probably why regular mortals can't use their sixth sense or see things like Glitter. Our frail bodies just aren't strong enough to handle it long term. The black-inked mark on my shoulder was burning like a white-hot brand, and I wondered if I'd have been dead by then if I hadn't been wearing it.

I ambled away from the mayhem of curious bystanders and nosy journalists. I caught a glimpse of Morgan arguing with the blonde reporter. Her cameraman had joined the party, aiming his lens at the angry detective like a sniper lining up a shot on an enemy. It served him right ... fine *me* for destroying public property, wouldja ...

I hailed a cab to get back home. I barely had the strength to stand, let alone drive. The car would just have to wait for another day. Maybe I could get somebody to pick it up before it got towed.

The shakes subsided on the way home. Between moments spent fighting to stay conscious, I tried to make sense of the case but failed. Damn, but that hellspawn in a dress had played me once again. She had to know what I'd be up against, yet she'd still sent me into the fray, blind and unprepared. Try as I might, I couldn't begin to make out the shape of what I was facing. All I did know was that she was swinging me left and right like a puppet, a feeling I hated. Well, this puppet wanted to know more about what he was being sent to do—time to let her know how I felt.

———

After I had got out of my wet clothes and snatched a few hours of much-needed sleep, I tried to get hold of her. She hadn't left me her phone number—it wasn't as if a being like her would ever stoop so low as to own a cell—but I had other means to reach her. The brand on my skin, which marked me as hers and protected me from death, was an energy link between us. And it was a two-way street.

I didn't possess any magic, so I had to resort to using some of earth's power to make sure my long-distance call would go through. I got five white candles out, pushed my coffee table out of the way, and sat cross-legged on the carpet. I placed the candles around me at equal distance from each other, the positions marking out the shape of the Seal of Solomon, aka a pentagram. I lit the candles and shrugged off my shirt.

Somehow I knew I would come to regret this. One doesn't simply call up Lady McDeath and expect to live to tell the tale. But the manipulative bitch had left me with no other choice, as I saw it. She knew something I needed to hear. After all, if she wanted a mindless soldier who never questioned her orders, she'd made the wrong choice.

I placed the palm of one hand over the black tattoo and thrust the other to the floor as I summoned her.

And nothing happened.

I blinked and tried again, pouring more of my will and desperation into the action. She had to come. I needed answers. I'd only tried this ritual once, but it had worked within minutes. I checked the position of the candles and made an effort to clear my mind. I dug deep within myself and tried to reach that strength that allows me to use the sixth sense.

The candles brightened, and the shadows in my flat

lengthened as an acrid smell filled the air. I kept the summoning going and willed her to appear.

The light wavered as the walls around me shifted and blurred. The room grew bigger, morphing into a long, rectangular marble hall. Candles adorned the walls, their pale light reflecting on the shiny black floor surface.

Amazed, I stood up on shaking legs. "The hells?" I whispered, thinking I'd somehow tapped too much into powers I understood nothing about. "This won't end well."

I let my feet carry me away from the candles, crossing the hall and turning left into a smaller, narrower corridor. The energy link leading me was almost like a tangible rope to follow ... like Theseus in the Labyrinth, but in reverse.

The corridor opened into a large room with an impossibly high ceiling—at least, I assumed there was a ceiling up there, though I couldn't make it out. Large bay windows stretched across one side, looking out on a black horizon. No —not black, not entirely. Faint hazes of red permeated the night, like the remnants of a sunset drowned in ink.

There was a large couch in the center of the room, and a fire was burning in a hearth set into the far wall. Two silhouettes stood in front of it. Lady McDeath was there, looking tense and so focused on the man facing her that I slipped into the room unnoticed, despite my special status as her pet flunky. Gone was the black silk dress. Instead, she wore black armor of iron and mail that gave the impression of being both light and sturdy, Joan of Arc gone goth. I'd never seen her in that kind of outfit before. But the worst part of it was the closed-up, almost contrived look she had on her face.

The second person in the room was a man ... tall, lean, and dark-haired, with locks that ran down the length of the back of his neck. He had his back to me and yet he noticed me before she did. With the swiftness of a snake, he whirled on me, his ink-black cape billowing and its edges slicing through the air like a knife.

The man raised his right hand as fury danced in his eyes, and the world went white. One second I was standing in that strange room, and the next, I was back in my flat surrounded by the candles. I was still sitting, but now with the familiar side effect of wanting to heave and finding myself drenched in cold sweat. The foul smell was gone, replaced by the faint aroma of snuffed-out candles.

The few times I'd called her, she had come to me, not the other way around. I raised a shaking hand to my face ... that man ... his eyes. I'd seen plenty of scary things in the course of working for my otherworldly mistress, but that one left me terrified. I didn't know who he was, but I'd somehow entered his home, and I felt he didn't take kindly to trespassers.

Another one of my brilliant plans had backfired on me yet again. I couldn't get those eyes out of my head, those two dark and unyielding black orbs that held no mercy in them ...

I dragged myself to the sofa and slumped down. I was screwed all right. But there was nothing for it. The blowback on that one would just have to find me later when I was better able to deal with it.

I was getting desperate to find a way out of this mess. And as I hauled myself up to get the milk from the fridge, I found myself hating what I was about to resort to. But after I had got a bit more rest, it would be time I had a chat with the late Mr. William Mallory.

5

DOWN THE RABBIT HOLE

I woke up before midnight and took a shower to help wake me up the rest of the way. The morgue was too far out for me to make it on foot before sunup, so I went out to see if my car was still where I had left it. Miracle of miracles, my Corvette Stingray was just where I'd last seen it, as if it had been a couple of hours rather than a couple of days since I'd parked it. I guess one of the custom features on this model was an ability to make people treat it like scenery no matter how long it had been parked.

The sports car hadn't been my first choice, believe it or not. I mean, Christ, I could never have afforded something like this in the first place, short of pulling a major heist. I just woke up one morning to find my battered old Honda gone and the Stingray in its place, keys in the ignition and registration with my name on it in the glove box. I suppose my boss had decided her envoy should drive something more becoming of her or something ... who knows what went on in that psycho mind of hers?

I drove to the city's largest hospital, Hidden Falls Center, where I pulled up in the parking lot of a nearby diner. I made the rest of the way on foot. Rule number one—when you plan a break-in, don't leave your car in the building's parking facilities.

Hidden Falls Center was a large, semi-circular structure that had been erected on a squared patch of grass. As hospitals went, it was pretty classy, all modern curves with glass windows and lean metallic structures. Some five years ago they'd blown up the old hospital and built a brand-new one on its cinders in the finest Cold City tradition.

The Cold City Morgue wasn't in the brand-new, secured hospital center, but in the old building next door. Actually, it wasn't even *in* the old seven-floor concrete office building that, due to some cosmic oversight, was still standing at this late date. Underneath it would have been more correct.

If you could see it, you'd understand why the people who work there aren't friendly. Most of the rooms don't have windows, and the ones that do have only small rectangular-shaped thick glass excuses for windows that stand a few inches above the sidewalk. But for people such as yours truly, these rusty old openings are a godsend when it comes to a little B&E.

I walked up the alleyway to the left of the building, stopped past a large dumpster and crouched down right behind it, beside a convenient window. It took me a grand total of four minutes to work the inside latch free with a piece of wire and a gentle push. I suppose it will come as no surprise to learn that I'd been here before.

I squeezed through the opening and lowered myself inside. At this time of night, most of the staff had gone home, with just two, maybe three people stuck with the graveyard shift. One of these three would be security officer Ray, a plump, middle-aged ex-cop whose retirement pension couldn't keep up with his bills. He was no problem to me. I knew from previous experience how he liked to spend his nights watching pro wrestling on a portable TV by the entrance desk.

I turned to my right, in the opposite direction to the front door, and made my way through the familiar, dimly lit corridors. I was aiming for the cold room where they kept the bodies, but I had to pass in front of the autopsy room first. With any luck, it'd be empty. Otherwise, I'd have to make sure to duck below the two large windows they had carved into the wall between the autopsy room and the corridor. But there wasn't a soul in sight, so I crossed quickly.

Like every other morgue in America, the bodies were kept in a large refrigerated room. All you had to do was follow the refrigeration system's constant wheezing to find it. I slipped in and fumbled with the light switch.

A bright white light came on, reflected by the white porcelain tiles on the floor and walls. I had to blink a few times to get used to the intensity of the glare, giving my sore eyelids a painful workout.

There were several rows of metallic drawers embedded into the wall facing me. None of them had name tags, just barcodes and a series of numbers that meant nothing to me. Nothing for it ... I set about opening each drawer until I found the one I was looking for. Third time was the charm ... or rather the very uncharming, mauled, and torn-up face of the late Mr. Mallory.

The body was clean, but it was a long way from pretty.

My brilliant detective skills saw a closed-casket ceremony in this corpse's future. I pushed the white sheet covering the body down and discovered that they hadn't performed an autopsy on the corpse, after all. It looked like the ME's office was siding with the official theory.

There were several large gashes on the torso, deep, angry red cuts that had torn the flesh beyond repair and to the point of exposing muscles and organs. On the side, two of them were so deep the white of the bones could be seen.

I thought my time in war zones had prepared me for everything, but this was a new one. The savagery, the brutality ... the wounds on this man confirmed my working theory that he had been killed with malice. The tears in his flesh had been inflicted with the clear intention of causing the maximum level of pain possible in a short amount of time. No animal kills like that, except the human kind.

I could have looked for the ME report, but I knew it wouldn't tell me much. Like most human beings, they'd stopped looking the second they found an answer that suited what they wanted to believe. In truth, there was only one person who could help me now. Time we were introduced.

I bent down and said, "Evening, Mr. Mallory. Sorry that we have to meet in such circumstances; my name's Bellamy Vale."

There was no answer ... not that I'd been expecting one. The guy was dead, after all. When it comes to my bag of tricks, nothing is that simple. No, it takes a little bit more effort to communicate with the dead.

I reached into my jacket pocket and took out a small amulet. It was about three inches long, two inches wide, and shaped like a short tuning fork. The two-pronged implement, which I called a "bident" for its two prongs, as opposed to the trident's three, was made from a black-and-red gemstone. I had taken it to a jeweler once, and he had told me, in amazement, that it was painite—one of the rarest gemstones on the planet. God knows where she had gotten it.

I swallowed as I held it between my fingers. I could feel energy emanating from the inert stone. This was one more tool that managed to function despite me not understanding how it worked. I think it's safe to say the hell she was from would freeze over before she took the time to teach her errand boy how to use her fancy tools properly or, God forbid, give him an instruction manual.

Previous experience had taught me that the stone came with a time limit in terms of contact: one complete revolution of the sun around our planet after the death of the body. Afterwards, the souls are over the Styx and out of reach.

I took a breath and readied myself for the ride of a lifetime. Leaning forward, I pressed the prongs on the dead man's brow. The moment the bident touched skin, I felt myself being sucked into a vortex of chaotic memories.

Images were swirling all around me, key moments repeating on a loop and displayed in no particular order—a young boy licking a chocolate-coated spoon, a thirty-something man in a suit proudly signing a contract, a child with curly hair falling from a bicycle, two teenagers walking hand in hand in a park. This was the life of William Mallory, son, brother, boyfriend, husband, and father. All of what he was surrounded me, the good, the bad, and the ugly.

It took me a while to sift through the jumble of recollections so I could find the more recent ones. They were a lot darker and more disjointed. I could feel the fear and the pain that was associated with these memories, and I dreaded touching them. No one in his right mind would ever want to get close to that particular kind of memory. I soldiered on and reached out for them.

The scene swallowed me whole, and darkness surrounded me. Rain was pouring down, and I was drenched to the bone. The headlights of a sports car blinded me, and I raised a hand to shield my eyes just as the car drove through me like a ghost. A second car was following the first, and I moved out of the road before it, too, drove through the ethereal entity that I had become. I mean, I could have stayed there—a memory of a van couldn't hurt me or anything—but I had some dignity left, and I drew the line at standing in front of speeding soccer-mom wagons.

William Mallory was on the sidewalk with me. He was wearing a suit beneath a long trench coat and balancing an umbrella in one hand and a briefcase and smartphone in the other. He rounded the corner of the street I'd been to yesterday afternoon and froze. I turned to see where his gaze was directed and felt a fear that bordered on panic rise in me. Mallory's emotions were oozing out like a toxin and infecting me. The hairs on the back of my neck stood on end as I gulped down bile.

Some kind of beast was waiting on the other side of the street, crouched in a darkened corner, massive despite the fact that it was on all fours. Its hindquarters were covered in thick, dark fur, and its skull flashed white in the gloom. I glimpsed its canines, sharp and ready.

Mallory screamed and made a run for the nearest door. He wasn't fast enough. The beast chased him down and pounced on him. Pain laced my back as the beast's claw ripped Mallory's skin. I screamed and forced myself to let go of the memory.

When I reopened my eyes, I was on the tiled floor of the morgue, panting, and I could barely hold onto the bident with my shaking fingers. A metallic noise broke the silence, and I clambered hastily to my feet. Someone was coming. I cursed and placed the sheet back over Mallory's face before closing the drawer.

I could hear the faint sound of heels on the cold, hard floor from the far side of the door. The sound was growing louder with each step, and it could only mean one thing— that someone was coming this way.

I was trapped, with nowhere to hide and only one way out. And that way out was also someone else's way in. Shit ... if they caught me here, I'd be arrested yet again. This time, Morgan would make sure I wouldn't see the light of day for a month or two. With my bad luck, Lady McDeath would consider this to be a breach of my contract and end me there and then.

I did the only thing I could think of. I moved to the side of the door, flattened my back against the wall, closed my eyes, and flicked off the lights. The steps kept coming closer until they stopped at the door. I held my breath as I waited for whoever was on the other side to push it open.

As soon as I heard the door opening, I snapped the lights on and re-opened my eyes. The woman who'd just entered let out a soft, pained moan as the harshness of the lights blinded her momentarily, and I seized the opportunity to push her out of the way and dash from the room. I was out of there in a matter of seconds, running like the Devil was after me. I never saw her face and caught only a glimpse of long blonde hair and a whiff of lily-scented perfume.

I was out of the building less than a minute later, squeezing out the same way I'd come in. I'd been expecting the security alarm to be blaring out by that point, but the streets remained silent as I got back to my car.

I pondered the situation as I waited in the Stingray for the adrenaline rush to subside. The memories had been hazy, disjointed and, for all I knew, inaccurate. I never got a good look at the beast as emotional resonance has a bad habit of exaggerating some details while ignoring others. Even if the time limit didn't apply, there was no way I'd ever agree to go back inside Mallory's head. I'd seen and experienced enough of the macabre for one night.

One thing was certain—it wasn't a wolf. It wasn't even an animal. Through the haze, I'd seen the thing stand on two legs as it lunged for Mallory and clawed at his back.

This creature, whatever it was, had killed twice already, and if Lady McDeath was telling me the truth, it wasn't going to stop. The attack on Mallory had happened during the day, while Nicholls had been gutted in the dead of night, so there was no connection there. Right now, there was no way of knowing whom its next victim would be. But it seemed certain that it would kill again and that it would enjoy every second of the experience.

As far as I knew I was the only one even looking for it. The rest of the city slept, oblivious to the threat, and there was no help coming. Thanks to that passive-aggressive game of phone tag I'd played with their answering service, it was clear that the Conclave wasn't going to do anything. They were the authorities in charge of this sort of stuff, yet they'd elected not to send anyone. So if I couldn't find this creature, more people would die.

That's when it hit me.

"I'll be damned," I muttered as I marveled at why I hadn't put it together sooner. If *I* couldn't find this thing, more people would die. A nervous giggle escaped my lips. That bunch of jackasses ... they *had* sent someone to deal with the situation ... me. I punched the steering wheel with what strength I had left.

"Well, shit!" I grumbled as I leaned back in the seat. "Guess we're screwed."

Damn deities and their twisted mind games. Couldn't they, just for once, be straightforward about something? Wait —didn't that also mean Lady McDeath was part of the Conclave? Once again, she'd left out critical information that I might have wanted to know about. It was almost as if she wanted me to suffer.

Well, if she didn't want to play fair, neither would I. I had one option left for getting inside info. She wouldn't like it, but it was either that or start roaming the streets saying, "Here wolfie, wolfie."

I turned the ignition on and drove down to the old docks, to the one place where I might get a foot in the door. Because, as they say on the streets, "If you want info, you best go to the Indigo."

6

THE INDIGO

The Indigo was a games arcade, one of the last, nestled in a warehouse by the docks. You wouldn't know it judging by its bland exterior of off-white metallic walls and darkened windows, but it's a real geek nirvana inside. The Indigo was one of those places that would never need to place ads on- or offline to draw in customers. It had a niche clientele, near all of them regulars. Word of mouth survives in the Internet age.

I pushed the metallic door, which had the arcade's name spray-painted on it, open. As soon as I was through, I felt like I'd entered another dimension. Throbbing bass-heavy music shook the walls. There were glowing neon lights everywhere. An S-shaped bar stood in the middle of the room, surrounded by dozens of tables heaped with various pieces of computer equipment. Tangles of wiring climbed up to the ceiling before coursing left and right.

As always, I stood out like a sore thumb amongst the regular clientele with their multi-colored hair and/or half-shaved heads. I was at least ten years older than the oldest gamer present and not showing nearly enough tattoos, piercings, or even bare skin.

A young girl with one half of her hair dyed blue and the other half pink gave me a look so full of subtext it made my pants feel a size too small. I gave her a polite nod and a smile and crossed the room without looking back. Sure, I'm a dog, but I've got standards. I wasn't interested in a fling with an underage wannabe hacker with daddy issues.

I headed straight for the door at the back of the room and punched in a code on the digipad. The door clicked open, and I took the stairs down to the real Indigo. The regular crowd called it "the Indigo Below."

The lower level of the structure was a study in contrasts with the upper floor. Here, everything was quiet, ordered, and clean. The people walking about the place were all employees. Each person was dressed in an immaculate suit with a golden pin on his/her collar in the shape of a caduceus, which consists of entwined snakes on a stick surrounded by a pair of wings.

A security guard stopped me at the foot of the stairs. He was one head taller than me and had arms the size of my legs. I reached inside my jacket pocket for a similar winged pin and put it on. He moved to the side without a word.

"Hi, Bob, is Zian in?" I asked him.

The bulky man kept his mouth shut but gave me an affirmative nod.

"Well, thank you very much, my chatty friend," I said, treating him to my most amiable smile. "Er, Tom, have you ever heard the joke about the Irish monk and the Swedish blonde?"

The guard remained silent, but I saw his jaw tense. I leaned in closer, gave him a pat on the arm and said, "I know, that one cracks me up every time."

His eyes screamed murder, but he remained unmoving, his lips sealed. Yes, I know it was childish, but I couldn't resist it. It was like poking fun at the guards standing watch in front of Buckingham Palace.

"You know, I'd love to chat some more with you, Steve, but I've got to go," I told him. "Have a nice day."

I walked past him, and I swear I heard him groan. I smiled. It was the most I'd ever heard him say.

I walked down the corridor, proudly presenting my silver pin. It was the rarest kind of accreditation for this place, meaning I was an authorized visitor in the secured zone. I turned a corner and carried on past the largest server room I'd ever seen. The guys in Cupertino would have wet their pants if they could have seen it. The next corridor I took conveyed me past several cubicles with people working at their desks. Finally, I came to the entrance of the room I wanted and started looking for a familiar bleach-blond mop of hair.

Zian was seated in the far left corner tonight. I made my way over to his desk. He brightened up when he saw me coming.

"Bellamy, my friend," he said in his rapid, faintly British accent. "What on earth brings you by at this hour?"

He pushed his chair backward and sprang to his feet. He was a good deal shorter than me, thin and with pale skin, but that was all right by him. In the information world, he was eight feet tall if you went by the standards of data collection.

"Morning, Zian," I said as we shook hands. He had quite

the vigorous and energetic grip despite the fact that it was two in the morning. "I need a favor."

His bright blue eyes widened as he peered up at me. "A favor, you say? And what type of favor would that be?"

"Information," I replied.

He laughed good-naturedly at that. "Information ... well, as always, Bellamy, you've come to the right place." He straightened his back, tugged at the bottom of his black t-shirt and passed a hand through his mess of bleached hair in a vain attempt to tame it. "After all, information is what I do best," he proclaimed in his most serious tone.

I smiled. Despite his best efforts and the fact that he was closer to thirty than twenty, Zian looked like a goofy teenager on a sugar rush. He was trying, though. Hells, he'd even put a gray vest on over his blue jeans and black t-shirt to try to make himself look more professional. But for all the effort he made to look like he meant business, the corners of his pale lips couldn't help but turn up in the beginning of a lopsided smile that told you just how much fun he had at his job.

"I know," I said with a nod. "I wouldn't settle for anything less than the best."

A full-blown grin bloomed on his face at that, and I had to admit it was contagious.

"So what can I do for you today?" he asked, clapping me on the shoulder.

"I need your help with a case I'm working on. I've got two dead bodies and a mysterious creature roaming the streets."

Zian's smile died a little at that, and he peeked apprehensively around the room. Then he steered me into the nearest private office available and locked the door behind us. He looked alarmed.

"I can't help you with that kind of stuff, Bellamy. We both know that."

"Story of my damn life," I muttered. "Look, Zian," I told him, rubbing the bridge of my nose, "I have no one else to turn to here. I promise you won't be breaking protocol this time."

He snorted at that.

I raised my hands up, palms turned towards him in a placating gesture. "I promise. Public domain."

"I won't do it, Bellamy," he said, crossing his arms over his chest like a petulant kid. "The rules are very strict on this. People like us can't get involved with people like you." He pointed an accusing finger at me. "Sweet Aphrodite, you shouldn't even know that this place exists in the first place! If the Conclave ever found out that I'd given you that pin you're wearing, they'd kill me."

"It'll never happen," I assured him. "We both know that in order to kill you, they'd have to stop sitting on their hands. See that happening anytime soon?"

Zian smirked. "True enough." Then he frowned. "But my father is a bit proactive, and it's never pleasant when he's angry. I'm sorry, Bell. I can't help you."

I shrugged, placed my hands in my pockets and laid down the last card in my hand. "Others can't, but you can. I mean, you're the king of information, right?"

"I'm not the king of information," Zian corrected me as he leaned over the desk to turn on the computer sitting there. "We both know who that is, and I'm telling you, for our mutual good, that he wouldn't be pleased to know what you're up to."

Then he moved to sit down at the desk as the computer booted up. His fingers start tapping keys at NASCAR speed.

"Thank you, Zian," I said with a smile, knowing I'd won. "You're the best."

"What are you thanking me for?" he asked as he stopped typing just long enough to glare at me. "I haven't agreed to help you yet."

"But you're typing."

"Yes, I'm typing," he retorted. "Of course I'm typing. I'm always typing. I'm the *prince* of information, aren't I?"

That he was, both figuratively and literally. In this place, Zian was the only one without a pin on his collar. He didn't need it. He was at home here on his father's property. I watched his fingers fly over the keyboard as I moved to stand behind his shoulder.

I knew there was no Web-connected system Zian couldn't break into. Given enough time, he could find out anything. It was in his nature, in his blood. Information was the preferred currency of his family. They'd used it to elevate themselves in society. The Indigo was just one of many similar outposts on the planet, and it was the tip of the iceberg of what Zian's father owned. He had shares in all the big Internet companies: Google, Facebook, Twitter, eBay, PayPal, and so on. He also had stock in the companies that built the computers and smartphones we humans were so keen to use, along with the optic lines that flew the data beneath our feet and along the bottom of the ocean. I'd even heard whispers that he'd become an angel investor for Elon Musk in recent years.

In other words, all the information that existed on this planet, all those zeros and ones, passed through the hands of Hermes, Zian's father, on a daily basis. In ancient times, he'd been known as the Messenger of the Gods, a position he still held all these centuries later. As a matter of fact, he was the only god left on this side of the border. Story had it that he struck a bargain with the creator of the Conclave himself, the Roman Emperor Aurelian, back in 273 A.D., to stay on Earth while the others got cast away. Why would a god-like him want to leave a world on the verge of so much? Some of the more outrageous whispers had him behind every major step humankind had taken since—he was the guy who *really* invented the Internet.

"Okay," Zian said as his typing slowed. "Two strange murders in Cold City within the same twenty-four-hour timeframe ... bet you that pin I gave you that's what you're interested in."

"I need to find out what did this," I said, leaning closer.

Ten seconds later, Zian pulled up a window for the official police reports and several pictures of the victims that could only have come from the ME office. By all the hells, this guy was good.

"Well, it says right here that a wolf on the loose did this," he said, pointing at the window of one of the police reports while his other hand kept typing.

"I got a good look at the thing that did this," I fired back. "Trust me, Zian, whatever it was is from across the border."

Zian's fingers froze over the keyboard in mid-stroke. That was never a good sign.

"Rules, Bellamy," he said again in a chiding voice. "I'm

not allowed to give you any information regarding matters not of this world."

"And like I said, I just want you to stick to the public domain," I countered. "I want copies of every official report you can find. Try to get footage from surveillance cameras too, if there is any. And find anything that connects the victims that you can. I can work out the rest from there."

Zian smiled, and both hands started typing again. "That I can do."

A small printer to the side of the desk started getting to work with a loud whirr. In less than thirty minutes, I had a binder's worth of documents to sort through. Zian found a plastic bag in one of the desk drawers for me to fill up with what he'd printed.

"Ah-ha!" Zian said as something on the screen got his attention. "Now isn't that interesting?"

I turned back to face him. "What is?"

His fingers were fan-dancing on the keyboard at such a furious pace I was afraid the keyboard would break. His eyes were darting left and right as he drank in the information that was zipping across his screen. I moved closer to him, trying to make out what he'd found.

Suddenly the screen froze. A panicked squeal escaped Zian's lips. "Oh, no, no, no, no, no ..."

He pressed a series of keys, but all that did was make the screen go blue. Now, I was no tech geek, but even I knew that wasn't good.

All of the lights in the small office shut off, and I heard Zian gulp.

"What's going on?" I asked, sotto voce, dreading the answer. It came quickly enough.

The wall on our left, which had been white until then, turned blue, making me realize that what I'd mistaken for large stone tiles was, in fact, a bank of flat screens displaying a picture of just that. The blue turned to black, and the face of a man appeared on each of the screens. At that, Zian whimpered.

The man facing us pressed a button off-camera, and the screens changed again. They coordinated to compose one single image to scale of a man in a Savile Row suit that fitted him so perfectly it had to be custom-made. He sat at an expensive mahogany desk placed in front of large bay windows. It was mid-morning where he was, and the sun was shining.

"And what have we here?" he inquired in a posh British accent that complemented his dress and surroundings.

When neither of us answered, one of his eyebrows lifted up. Though small, almost insignificant, the motion carried with it palpable weight. It prompted Zian to speak up, making him utter a weak, almost inaudible, "Just helping a friend, Father."

I felt all the air get sucked out of my lungs ... Father? That meant ... uh oh.

Hermes, son of Zeus and Mother Night, the god of trade, thieves, and travelers, didn't look too pleased with his son's answer. He stood up from his desk and moved closer to the camera. The screens on the wall followed his movements and adapted the ratio, giving us an up-to-scale view of Zian's father. He was as tall as I was, maybe early fifties, with short ginger hair and the same blue eyes as his son.

"Bellamy Vale, I presume," he said, though his tone told me he didn't "presume" anything—he knew. "We meet at last," he added. I couldn't tell if that was a good thing or a bad thing from where he stood.

I wasn't sure how one was supposed to address a god thought to have been dead for centuries, but the guy sounded British, so I inclined my head a little and said, "Sir."

Hermes turned his attention to his son and, out of the corner of my eye, I saw Zian hunch his shoulders as though trying to make himself smaller.

"I thought I'd been clear on the subject, Zianyon," Hermes muttered, the use of his son's full name universal parental code for "You're in deep shit right now."

"Even my patience has its limits, and you're getting far too old to behave like a brat."

Zian bowed his head further. "Yes, Father."

"Wasn't I clear when I told you that this ..."—Hermes waved a hand as if he was searching for the right word, lips pursed—"... *friendship* was to be terminated at once? I don't take kindly to my son 'hanging out' with a PI with a rap sheet a mile long, methods I loathe, and an utter disregard for the quintessential beauty of gardenias."

That got my attention. How could he know this story already? The man really *was* the information center of the universe.

"If you know so much about me, then you know who I work for," I said, deciding to place my chips on *her.*

Hermes transferred his attention to me with a bemused expression. "Of course I do, Mr. Vale. But the real question is ... do you?"

I gulped. Something in the set of his eyes told me he wasn't joking. He knew more about my situation than even I did. But as tempted as I was to press the matter, time was running out on why I'd come here in the first place.

"What do you know of the creature I'm after?" I asked him.

"Everything," he said in that same tone.

"Care to share?" I asked as I attempted to offer him a ghost of my usual Cheshire Cat grin.

Hermes' smile grew as if my gall amused him. I couldn't shake the image of a cat toying with a mouse before going in for the kill.

"Unlike my son, I abide by the rules, Mr. Vale," he said. "Mankind's destiny is set on its own course, and I dare not interfere. Need I remind you how those rules were set in stone long before you came into the picture?"

I took a step closer to the screen. "People will die if you tell me nothing—good people."

"I'm afraid that is what people do," Hermes said in a flat voice.

I thumbed quickly through Zian's printouts and, almost at once, saw what I was looking for. "William Mallory had a wife and a son. Ethan Nicholls had two girls and three grandchildren. All of them are going to miss the men who got killed over the last two days—and that's just the kills by this thing that I know about right now." I pointed a finger at the screen. "Something from your world did this. That makes it *your* problem. The least you could do is give me a nudge in the right direction."

Fury passed through Hermes' eyes for an instant. It had probably been a long time—centuries, maybe—since someone had dared speak to the Messenger of the Gods like that. I half expected to be disintegrated where I stood at a snap of his fingers for mouthing off.

But the moment passed, and Hermes just sighed instead. "I wish I could do more for you, mortal ... I swear to the Styx. But these are the rules that were set down by *your* people. That old fart Aurelian was very clear on the subject. As for your 'nudge,' as you put it, I believe it has already been given."

I frowned at that. "What?"

The annoying know-it-all smile returned to Hermes' lips. "Who do you think gave you this assignment, mortal? Think —whose brand is it that you carry?"

My hand came up to scratch at my shoulder, an almost unconscious gesture. A long time ago, I had found out the meaning of the symbol on my back. A quick search on the Internet had revealed it to be the Greek symbol of Hades, king of the Underworld and guardian of the wealth of the Earth.

But I'd always thought that symbol was ... well, symbolic. Something *she* had chosen because of what the concept of Hades represented—death and judgment—not a brand. Death couldn't be ruled by him or by any of the other Under-world crowd these days. They'd all been banished with the rest, so he couldn't still have ties to our world ... right?

Hermes took notice of my growing understanding. "And to think you call yourself a private investigator. Yes, I did mean my dearest Uncle Hades. It is his daughter whom you serve."

Hermes' smile grew with my uneasiness. "He's the funny uncle; did you know?"

I gulped as the realization hit home. I was working for the daughter of the god of the dead, destroyer of Titans and proud owner of Cerberus. My heart missed a beat or two. I couldn't begin to wrap my head around the implications of that statement. But I did put this much together—just because he wasn't on Earth anymore didn't mean that he didn't have agents doing his bidding ... and, lucky me, I was one of them. Hells, no wonder my death kept getting canceled until further notice.

"There is a lot you do not understand yet, Bellamy Vale," Hermes went on. "Your path treads across a tapestry that was woven centuries ago, and many events are yet to unfold." Then he shrugged. "But it is not my place to tell you more at this time ... perhaps when next we meet. For now, I shall only tell you this: the information you seek is already at your disposal in the archives Zianyon has bequeathed you. You only need to look for it."

I had no idea what he meant by that, but I nodded anyway. It felt like the right thing to do, considering what he could have done instead of being civil.

My phone started to vibrate in my pocket. I fought against the reflex to get it, forcing myself to remain immobile so that my attention could stay fixed on the god standing before me.

"You should get that," Hermes told me. "It is urgent news."

With those words said, he turned back to his son, as though dismissing me from his awareness. He addressed my friend in another language that hadn't been spoken since the Parthenon was still in one piece. Though I didn't speak a word of ancient Greek or whatever the hells it was, I could tell Hermes was tearing Zian a new one.

I pulled my phone out of my pocket and pressed the answer button without looking at the display. "Hold on one second," I said into the receiver before taking a step forward so as to place myself between Zian and the wall of screens.

Hermes broke off his harangue so that I could speak.

"Will you be okay?" I asked my friend.

He nodded, the gesture a little too nervous for my liking. "Yeah, don't worry about me. See you around sometime, yeah?"

I returned his nod and stepped out of the room to the sound of the lecture continuing. Once outside, I raised the phone to my ear. "This is Vale."

A woman's voice with a Latino accent greeted me on the other end of the line. "It's me," said Ramirez. "I've got a tip for you."

I smiled to myself as I made my way back upstairs. "I'm listening."

"Go to 6 Plymouth Road," she said, speaking low and quickly. "Crime in progress ... and you didn't get that from me."

"I never do," I said, ending the call as I stepped back into the main part of the Indigo.

7

NIGHT OF THE BEAST

I all but ran out of the Indigo, making it to my car in record time. The sleek, dark-gray Stingray looked black in the dim light. I unlocked it at a distance, threw myself inside, and floored the gas pedal the second the key had started the engine. I had no idea what I'd find at the address Ramirez had just given me, but it was essential that I beat the cops there.

Luckily, I had two advantages over them. First, the CCPD precinct was in the lower eastern part of the city, near the coast. My starting point was near the far west coast, much closer to Plymouth Road. I'd been down that way before. It ran through a small residential area north of the city, right at the foot of the mountains. It being towards the western end of Cold City meant that, unlike my friends in blue, I wouldn't have to cross through the entire city to get there.

My second advantage? Well, I was sitting in it: a

Corvette Stingray with a V8 engine that could go from zero to sixty in four seconds.

The Michelin tires left rubber marks behind me as I sped out of the parking lot and onto Eighth Avenue. It was the quickest way north, a long, linear stretch of deserted asphalt that might as well have been a racetrack. The Stingray was loud in the quiet night, its four-hundred-plus horses roaring underneath the bonnet.

It took me less than ten minutes to get to number 6, a small, cottage-like house at the end of a private drive. Light was pouring out of the ground-floor windows, and I ran for the entrance door as soon as the car's engine flicked off. I unholstered my pistol, a SIG-Sauer P226, when I found the front door had been busted open.

Gun in hand, I crossed the threshold and entered the living room. It was cozy, with a neatness that made it look like a page taken out of an interior design catalog. The only false notes were the shards of a broken table lamp in one corner and an upturned armchair. I tightened my grip on the pistol and continued forward. Pictures on the coffee table gave me more information about the house's residents—a family with two kids, a boy and a girl ... four potential victims by my death math.

A scream ripped through the air, and I quickened my pace in its direction. That led me to the kitchen, which was just as empty as the living room had been. There was a faint smell of curry in the air. There was also a half-open back door. The scream had to have come from out there.

Unsure of what I'd find, I stepped outside. There was a small garden behind the house, with high bushes on all sides and a small garden shed to the left. I spared no mind to the flower arrangements, however, but focused instead on the furry beast that was circling the shed. It looks like I've found my monster, I thought.

I paused and tightened my grip on the pistol while adjusting my aim. The creature's bulk made it impossible to miss, even in the low light. It was standing on its back legs, a good six and a half feet tall and covered in dark fur.

Whimpers came from inside the shed, and it wasn't hard to guess where the family had gone to hide. If the claw marks on the door were any indication, the creature knew it too. Even as I watched, it threw itself at the door, and the whole shed shook under the impact. The rusty old hinges weren't going to last long.

"Hey!" I yelled.

The beast's head swiveled towards me. I found myself staring at a skeletal cranium, its white bone reflecting the glow of a nearby streetlamp. I wasn't sure, but it looked like it had belonged to a bear. I took two steps closer, my weapon aimed at the creature's bulky torso.

With a low, guttural growl, the creature turned its whole body in my direction. It stood tall, menacing, a nightmare silhouette against the backdrop of sodium light.

"I don't know how you got to this world, but it's over," I said, trying to project courage I didn't feel. "The killings end ... tonight."

"Die," the creature grated in a voice that was the audial equivalent of a stinky breath. "Human!"

My finger pressed hard on the trigger, all by itself. The gun fired, but instead of a loud wail and the sound of flesh being torn apart, I heard only a metallic clang as the nine mil round ricocheted off the creature. I swore as I realized the thing was wearing some kind of body armor that I hadn't made out in the dim light.

It made no sense. What kind of beast wore armor? And spoke?

But there wasn't time to consider that now. The creature took a heavy step towards me, snarling. I shot at it again, three bullets in rapid succession this time. One round ricocheted off its bicep, another one off its leg. The third one grazed its elbow, drawing blood.

Never mind what it is, I thought, as I took aim once more. If it bleeds, you can kill it. It wasn't wearing full body armor, that was clear. More like protective plates tied to selected parts. All I had to do to kill it was to be careful with my remaining shots.

The beast took another heavy step towards me, then another. It took me one second too many to realize it was launching into a charge. A good three hundred pounds of mean muscle was heading my way, and I had my back to the house.

I fired again, but the bullet didn't even slow it down. I had to dodge before it crushed me like a freight train. I waited until the last second and threw myself to one side, rolling on the grass.

The beast crashed into the house. Somehow the wall survived the impact, though wooden boards were sent flying everywhere. I fired again, aiming for the base of the neck. It was too bad that I missed, especially since the beast proceeded to throw itself at me once more.

I escaped the bulk of it, but I wasn't quick enough to get out of range of its long, lacerating claws. They etched burning lines deep in my side, and I cried out in pain.

I fought to keep my grip on the pistol as I got back to my feet. The creature snorted with contempt and threw a massive punch at me. My ribs took the full brunt of the impact, and I went soaring, landing a good two feet away from where I'd been standing. The Sig, however, was still in my hand.

When the beast came at me again, I fired two wild shots as I fought to get back to my feet. What with the wind that had been knocked out of me and the droplets of sweat in my eyes, it was wasted ammo.

This time, I had the streetlamp at my back, and I could see the creature facing me more clearly. It had no fur on its front, and now I saw it was a hairy pelt it was wearing on its back, like a cape. The claws were fastened to leather arm bracers, and the rough, callused features of a man poked out from underneath the animal skull.

Old stories from Norse mythology came back to me, tales of an elite troop of warriors thought to be undefeatable; comprising furious, bloodthirsty men who were more animals than humans, they were thought to be immune to pain from edged weapons.

"Berserker," I addressed the creature, forcing a calm I was barely hanging onto, "you're not welcome here. Go back to your own realm."

Since I was almost out of bullets anyway, I dropped my pistol and reached for the blade I always kept at my ankle. Immunity to edged weapons or not, this fight would have to be won at close quarters.

Feet planted on the ground, I waited for the Berserker to come at me again. He didn't disappoint, and I rolled to the ground at the last second to avoid the impact. But the man-beast had been expecting me to do that. He stopped dead in his tracks the instant he missed me, adjusted his course, and charged my way again.

With one knee on the ground, I had only a fraction of a second to get him with my knife. I stabbed the creature behind the knee, where I hoped the blade might find a small expense of vulnerable flesh. My knife had just enough time to draw blood before the beast knocked me down again.

I saw stars as I started to get up again. The Berserker was already turning back for another charge. He was quicker than I'd guessed. Worse, the wound I'd just inflicted on him wasn't doing anything to slow him down.

I braced myself for the impact as best I could. I used one arm to deflect the claws while I stabbed at the Berserker with the other. I put all of my strength into that attack, but it still wasn't enough for the blade to penetrate.

The man-beast head-butted me out of the way. I felt my cheek split open as it connected with one of the sharper edges of the bear's skull. I reeled backward with a scream.

Blood was streaming down my arm, making it difficult to keep a good grip on the blade. I was in bad shape and getting worse with each round—and I'd barely managed to do more than scratch the bastard.

The creature stood tall and readied for another charge. He took a step forward, and I braced myself for what was likely going to be my last stand. But just as quickly as the man-beast started, he stopped, head cocked as though he heard something in the distance.

I waited, thanking whatever had caught his attention for the small reprieve. I took in a deep breath and passed an arm over my face to clear it a little of blood, sweat, and dirt.

Then I heard what the Berserker had heard, the familiar wail of sirens in the distance —faint but growing louder with each passing second.

There was probably one patrol car in front, with Ramirez right behind it and Morgan in tow. That was four people, maybe six if they'd sent two units. It wouldn't be close to a fair fight when they got here. The cops wouldn't be taking any of the chances I had. And it looked like the Berserker was coming up with the same death math that I was.

Even so, he stood frozen in the half-light, his breath coming out in ragged puffs. He looked at the shed, then at me, then back at the shed one more time.

"Not over," he hissed, taking a step backward. "Human!"

With a growl, he jumped over the bushes and out of the garden. Once the rustling had stopped, I let out a deep sigh of relief, thanking my lucky stars that the Berserker's orders had been to be discreet. I put my blade back where it belonged and went to look for my gun.

————

I didn't have much time before the cavalry's arrival by the time I found my Sig. I rushed over to the shed and knocked on the door.

"Hey, it's safe," I called, panting. "You can come out. That thing's gone." I didn't get a reply, so I knocked again. "The police are on the way," I said, confident that they could hear the sirens too. "My name's Vale. I'm a PI. I'm working with the cops on this case."

Sure, I was stretching the truth. But the last thing I

wanted was for the would-be victims or the cops to get the wrong idea about me on this.

I heard the door unlock. It pushed open just a fraction. I stepped back. I had no doubt I looked like I'd just been trying to juggle chainsaws, and I didn't want to scare whoever was on the other side of that door ... well, worse than they already were.

"Is it gone?" a woman's voice stammered.

"Yeah, it's gone. You're safe."

The door opened a little wider, and I recognized the woman from the photo in the house. She was in her night-dress, and her short brown hair was a real mess around her dark ebony face. The light from the streetlamp was just enough for me to make out the fear that stretched her eyes. She was just a couple of degrees short of petrified.

"What's your name?" I asked her. When she didn't answer, I added, "I'm Bellamy."

"Ni-Nicole," she volunteered.

Something moved behind her.

"Are your kids in there with you, Nicole?" I asked.

At the reminder of her children, she closed the door a little. The reflective gesture of a protective mother ... Given the state I was in, I couldn't blame her.

I raised a hand, palm up. "It's all right, Nicole. You can all come out. It's safe. Hear those sirens?"

They were deafening by now. Judging from the noise, they were almost in the driveway, but I knew they wouldn't come rushing in right away, not till they had checked the place out.

"Why don't we go inside the house?" I suggested, holding out my hand.

I think it was the promise of official help arriving more than anything else that convinced her to come with me. She stepped out of the shed, two sets of tiny hands grabbing at her own. I let the three of them into the house and closed the door behind them.

"Where's your husband?" I asked as soon as Nicole had sat her kids on a kitchen stool. The sirens were loud outside, and I had to raise my voice to be heard.

The boy looked to be ten, the girl a year or two younger. Once their mother let go of them, the boy reached for his sister, wrapping her in a protective embrace. I made sure to stand as far away as possible and placed my pistol back in the holster I wore at my hip.

"Mark's at a convention out of town," Nicole replied in a shaky voice. "How to diversify the agricultural system, I think ... he's a biologist."

"Do you have any idea why someone would want to hurt you?"

She seemed baffled by my question. "That thing ... what was that thing?"

"Werewolf," her boy whispered from behind her.

"What *was* that thing?" Nicole repeated, staring at me.

I couldn't give her the answer she wanted, so I went with the one everybody else had been going with. "It's the animal the local news has been talking about ... it's killed two people over the last couple of days."

"Werewolf," the boy repeated.

"There's no such thing, Kevin," her mother responded, turning to him with a stern expression that was less about convincing him than it was herself. She'd gathered herself since getting inside and seemed more focused now. "Why did you ask me if someone wants to hurt me?" she demanded, turning back to face me. "I thought the attacks were random."

I told her the truth this time. "I'm not so sure anymore."

"But there's no reason for this," she said, throwing up her hands as the words rushed out of her. "We're nothing special. I work for the city, and Mark's a biologist. Our kids go to school. We're nothing special."

"CCPD!" someone shouted from outside the house. I recognized Ramirez's Latino-tinged voice. "Anybody home?"

I opened a window to call back. "In the kitchen."

The arrival of the cops had come a little too quick for my purposes. Yeah, okay, they'd saved me from getting mauled by that prehistoric slasher, but they'd also gotten there before I could get anything useful out of Nicole.

Ramirez entered, weapon in hand and her hair tied in a slick ponytail. She lowered her gun when she saw me.

"Vale?" she said, lowering her gun. "What are you doing here?"

The word "Clear" was repeated several times as the other officers checked the rooms one by one.

I raised my hands in a show of goodwill. "Well, I was driving by," I told her. "I heard a scream from the house, so I came to take a look."

"Driving by," echoed the scornful basso voice of Jeremy Morgan from the living room. The man himself made his entrance a moment later. "We're supposed to believe that?"

He glanced around the kitchen, taking in the huddled forms of the children, the slightly more relaxed Nicole and then me again.

"Any sign of the animal?"

"It's gone," I said. "It was in the garden. I fired a few shots in the air and scared it off."

"What aren't you telling me?" Morgan asked, coming near enough for me to smell his halitosis working overtime.

I raised my hands a little higher, despite the pain lancing me in my side. "Look, it was dark out there. I didn't see it that well. It went after the family. I got in its way, and it attacked me. That's when I fired off a few rounds to scare it off."

"And you just happened to be driving by ... at just the right time."

I smiled. "Got lost on my way to the Redbox kiosk."

A flashlight reflected from outside, and a uniformed cop popped his head through the back door.

"Signs of a fight, LT," he said to Morgan. "Blood drops and a large dent in the side of the house. No signs of the wolf, though."

The young man disappeared back outside, and Morgan cast an accusatory gaze at me.

"Like I said, it attacked me," I repeated, dropping my hands and letting some of the weariness I felt show on my face. "I fought back. That's why it's gone now. So if you don't mind, I'd like to go home and get some rest. I'm not feeling well after this."

"This has to be the thickest bullshit you've ever served me, Vale," Morgan said, his dark eyes glinting with menace. "And that's saying something."

I couldn't resist one last jab. "I saw a family in danger, so I stepped in to intervene and saved them." I took a step closer and dipped my fingers in my wound, then showed him the blood and smiled. "I'm a bloody hero."

Morgan lost it at that. He lurched for me, much like the

Berserker had moments before. Guess I was lucky he had holstered his gun, or he might have shot me where I stood.

Quick as he was, Ramirez was quicker. She caught Morgan's arm and pulled him back. "He's not worth it, sir," she said calmly. "Let it go."

That seemed to do the trick. Morgan threw off her hand and retreated, rage coursing through his face. Ramirez made a point of staying between the two of us until he was all the way into the next room.

"Get out of here, Bell," she muttered to me. "Just go."

As I headed for the front door, I heard Morgan call for an Anderson to keep an eye on me. Like I needed another reminder of why I needed to be gone! Even as I crossed the living room, a young uniform—the one who'd poked his head in earlier and who I assumed was Anderson—caught up with me.

"This way, sir," he said, gesturing for me to follow him outside.

I was too tired to do anything but go along with it. Another uniformed officer out on the front lawn was unrolling the yellow tape to set up a perimeter. The guys from CC News had arrived, and the Headliner channel's van was just coming up the drive. The whole place was going to turn into a media circus fast ... yet another reason to get out of here.

"Look, kid," I told Anderson, "this has been a shitty week for me so far. Why don't you just let me go home?"

Anderson scowled. "Sorry, sir. No can do."

I groaned as I sat down on a small boulder that had been placed at the edge of the lawn. Even though it wasn't as bad as what Ragazzo had put me through, the Berserker had done a number on me. I could feel blood trickling down my side. I pulled my jacket closed over it, hoping it wouldn't show.

The people from CC News started taking stock footage of the house and the neighborhood as the ones from the Headliner unpacked their gear. They were waiting for Morgan to show up so they could pester him for more details. That was the only consolation I had for being detained. I looked around for any sign of the Berserker but came up empty. The street was deserted, except for the camera crew milling about and the two patrol cars parked behind Ramirez's green Chevy.

The first neighbors had started to come out of nearby houses. With glazed eyes and wearing their nightclothes, they scratched their heads as they tried to figure out what was going on.

"And we're live from Plymouth Road, where there has been another attack minutes ago," a female voice piped up. "The same beast that attacked and brutally murdered two people this week was seen earlier in this quiet residential area."

There was no mistaking Candice Kennedy from the Headliner news channel. She was standing with her back towards the house while her cameraman filmed her with a camera that had a built-in lamp. She'd let loose her long blonde hair for the occasion.

"We are waiting for the official police report," she went on, "but witnesses indicate that the house belongs to Mark and Nicole Thricin. They live here with their two young children. We do not know, at this time, if there have been any victims in this latest attack. Mr. Thricin is a biologist for

AgroCorp, and his wife Nicole works for the city council, where she holds a seat on the board for infrastructural development in Cold City."

I watched the blonde through narrowed eyes. She was good; you had to give her that. I had no idea how she'd gathered her facts that quickly. I listened in, committing the relevant details to memory. Might as well get something useful out of this.

"In a troubling new development, this marks the second victim related to real estate. Which begs the following question: are these the random attacks of a wild animal, or is there more to the story? This was Candice Kennedy, live, for the Headliner evening news."

She signaled to her cameraman to cut the feed before turning to face the house again. Our gazes met for the briefest instant, and I saw her raise a thin eyebrow. Then Morgan came out of the house, and Kennedy focused all her attention on him.

"Detective Lieutenant Morgan, any comment? Can you confirm this attack was connected to the deaths of Ethan Nicholls and William Mallory?"

Watching Morgan coming down the porch steps was like watching a documentary on allergies. "No comment," he said, voice taut, a hand going up to shield himself from the prying eye of the camera.

"Have there been any new victims or an ID of the animal that did this?" Kennedy continued, relentless.

"No comment," Morgan repeated, taking two more steps towards his car. Sweat had begun to pearl on his brow, and his jaw was tight as iron. He ducked under the yellow tape, damn near tearing it off in frustration.

"William Mallory and Mrs. Thricin both worked for the city ... is there a connection?" Kennedy asked, right in Morgan's face.

"No comment, Ms. Kennedy, means no comment. Now piss off before I book you for harassment, obstruction of justice, and any other charge that I can think up on the spot!"

With that, Morgan got into his car and gunned the engine before driving away as fast as the speed limit allowed him. I smirked. It was nice to see that I wasn't the only one who got under his skin.

"We can now confirm that the detectives investigating this attack are the same as those for Ethan Nicholls and William Mallory's cases," Kennedy said into the camera. "While Detective Lieutenant Jeremy Morgan has not confirmed if there have been any new victims, he hasn't denied that there could be a connection between the three cases."

The journalist's last line got a chuckle out of me. She had better pray Morgan didn't catch sight of her news report tonight or he'd book for her the cell next to mine in the morning.

The blonde seemed satisfied with her performance and handed the microphone back to her cameraman, who packed it up with the rest of the gear. They'd got what they came for, apparently. A little further down the drive, the crew from CC News was capturing footage of the area.

"You all right, Bell?" Ramirez said behind me.

I turned to face her and winced at the motion. She frowned and came to sit next to me.

"Just got banged up a little," I told her, hoping it was the truth. "Nothing to write home about ... get anything more out of the Thricins?"

"No, they're all too shaken up to make sense," Ramirez said with a sigh. "Mrs. Thricin doesn't even remember how she and the kids ended up in the shed. Something about animal cries and her wanting to run away with the kids and how that animal backed her out into the garden. After that, it just becomes terror-stricken gibberish."

I nodded before I asked her the one question that interested me. "Did she get a good look at what it was?"

"No. It was too dark, and it happened too fast. Which is why"—she crossed her arms over her chest and looked at me —"I'm asking you."

"Can't help you there, Mel," I croaked as I got to my feet with the last of my strength. "I saw claws and fur, but there wasn't enough light for me to make sense of it either."

I hated having to lie to her, but it wasn't like I had a choice. For everyone's safety, it was better she stayed in the dark.

"Now," I added, rubbing my face. "Can I go home, or do I have to spend the night on this rock?"

Ramirez narrowed her pretty brown eyes at me, lips tightening into a thin line. She wasn't buying it, but she had no way to prove I was lying either. She knew it, I knew it, and she knew that I knew that she knew. This was a game we'd played before.

"Just piss off already," she said before turning her back on me.

Sorry, Mel, I thought. *I'd tell you if I could.*

Cursing under my breath, I turned to where I'd parked the car and started to walk away from the house, one hand draped over my chest. I hadn't had a chance to look at my wounds yet, but every step was sending jolts of pain through my side. There was no way it was going to be pretty to look at. But however much it hurt, it wouldn't be fatal —that much I was sure of.

The Stingray was where I'd left it, parked half on the drive and half on the grass. I swung the door open and reached for the keys I'd left in the ignition. My fingers caught only empty air.

I frowned as I sat down and turned on the interior lights to check if they'd somehow fallen on the floor.

"Lost something, hoss?" a familiar voice with a Texan accent said.

The blonde journalist, Kennedy, was standing near the hood. She'd hooked one finger through the key ring and was twirling the keys around in a taunting fashion. I took her in, her thin frame encased in tight blue jeans, short white blouse, and brown leather short-crop jacket. She wore little makeup, just enough to look good on camera without it being too much. Her smile was flirtatious, and she had her free hand resting lightly on her hip. I don't know if it was the accent or the posture, but the image of Daisy Duke standing in front of her yellow Plymouth flashed through my brain.

I shook the thought out of my head and took a longer look at the woman facing me. There was a steely determination in the set of her mouth and in the gleam in her eyes. She was like a dog with a bone or, rather, like a shark with a leg.

My leg.

8

UNHOLY ALLIANCE

Before I had time to utter a word, Kennedy slid inside the car and closed the passenger door after her. I stared at her sitting next to me, dumbfounded.

"So," she said, as if talking to an old friend, "where are we going?"

"*We*"—I let my voice rise in volume—"are not going anywhere. *You* are getting your ass out of here before I make you."

One of her carefully trimmed eyebrows shot up. "Make me? You and what army, hotshot?"

I tried to cross my arms over my chest and winced when it pulled at my wounds. I gave up and rested both hands on the steering wheel.

She was smiling at me now. "You don't look too good. The state you're in, I bet you couldn't even swat a fly."

She was right, of course, and she knew it. She still had my keys around her finger, and I took advantage of her distraction to reach for them. Any other day, it'd have worked. But banged up as I was, I winced midway, muscles cramping bad enough to prevent me from completing the motion.

Kennedy took notice and reached to pull open my jacket. Her eyes widened at the sight of blood. "You need to get to the hospital," she said with alarm in her voice.

I clenched my teeth, brushed her hand away and closed the jacket. "I'm fine."

"You're anything but fine. Look, I'll drive, and you can fill me in on the details on the way."

From the ferocity in her blue-eyed gaze, I realized she wasn't going to be dissuaded that easily.

"Stubborn Daisy Duke knock-off," I muttered, getting my P226 out of its holster. I was out of ammo, but she had no way of knowing that.

I cocked the hammer and pointed the gun at her. "Give me my keys and get lost."

The corners of her cherry-red lips arched up. This wasn't the first time this kind of thing had happened to her.

"I don't need to be at my best to pull a trigger," I said, waving the Sig about for emphasis. "At this range, there's no way I'll miss. And given the lousy couple of days I've had, I might just do it."

She gave me a mirthless laugh, which creeped me out more than it should have. Gone was the flirtatious girl next door. I had one hard-headed businesswoman facing me now.

"Or maybe I'll just send this interesting video that I have," she replied, shaking her phone for emphasis, "this video of you breaking into the morgue, to the cops? Maybe I could even exchange it for a favor or two."

Goddamn. The reality of her words sank in fast. The

woman who'd interrupted me that night—it had been her. Shit, I was way too tired to keep putting up a fight.

"All right, I'm involved in the story you're chasing. I don't know how it's going to end yet. Hells, I haven't figured out half of how it started yet."

"But you'll let me know when you do, right?" Kennedy countered as she produced a white business card that she held out for me.

I took it grudgingly. "Yeah."

"You better, hotshot," she said. "Otherwise Detective Lieutenant Jeremy Morgan will need to start making popcorn."

She reached forward, sliding her lithe body halfway over me to pluck the card from my hand and put it in my breast pocket. I still had the gun trained on her, but she didn't seem to mind.

She drew closer still, distractedly rearranging my collar with one hand. Her long, wavy blonde hair cascaded over me, and the smell of lilies engulfed me.

"By the way, I grew up with three older brothers and learned to shoot a rifle by age ten," she told me, her lips an inch from mine. "It's gonna take more than a bleeding, banged-up PI to scare me ... a whole lot more."

She pulled away, then slipped out of the car and tossed the keys back to me with a flourish. I watched her go, not quite sure what had just happened. But it felt as if the invisible noose I had around my neck had just tightened an inch or two.

It took everything I had left to drive back home, where I collapsed on the couch. No making it all the way to the bedroom tonight. No looking at the wound in my side either. It looked like it was going to be one of those weeks ...

———

I woke up as the sun rose, feeling considerably better. The bleeding had stopped overnight, and I was able to stand without the world blurring around me. I took a shower, downed some coffee, and I more or less resembled a human being when I looked at myself in the mirror. It was another perk of being Lady McDeath's errand boy—I recuperated quicker than your average Joe. The swelling in my sore eye was almost gone, even though I had a patchwork of yellow and purple bruises around it.

I moved to the bookcase in the living room and pulled out a book on Norse mythology. Flipping through the pages, I found what I was looking for: Berserkers.

These Norse warriors were old creatures, but documentation on them was sparse and often contradictory. One text presented them as humans who drugged themselves with magic mushrooms before going into battle, during which they fought in uncontrollable trance-like fury. Others recounted the tales of ruthless, wild soldiers who fought with such rage that they lost all humanity and became the creatures whose pelts they wore. One text even described them both as "fire-eating" and "possessing an immunity to edged weapons."

All the stories seemed to agree that the Berserkers' fame grew until finally, they joined King Odin's personal guard. This confirmed where my lone wolf killer came from:

Valhalla. No illegal crossing of the border to report, the Conclave had said—yeah, right!

Massaging my sore neck, I flipped the book closed. The beast I'd fought the previous night may have been a man a long time ago, but it sure wasn't anymore. There'd been no sign whatsoever of any humanity in its eyes. I wasn't sure where to stand on the fire-eating issue, but there was no arguing that my blade had wounded it.

I passed a weary hand over my face and glanced at the pile of documents I'd brought from the Indigo. The killings weren't random. This man-thing was working off some kind of list, and I had to find the connection. It was the only way to pick up its trail again.

"Let's see who's pulling your strings, Fido," I muttered, reaching for Zian's documents with a second mug of coffee in hand.

PI manuals say there's no such thing as too much information. Well, I beg to differ. Zian had printed everything the victims had on file, from phone records and bank statements to Netflix accounts and dentists' bills. And it was all written in very small print.

An hour in and all I had to show for it were burning eyes and a headache. The first two victims and the Thricin family led very different lives. I could sometimes find connections between two of them, but never anything linking all three.

Candice Kennedy had had it right when she said both Nicole Thricin and William Mallory had ties to real estate. She was part of the city council, which granted construction permits, and he was a municipal worker on some development plan committee. This was the strongest link I could find between any two of my victims, but Ethan Nicholls and his little cinema didn't seem to fit anywhere in this.

I looked into Nicholls' life more closely. It came as no surprise to find that he was close to bankruptcy. His little cinema was no match against the giant multiplexes with their 3D releases and curved screens. It was a wonder he hadn't sold the building yet.

I frowned. Maybe there was something to that. I flipped through more pages and found he'd received several buyout offers, all of which he'd declined. There was a newspaper article from last year in which Nicholls declared that he saw his job as his duty to preserve history and that the day hadn't yet come when he would watch his beloved movie house be transformed into tacky, useless condos.

I paused after that last sentence and re-read it. Was this the link? Was there a new real estate project involving Mr. Nicholls' property? I kept reading and found several mentions of a project called Orion. The name rang a bell, so I went back to Mallory's file, turning pages until the name popped up again. There. Orion. It was in his mailbox. His office had reviewed the project and given it the green light.

I jumped to the third pile and rummaged through Nicole Thricin's documents until I found what I was looking for: Construction Permit request number 100152-BC/ORION. Skimming through the details, it became obvious that the project would have to include the cinema that Mr. Nicholls had devoted his life to in order to go forward. Another interesting fact: this project was opposed by Nicole Thricin, who seemed to be working towards getting Cinema Leone historic landmark status. It looked like a good motive for murder for anyone who happened to be betting all their chips on the project coming through. Something about the appearance of Thricin's name in the record started nagging at me. I couldn't put my finger on it, though, so I shoved it aside. If it was important enough, it'd come back to me.

On the surface, Project Orion looked about the same as all the other condo proposals that Mr. Nicholls had spent his last year turning down. Sure, maybe it was a bit ritzier than the others—the sketches and blueprints looked like it stole most of its design ideas from ancient Greece—but still ...

My thoughts stopped cold. Ancient Greece! Hermes would surely still have an intimate connection with the old country, even after all these centuries of slumming with us mere mortals ... was this how he knew what I was up against? He had intimated that he could not talk to me because of the old compact he had with Aurelian, but could the real reason be that he was involved?

I stared at the name of the project, Orion ... It was one of the better-known constellations but not one of the better-known stories from Hermes' heyday. Like everybody who's ever done a basic astronomy class, I knew Orion was a hunter, one of the best. He was also a stupid, arrogant prick who made the all-time mistake of pissing off Hera, step-mom to Hermes. Vengeful bitch that she was, Hera sent a scorpion to deal with him. Orion was too good a hunter not to see it, however, and squash it ... but not before Little Poison Tail had his own fatal say.

After that, for reasons never explained, Orion went on to become a constellation of stars. Hera made sure her tiny assassin got the same honor and it, in turn, became the constellation Scorpio. The rest of Olympus didn't take any chances, though. The two constellations were sent to opposite ends of the sky.

Armed with my new information, I dug back through the piles of paper. It didn't take long to find the victims' final connections through the phone records. Mr. Nicholls had been in regular contact with Mrs. Thricin right up to two days before his death. Our intrepid councilwoman had also been pretty chatty with the late Mr. Mallory on a near-daily basis. Add in the emails that had been traded back and forth between all three parties, and it was obvious that they were working night and day to keep that old movie house standing.

But it was obvious from the tone of the emails that they were fighting a losing battle. Mr. Nicholls had suggested that he could find a way to get some reinforcements, but he was vague about what kind he meant. Since there was nothing else in the emails that could tell me what he was talking about, I went back to the phone records.

By the time I put down the papers, I realized that it was half-past noon. Right on cue, my stomach started growling. With all the shit that'd been thrown my way in the last three days, I hadn't had time to get groceries. Hells, I couldn't even remember when I had my last real meal. It was a good thing I knew a decent greasy spoon just around the corner.

I was just putting my shoes on when that nagging feeling told me why it was bugging me in the first place. Zian had given me a complete work-up on all three people attacked: Mallory, Nicholls, and Thricin. But ... he'd given me that information just *before* the Thricins were home-invaded by Grizzly Adams' psycho Norse cousin. That was the real reason why his dad had paid him an unfriendly call. Insider trading is frowned on by more than just the FCC in that world.

That led to another unwelcome thought ... the tip from Ramirez that had put me on the scene just when the shit was hitting the fan. "You didn't hear this from me." Maybe it was someone's way of saying that the voice on the other end wasn't Ramirez at all. I'd been too wiped by the fight with the Berserker to put it all together before this. Now I recollected that Ramirez had been as surprised as the rest of her fellow cops about the attack, never mind the fact that I was there. Trust me, if she was that good an actress she wouldn't be working for a prick like Morgan. So who tipped me off?

The more I thought about it, the more my gut burned from the lack of food. The hell with it ... I needed to get down to the Tombs for a bite to eat if I wanted a head clear enough to do this job.

9

FATHERLY ADVICE

The Tombs has been around since the early 1980s. Everybody I've ever talked to about it tells the same story. One day, the place was just a vacant lot with a For Sale sign in front of it, the apartment building that had been there having long since become a victim of the wrecking ball. The next, a magnificent old school diner out of Dash Hammett appeared seemingly from nowhere like a mutant vegetable, doors open for business. It even had a catchy slogan: "Where hunger goes to die."

Cold City dirties up every building within the city limits eventually, except for the Tombs. Even now, the outside was all gunmetal chrome and neon lights, a train car from the Orient Express that took an inter-dimensional detour through Vegas. The inside was all posh seating, bar stools, black-and-white checkerboard floors, and ceiling fans. No matter what time of year, the inside always provided its customers relief from the elements. During summer, the chill was just enough to take the edge off the heat. During not-summer, you'd swear you were around a campfire. Add to that the novelty of it being squashed between two towering apartment complexes and word about the place was guaranteed to get around.

The place did brisk business in any given week, but it wasn't a hangout joint. It was your classic diner pattern: full during regular meal hours and dead—as I should have been by now—in between. I was catching the tail end of the lunch hour when I walked in the front door.

The last batch of customers was finishing up their meals as I went to sit in my booth. I mean, other people sit in it when I'm not around, but I like to think of it as mine. Somehow, it always winds up being empty every time I come in the door. That's why I have meetings with some of my clients here, like the Townsends when they asked me to grab Marion from that Mafiosi piece of shit Vitorini.

I heard barked instructions in Cherokee behind the counter—another rare treat exclusive to the Tombs. More than English is spoken in Cold City these days. Spanish, of course, but there's also been a recent increase in less typical native tongues like Indonesian, Croatian, and Korean. Contrast that with any language originally spoken by what we call Native Americans these days—they're near extinct. Maybe because they'd had a written language to go with it, Cherokee is one of the few that has survived into modern times, and the owner makes a point of making sure all his employees know it. I'd even heard one or two of them talk about how he'd insisted on teaching them how to read the written version.

Speaking of the owner, the man himself came out from

the back with one of his typical big grins on his cracked leather face and a glass of water for me. We shook hands, and then he set the glass down on the table and himself in the seat opposite. The stained whites of his chef's outfit were a stark contrast to the dark bronzed tan of his skin.

"Bell," he said with that always hard-to-place accent, "how are you, son?"

"Been a rough three days, Tommy," I said with a sigh.

"So I heard." Tommy ran a gnarled hand through his thick, still-black hair. "A bunch of flowers giving their lives so that you might live ..."

"God, is anybody going to let that one go?" I snapped. "It's not like I get to choose what happens when my death insurance kicks in."

Tommy gave me one of his hearty chuckles, which always sounded about an octave higher than his normal speaking voice. "Not trying to give you grief, son ... well, maybe a little. You need to think about investing in a Shiatsu massage sometime. You get way too tense."

"Consider the way I live, Tommy," I said, picking up the glass of water. "You blame me?"

Tommy's face darkened a bit as he shook his head. For all his good-natured clowning, this old man—nobody seemed to know how old—was as tapped into the world *she* had thrust me into as anyone in Cold City. What Zian was to raw data metrics, Tommy was to street contacts. Everybody knew him, respected him, and even hired him to do a discreet job or two. I had enough sense never to pry into that last part, by the way.

"Hear you had a bad one last night," Tommy said, suddenly serious. "A man of the bare shark."

"Huh?" I grunted in confusion as I sipped from the glass.

"What you call a Berserker," Tommy explained. "Subtle as a cannon, mean as a rattlesnake ... you're lucky to be alive."

"If I hadn't been there, he would have gotten his third kill that I know about."

"So you're on a case?"

I hummed in the affirmative as I took a deeper pull from the glass.

"You getting paid?" Tommy asked.

I put the glass down. "It's ... not that kind of case."

Tommy gave me a disgusted groan as he leaned his head back and looked upwards. My guess was that he was asking the Great Spirit or whoever why I had to be so bad at business.

"So this one's for *her*," Tommy said, the disgust in his voice getting even stronger.

"Yeah, well, Tommy, it's like this," I said, sounding a bit more defensive than I would have liked. "For the amazing privilege of having guns jam in my face and flowers break otherwise fatal falls, I have to do this. I buck, she reminds me who's the boss."

"No wonder you and Ramirez can never stay in the same bed for too long," Tommy murmured.

"What was that, Pops?" I asked, using the nickname to signal to him that I didn't appreciate him prying into that part of my life.

"Nothing worth repeating, Bell," Tommy responded, the bemused grin returning to his face. "But you'd think that someone with *her* connections would hook you up with a sweet pile of cash every once in a while."

"Hey, she gave me the car."

"That was for her, not you." Tommy got up. "Okay, I've fussed over you enough for now. Want your usual?"

"You know it," I said. My usual is a burger done Philly-Cheese-sandwich style with salt-and-pepper fries. "Salad for an appetizer too much to ask?"

"Since when? This kid I just hired, he's got a healthy alternative to Italian dressing I'd like to try on you."

I frowned. Before Tommy unleashed a new culinary feature on the public, he always tried it out on me first. Sometimes it was great, like that fantastic soy burger that had been made up to taste like turkey. Sometimes, however, it was an ordeal, like that ungodly blend of different juices that Tommy had the gall to call a drink. But considering he ran a tab for me between paydays, it was a small price to pay ... some days.

The dressing that the kid in his kitchen had whipped up qualified as one of the great ideas. Tommy just gave me a knowing chuckle when I told him as much.

"All right, now that you've had time to settle in, you ready to tell me why you dropped by today?" Tommy asked finally after he had finished chuckling and sat down opposite me once more.

"The food, of course," I said with a shrug before stabbing a tomato slice with my fork.

"If that was all you wanted, McDonald's drive-in could have handled that problem," he pointed out.

"C'mon, Tommy. The corporate board of McDonald's would sacrifice several quarts of human blood to get what you have."

Tommy shot me a stern look. "If you're done with the suck-up routine ..."

I sighed. "Sorry, Tommy. I don't mean any—"

"You're just being you, Bell," Tommy told me with an offhand wave. "But goddamn if it ain't like pulling teeth to get you to tell me how I can help you."

There was a reason for that. Tommy was one of the few people in my life who was constant, steady, and somebody I knew would help me out of a jam if it got too hot. But I never wanted to rely too much on him. There was always a fear in the back of my mind that one day I'd ask for too much ... and that would be that.

What I said to him was, "I need to arrange a meet with Vitorini."

"Holy shit," Tommy said as he buried his face in his hands. It was a good ten seconds before he came up again. "You take away a payday from him, you kill three of his people, and now you need to talk to that little Frank Nitti wannabe?"

Between bites of salad, I said, "Pretty much, yeah. It's to do with the case. I think he might know something that could help me."

"Sure," Tommy said, sounding less than convinced. "And maybe I might know what tomorrow's winning lottery numbers are. C'mon, kid, isn't there another angle that doesn't involve somebody who would like to test your death insurance to the max?"

"Know Cinema Leone?"

"Yeah," Tommy said, his voice warming back up. "I got fond memories of that from-dusk-till-dawn Hitchcock marathon that ran there last summer. Shame what happened to Old Man Nicholls ..." Then he blinked and realized. "By the Great Spirit ... he's part of your case, isn't he?"

"Yeah. Far as I can tell, he was the first one to get done by the Berserker."

Tommy let out a breath as I finished off my salad. "And you're sure that it's not random?"

"Looked that way at first, but no," I confirmed, wiping my mouth. "This Jason Voorhees clone is working from a hit list, and it's got something to do with that old movie house."

Tommy leaned back in his seat and hmmed.

"That means you know something I don't?" I asked, pushing my salad bowl away.

"No, it means 'hmm'." Tommy got up again. "I can do a little poking around to see what's been going on with the cinema. But if you want to get close to Vitorini again, you're going to have to ask somebody else."

"Anybody you'd recommend?"

"De Soto."

I felt the room turn into a meat locker at the name. "No, no, no, no—"

"Ah–ah," Tommy said, wagging a finger at me. "You said you wanted to arrange a meet with Vito, that's how you do it. And it's not like De Soto won't make you pay for the privilege, right?"

I didn't have any snappy comebacks to that. When the subject of Ramon De Soto came up, my brain went into fight-or-flight mode.

Tommy sniffed the air. "That burger oughta be done by now. You are getting money for the Townsend job, right?"

"Huh? Oh," I said, shaking myself out of my fear, "yeah,

the Townsends should pay me the rest in a couple of days. I'll settle the tab then."

Tommy nodded and went to get my food. Meanwhile, the ice ball forming in my stomach was telling me that I might want to appreciate every bite of the food coming my way.

10

NO GOOD DEED

T he Tombs wasn't the only place I needed to go to that day. While it was still daylight, I figured a return visit to the Thricin family would be in order. Sure, they would still be pretty shaken up from last night, but maybe somebody saw something which could help put me on the track of which player I was dealing with on the other side of the chessboard.

Imagine my surprise when I saw a couple of black-and-whites in front of the house as I walked up to it. I had my Stingray stashed at a Walgreens three blocks away. The plan had been for me to inquire after the family and see what kind of info I could get for my "client." That plan just got a lot more complicated with the uniforms in the picture. There was no way word of what I was about to do wouldn't get back to Morgan.

"Just happened to be driving by," a familiar voice said behind me. "Really?"

Ramirez was standing right behind me with her arms

crossed across her rather attention-grabbing chest and tapping her foot on the sidewalk. She looked like a fed-up housewife who'd caught her husband cheating on his diet plan.

"Nice to see you too, Mel," I said, the sarcasm running heavy in my voice. "Yeah, I'm feeling a lot better today, thanks for asking. Good to hear you've had a great morning too."

Ramirez just gave me a disgusted sigh and looked pointedly aside. I tried to ignore how cute that made her look.

"Isn't this a bit of overkill for a random animal attack?" I asked, waving my hand towards the prowl cars.

"That's the thing about live witnesses," Ramirez said, uncrossing her arms. "They tend to contradict whatever pet theory you might have with fresh details."

"What kind of fresh details?"

"*Madre de Dios!*" Ramirez spat out, throwing up her hands in disgust. "Do the words 'ongoing police investigation' mean anything to you, Bell?"

"Yeah," I said without missing a beat, "they tell me how soon I'll have to deal with a prick like Morgan again."

"Don't start," she warned, jabbing her forefinger in my face. "Morgan wants to throw your lying ass into jail on obstruction of justice charges. I had to do a lot of talking to make sure that didn't happen first thing this morning."

"So I can expect him bright and early tomorrow?" I asked, inching my way towards the house.

Ramirez knew enough of my tricks to put herself between me and where I wanted to go. "No, you can agree to be interviewed by yours truly. After all, in the heat of the moment, maybe you forgot a few details that your mind has just now got around to telling you about."

I sighed and thought about it. It'd be nice to have one less excuse for Morgan to lock me up. On the other hand, if this was now an official attempted murder investigation, I wasn't likely to get a better chance than this to talk to the Thricins.

"Tell you what," I said. "Give me a chance to talk to Mrs. Thricin alone, and I'll sit for that interview right after I get done."

"And why would I do that again?" Ramirez countered, her eyes narrowing in suspicion.

"Maybe she's willing to tell the guy who saved her life something she didn't want to share with the guys who got there after the party."

I could almost hear the wheels turning in Ramirez's head. They were busy weighing the possibility of finding out something useful against the fact that I was a lying, scheming son of a bitch with his own agenda.

"I sit in on the interview you have with Mrs. Thricin," she said at last. "Any leads you get from what she says, you share them with me. I find out that you kept one piece of critical info from the department, I'll lock you up myself."

That was as straight a deal as I was going to get. I nodded.

I'd gotten halfway through my greeting when Nicole Thricin gave me a hug. I suffered awkwardly through it until she broke away and apologized. After that, she invited us in and offered us coffee. We both took her up on it.

"As you can imagine, I'm taking the day off after last night's ordeal," she said as she handed us our mugs. "I'll have a pile of work waiting on my desk tomorrow morning, but ..."

She was different from the frightened woman I'd met the night of the attack. Today, she stood tall in a light pink designer blouse; her straightened hair was brushed into a perfect bob, and her makeup was neatly and firmly applied.

She sighed a bit before going on. "You know, it's a shame that it takes something like ... *this* ... to appreciate your regular life."

"What about your kids?" I asked.

"I talked it over with Mark last night," Nicole said with a wistful expression. "We decided that it'd be best if they gave school a try today. Sure, they'll tell a lot of wild stories about last night maybe but ..."

"You want them to know that the world still works," Ramirez said in a gentle tone.

Nicole gave her a quick nod. "Yes, Officer, that's it. I never want them to think that something like what we went through is ... normal."

"I know you've been over this with the authorities quite a few times already," I broke in, "but I was hoping you could tell me something more about what happened last night."

Nicole's expression tightened. She looked reluctant to say anything.

"I was face to face with that animal, Mrs. Thricin," I added, stretching out a gentle hand turned palm-down. "I just want to make sure that it never comes back to your house again."

A taut but grateful smile appeared on her face at that. Then she gave me a more definite nod. "It was just an ordinary night for us at the start. We were watching that new version of *Alice In Wonderland* when there was a knock on the door." She frowned. "Come to think of it, those knocks were quite a bit heavier than what you'd usually expect ... almost like someone was trying to bash through the door with their fist."

"So you answered the door," Ramirez said. "And ...?"

"I couldn't describe the man who was on the other side," Nicole went on. "Not because of what happened next, you understand. It's just that he was so ... ordinary-looking. You might remember, Officer, that I had a great deal of trouble describing him for your sketch artist this morning."

Ramirez nodded.

I leaned forward. "Were there any details about the man that stuck out? What was he wearing? Did he have a vehicle of some kind?"

"He was dressed like a deliveryman, but I didn't see any kind of vehicle," Nicole said, tapping her chin in thought. "Then again, I thought they looked like some kind of auto mechanic's coveralls at the time, so maybe I'm misremembering it altogether."

Or maybe our would-be everything-but-the-kitchen-sink hitter was using low-quality Glitter that didn't give a consistent-enough camouflage to maintain the human illusion up close. Worth remembering for later.

"Did he say anything?" Ramirez asked.

"Like I said, Officer," Nicole responded, her hands starting to shake a bit, "he only had one thing to say—'You.' That's when ..." She suppressed a shudder. "That's when he tried to barge his way into the house."

"Tried?" I asked.

"I always carry a stun gun with me, even at home," she explained. "Political life can be a bit ... rough, and my husband isn't always in town. I jabbed it dead center in his chest as he moved forward and ..." She cleared her throat. "I had to use it once before, and they just went down like a sack of potatoes. Couldn't get up either. But this time ... I could tell it hurt him because he fell back a couple of steps. But then his eyes got this ... fire in them. I got so scared, I slammed the door in his face and locked it."

"And that's when he knocked down the door," Ramirez said.

"Not straightaway," Nicole corrected her. "It was a stout door with an iron frame. Anyone else trying to knock it down would have been breaking their own bones instead. It gave me enough time for me to get my kids and reach my phone to dial 911."

"Did you have the phone on you when you got to the shed?" I asked.

"It ... it slipped right out of my fingers when that ... that thing burst into my house," Nicole told me. "Would you believe that it managed to—"

"Wait," Ramirez said, raising a hand. "Every time you get to this part of your story, you always describe your assailant as a 'thing' rather than a 'man.'"

"I know, I know," Nicole exclaimed in exasperation. "Obviously it was the same person I saw at the door, but I swear it was a ... a thing. You said to tell you the story how I remember it; that's how!"

"We don't mean to upset you, Mrs. Thricin," I interrupted, cursing Ramirez for pushing too hard. The story made sense to me, but I couldn't explain to the good sergeant that the taser shot must have interrupted the Glitter flow and allowed Nicole a good look at the Berserker. "We're just trying to be clear on details. Would I be right in saying that this is the part where you and your kids fled to the shed?"

"With that monster right on our heels," Nicole confirmed. "It was a minor miracle that it didn't take down that door like it had the front one. You ... you pretty much know the rest, Mr. Vale."

Did I ever. "Okay, thank you for agreeing to speak with me, Mrs. Thricin."

Nicole gave a short bark that didn't pretend to be a laugh as we all got up. "I'm the one who should be thanking you, Mr. Vale ... for the lives of my children, if nothing else."

"Just glad I got here in time," I said, letting the stone truth shine through.

"I believe you said that you were a private investigator, Mr. Vale?" Nicole asked as we approached the shattered front door.

Ramirez gave me a look, but I ignored her. "Yes, ma'am, I am."

"If I'm not out of bounds for doing so ... I'd like to retain you," Nicole went on. "May I ask what your rates are?"

"Typically, they're eighty dollars a day plus expenses," I said as we paused in the doorway. I did my best to disregard the burning stare directed towards the back of my neck by Ramirez.

"If you can give me an additional day, would a five-hundred-dollar retainer be adequate for you to work for me?"

"Mrs. Thricin, with all due respect," Ramirez protested, suppressed panic cracking through her voice, "the department takes your safety and that of your family very seriously—"

"While I don't doubt that for a moment, Officer," Mrs.

Thricin conceded, "the fact remains that your department was too far away to help me last night. Therefore, having Mr. Vale supplement your efforts makes sense, doesn't it?"

Ramirez gave me a look that I knew too well. She gave it to me whenever she thought I'd pulled a fast one on her.

To give myself some cover, I gave Nicole a chance to change her mind. "Are you certain that you want me to look into this for you, Mrs. Thricin? We both know that we're dealing with a dangerous customer."

"I'd much rather you find out who did this before he finds us again," Mrs. Thricin said, clasping my hands with her own.

What could I say other than "Yes"?

Ramirez, on the other hand, had a lot to say as soon as we were out of earshot of the lady of the house. Most of it was in Spanish and, judging from her tone, none of it was complimentary.

"You planned this!" she accused me as soon as she had run out of vile things to call me. "A little face time with the *Señora,* and suddenly, Bellamy Vale's current financial situation improves!"

"Look, I'm as shocked as you are," I said, meaning every word of it. "If you and the rest of the boys and girls in blue hadn't turned up, I'd have become one with the wallpaper. So Mrs. Thricin asking me to find that beast again, despite the fact that I've proven to be lousy in a fight against him, was the last thing I had in mind."

"I notice you didn't take the time and trouble to point all this out to your new client," Ramirez said, gesturing towards the house.

"Money's money," I said. "I'm sure hers will spend just as well as anybody's."

"Ahh, *cabrón!*" Ramirez muttered. "This case makes no sense: first a wolf, now a man and an animal ..."

We didn't say anything else to each other as we walked back to her car on the corner. By the time we reached it, her mood had changed. "Look, Bell ... just promise me that you won't go out of your way to get yourself killed by this animal. We fight, sure, but that doesn't mean that I want to see you be my next homicide investigation."

"Can you promise me not to tell Morgan about how Mrs. Thricin's my new client?"

"Well, seeing as I was already never going to mention how you talked me into granting you your own personal interview with Mrs. Thricin in the first place ..."

"Yeah," I said with a nod. There was no upside for her in telling Morgan anything other than the fact that I had come by for a visit. He'd be suspicious, but there'd be nothing he could prove without pissing off a councilwoman.

"Guess we should get that interview out of the way," I said.

Ramirez pulled out her smartphone. "Give me a minute to remember how to get this thing to record, and we'll be out of each other's hair for the day."

11

PRIME SUSPECT

It was getting close to sundown by the time I wrapped things up with Ramirez. I had her drop me off at a bus stop about a block from the Walgreens. A quick hike later, I was back behind the wheel of my Stingray. I had a lot to think about during the ride home.

One thing the texts and my own information agreed on: Berserkers don't do subtle. They were the Big Bad Wolf a real long time before the Big Bad Wolf came knocking on Grandma's door. Then again, maybe that wasn't the right metaphor. Red Riding Hood's nemesis was smart enough to eat and impersonate her grandma before making his play. This Berserker was more like a mugger—smash and grab and squash. His first victims had been done on public streets. Yet with Mrs. Thricin, he had made a home invasion play that deviated from the established MO. Why the big change?

I could understand it if he did it to throw someone tracking him off his trail. Brutal doesn't mean stupid. But he'd had a good cover with the rogue-wolf story that the authorities had bought before this last attack. Surely taking down a member of the council out in the open wasn't that much more complicated than doing it to an old theater owner or city worker. So, yeah, maybe somebody was tracking him before I caught his scent ... somebody who had decided to slip me a hint by impersonating Ramirez.

Could it have been Hermes? He had both the info and the means to pull it off. But seeing at how pissed he had got at Zian for giving me the edge on the Thricins, that didn't seem to fit either. My guess was that he'd stopped having to answer to anybody a long time ago. Why bother pulling an act on my behalf?

Then there was the Glitter as described by Nicole Thricin. Like anything else, quality on Glitter varies for any number of reasons: source material, manufacture, individual components in the recipes used to make it. Valhalla, I knew, had access to a decent supply of the good stuff, yet here was this guy walking around with stuff that kept his form shifting like the fog closing in around me. It was easy enough to rule out a good many of the major players on the basis of that alone. Somebody had gone to the trouble of getting this man-monster to my side of the border, somebody with either enough pull or the right access to get him here with what he needed to do the job.

I did what I could not to look annoyed when I saw *her* leaning against the side of my apartment building, smoking a cigarette in a very long holder. Tonight she was dressed in a short leather top that stopped well above her rib cage, matching leather skirt, and fishnets with heels. Her hair was cropped into a bob, with black eyeliner, red lipstick, and a pale complexion completing the package. She looked like a

1920s flapper who had got back from a fashion expedition through Hot Topic.

"I'm working on it," was all I said as I killed the Stingray's engine.

"I am not here for that," she replied as she walked up to the driver's side door. "You went somewhere the other night where you were not supposed to be."

"Yeah, I kind of got that impression," I said, shuddering at the memory. "He got anything to do with what I'm looking into?"

She ignored the question. "It is because you are mine that you managed to walk away from that. Never be so foolish as to attempt what you did again."

"Don't call us, we'll call you—got it," I snapped, my irritation getting the better of my good sense. "Now if you're done with the lectures, I'd like to go back to the job you wanted me to get done."

"You're going to see De Soto," she remarked as I got out. It wasn't a question.

"Yeah. Tommy wouldn't play ball on something so—"

My head was against the hood of my car before I even knew what was going on. No black eyeballs tonight, but there was a fire that surged through them as she pinned me by the throat.

"How truly stupid are you?" she asked in amazement. "De Soto is an amoral monster who knows far too much and gets away with even more."

I tried answering, but it's hard to talk when your trachea is being squeezed. I pointed to my throat as I made choking noises. With a look of utter disgust, she released me, and I slid down the hood to the ground.

After a couple of seconds of coughing, I managed to find my voice. "Yeah ... huhh ... I know it's dangerous. But for some reason, the guy has taken a liking to me. Not enough to put his neck out for me, sure, but he's the only guy I know who can make something I need done happen."

"It will not be free," she observed, unimpressed. "Sacrifice runs in his blood."

"Yeah, but never anything you can't pay and walk away from after," I said, getting up. "He's better than his ancestors were."

"He is as his ancestors were," she contradicted me. "The only true difference is that he lets most of his victims live."

I rounded on her to deliver a stinging retort, but once again found myself staring at empty air.

"Good talk," I muttered as I went inside.

There was no food in the house, but I did have a quart of milk in the fridge. I treated myself to a swig of that and then went digging through my books. Today had been easier than yesterday and especially the day before yesterday, but it had still been a long way from easy. And the fact that I was going to visit De Soto while he was holding court at his club in a few hours looked likely to ratchet the ugly factor up a few notches.

12

SMOKE & MIRRORS

S moke & Mirrors had been open for a couple of hours, but the line outside it already stretched around the block. Cold City has its share of nightclubs but nothing like this place. While the exterior is your run-of-the-mill club façade, the interior is a mixture of ancient Central American architecture, most prominently Aztec. The bar is stocked with every form of liquor known to man, along with a few specials that you have to know the right people to ask for. There have been whispers about in-house designer drugs that you can score nowhere else, pit fights with heavy gambling action, and a connection to a brothel where the customer's sexual tastes are always right, whatever they happen to be.

Not that I've ever tried to verify any of those rumors. Sticking your nose in Ramon De Soto's business can shorten your life span down to seconds ... and that's if he's in a good mood. A few years ago, his business and my business crossed paths, and I managed to be one of the few people he ever let live to tell the tale. I'd done an accidental service for him that was so big that he had left a standing offer for me to come to him with any problem I might have. This would be the first time I'd be taking him up on that.

I ignored the line and went right up to the front door. A doorman with a bald head and mirror shades held up a hand as big as my chest to stop me.

"Back of the line, sir," he rumbled, making it clear it wasn't a request.

"I need to see *El Jefe*," I replied. "That's the reason I'm here."

"Back of the line, sir," the doorman repeated.

Shrugging my hands in my pockets, I complied and prepared myself for a long wait.

I was just about to gain entrance when I heard a female yelp right behind the walk-in vault door. Everyone's eyes turned to the source of the noise as the door opened. After all, it's not every night that you see a six-foot-plus Amazon carrying a pretty girl over her head.

The Amazon in question was of Latino stock, somewhere in her forties, with a pretty enough face to pass for younger. She was wearing a sheer crimson dress with spaghetti straps that matched her lipstick. Her bronzed skin seemed to match the color of her permed, curly hair in the dim light. But you noticed those details afterwards. The first thing you saw and couldn't quite believe was her muscles. They bulged out from her arms like a mass of coiled cables, as mesmerizing to watch as a cobra preparing to strike. She looked like a cross between the She-Hulk and Sofia Vergara.

"I caught this little mouse trying to sneak in," she told the doorman with a hint of reproach, her mid-alto voice carrying no trace of an accent.

Having said that, she dumped the girl she was carrying in my general direction. The former human cargo landed on top of me hard. I shook my head a couple of times before I realized whose face I was staring at: Ms. Kennedy. How she thought she could sneak into a club like this with her face plastered all over television on a regular basis would take a better detective than me to figure out.

The Amazon grabbed Kennedy by the hair and pulled back her head. Bending down to whisper in her ear, the Amazon told her in a low voice, "The next time I catch you in here, mouse, prepare to be eaten."

Then she lifted Kennedy back onto her feet. The crowd howled with laughter as the humiliated reporter ran off into the night.

The Amazon then turned her attention to me and offered me a more conventional hand up. My impression of her strength hadn't been wrong—she lifted me off the ground like I was a bag of groceries.

"I must apologize for using you as an airbag, *Señor*," she said in a much kinder tone.

"This man wanted to speak with your husband, Mrs. De Soto," the doorman said.

"*Si?*" she asked, raising an eyebrow at the bodyguard then at me. "And what business have you with my husband?"

"I'm ... Bellamy Vale, Mrs. De Soto," I explained, my mind still reeling at the extraordinary figure in front of me. "Your husband and I—"

"Ah, of course—*Señor* Vale," she said, laying a hand

softly on my shoulder. "Ramon speaks highly of you. Won't you come in?"

With a last death stare of disapproval to the doorman, she herded me into the club proper.

That architecture I mentioned before was hard to make out in the dim lighting of the club. As well as the colored lights and strobes playing on the usual party crowd, wall mirrors and smoke machines were doing their bit to add to the atmosphere. The easiest place to spot any Aztec touches was the DJ's booth, which was made up like a mini-Mayan pyramid. Right then, the DJ was blasting out a techno track via wall speakers in Too-Loud-Around-Sound. The sheer volume near deafened me; I could hear nothing else. I saw hearing aids in a lot of these kids' futures.

Even with all the activity and noise, everybody gave Mrs. De Soto a lot of room. Her size and poise were enough to intimidate even the most strung-out raver. I walked in her shadow, knowing that nobody would even know I was there with her around.

We got to the back right booth of the club, where the noise was muted enough to have a regular conversation without having to shout at the top of your lungs. Bodyguards flanked it on either side, looking like Secret Service men on steroids. They moved aside for Mrs. De Soto just like the clubbers had. Somebody rose from the shadows of the booth to give her a deep kiss.

Stepping into the light was a ruggedly handsome guy somewhere in his late forties. His black hair was styled and gelled in a 1950s pompadour, while his clothes were the cutting edge of fashion and looked more suitable for a senior vice-president than the most feared criminal overlord in the city. His dark eyes caught sight of me as he broke off kissing his wife. The bright, even smile that creased his lips didn't thaw out the cold in those eyes one iota.

"*Mi amigo!*" he exclaimed, giving me a hug and a kiss on the cheek. "How are you?"

"I'm good, Mr. De Soto," I replied. "Better than I've been in a couple of days anyhow."

He patted my shoulder twice. "Ramon, *mi amigo*, Ramon ... how many times must I tell you that there need be no formalities between us?"

"It speaks well of him that his first instinct is politeness, Ramon," his wife said as she took her seat. "Too many *Norteamericanos* forget that critical survival skill."

The way she said it made me glad that all that had happened to Kennedy was that she was thrown out.

"Ah, you have never met my wife Estella, have you?" De Soto asked as he draped an arm around my shoulder.

"Never even knew you were married," I admitted, as the wall of bodyguards closed behind me.

"In our hearts since we were eight," Mrs. De Soto said, shaking my hand with a firm but friendly grip. "Legally for slightly less long."

Her husband gave a hearty laugh and steered me to a seat. Then he sat beside his wife, who gave him an affectionate sideways hug and a nibble at his ear.

"One unusual thing about Mr. Vale," she said as she looked at me again. "Despite his profession, he has made no effort to inquire as to how a mere woman acquired my quite impressive musculature."

"Chalk up my lack of curiosity to that critical survival skill you mentioned before, Mrs. De Soto," I told her.

This provoked a huge laugh from both the De Sotos, like I'd told the best joke of the night. It made me wonder if an audience with Lucifer would make me as uneasy as I was beginning to feel.

"I'm afraid this ain't a social visit, Ramon," I said with a sigh.

"So I would assume," he acknowledged. "Please speak freely."

"You heard about what went down with Vito a couple of days ago?"

Mrs. De Soto broke in before her husband could answer. "I remember going over to that *puta's* place and reminding him why he wound up having to give up all his profits for the last month." She all but spat the reply.

I did a double-take.

"A true marriage shares everything, Bellamy," Ramon explained. "In our case, part of that sharing is in power. I oversee the overall picture while mi *corazón* Estella handles the day-to-day."

"So losing all his profits was the reason why he kidnapped that girl in the first place?" I asked.

"No, he took that poor *niña* from her home to make himself feel strong," Mrs. De Soto said, the hate coming off her in palpable waves. "The money was a bonus. It is only by my husband's continuing grace that the *bastardo* continues to walk this earth."

"Estella, please," De Soto said, rubbing his wife's left forearm. "You are frightening our guest."

"No, it's all right," I assured them, glad that he'd picked up on that. "It's just ... Vitorini may know something I need to know myself."

"For a case?"

I nodded. "It might ... cross into some private areas. I'd ask him directly, but after what I've done—"

"Say no more," De Soto said, holding up a hand. "A conference will be arranged where you two may speak privately."

"However," his wife put in, "we cannot guarantee your safety at this conference."

I glanced at De Soto.

"Sadly, she is right, *mi amigo*," he said with a shrug. "However much we despise Vito's practices of late, he is a member of our organization. To favor an outsider over one of our own sends ... the wrong type of message."

His wife looked thoughtful. "Nevertheless, Ramon, as Vitorini is an utter and complete piece of shit and *Señor* Vale an old friend, I believe that we may be able to come to ... an arrangement."

Her husband opened his mouth to speak and then closed it. Another easy smile climbed back onto his face. "The changeling?"

At his wife's nod, De Soto looked at me. "How would you feel about doing a small but vital job for me, Bellamy?"

"Depends on the job," I said with uncertainty.

"It will be well within your skill set to accomplish," he assured me. "After all, one does not expect a plumber to know how to build a complete house."

"Perhaps part of a house," Mrs. De Soto joked. "But we jest when we should be explaining what we wish of our dear friend."

De Soto pursed his lips. "We have reason to believe that

some of our more ... exotic mixtures are being sold outside the purview of this club, which is forbidden."

"Could the dealer be taking it from the club's own supply?" I asked.

"The very first thing we thought of, but no," Mrs. Do Soto answered. "Therefore, the substances are being made elsewhere, and the raw materials are somehow being supplied from Atzlan, impossible though that may sound."

"Not really," I said, remembering that frustrating game of phone tag I'd played at the start of this case. If a Berserker could cross the boundary with Valhalla, why couldn't somebody else be getting controlled substances from the Aztec part of Alterum Mundum?

"The dealer has a contact he has cultivated among the earthbound Arcadian court," De Soto confided. "All we know is that this contact is a faerie changeling. Beyond that, we have no further details, not even gender."

"So my job is to find them, ID them, and tell you where they are?" I asked.

"You do catch on quite quickly, Señor Vale," Mrs. De Soto teased as her husband slid out of the booth so that she could do the same. "We both realize what a difficult task we are asking of you, but still ..."

She ended the thought with a shrug as she rose to her feet. That's when I noticed that she was wearing flats.

"Nor do we expect you to take such risk without financial compensation," De Soto added. "Would five hundred dollars be an adequate start to this task?"

"I wouldn't say no," I said.

"Are you, therefore, saying 'yes'?" Mrs. De Soto asked, leaning down so close that her top exposed her breasts.

Doing my best to ignore them, I nodded. "Yeah."

Mrs. De Soto clasped my head in both hands and gave me a kiss to the forehead. *"Bueno."*

The bodyguards parted one more time as she went out onto the dance floor.

"Look, Ramon, no disrespect," I said, choosing my words very carefully, "but your wife seems ..."

"A bit flirtatious? *Si*, she often is with those she takes a liking to."

"I'm a little surprised that she's this much a part of your world."

De Soto shrugged. "Too many men in my profession have the wrong ideas about the fairer sex. To them, women are arm candy, easy lays, or wives whom they surround with enough luxury to paper over the blood and sweat of what they do. Estella has never, and would never, consent to being so used."

"Is that a lesson you learned from the family founder?"

"Not so much," he replied. "He demanded that all of his blood seek the truth in all things that we do. These many centuries later, the wisdom of Tezcatlipoca continues to be relevant."

"Well, the truth I'm seeing is that your wife is an extraordinary woman," I told him.

"You honor us both, *amigo*," De Soto said with a half-bow from his seat. "Now, I must insist you have something to eat. No sense in beginning your work on an empty stomach, is there?"

I nodded and hoped that my meal would come from something I would have recognized.

13

A FRIEND IN NEED

I was driving the Stingray home from the club when my phone buzzed. I waited until I came to a traffic light on red before checking it. It was Mr. Townsend, letting me know that my money would be available tomorrow morning, and could I please swing by his office? I would have texted him back, but the light turned green.

Once I started driving again, my mind went back to what I had been thinking about for the rest of the way: changelings. They were Arcadia's dirty little secret, a clear violation of the compact between humans and gods that kept coming up. The Fae had been notorious border-crossers for centuries, and more than a few of them found the time to have kids by us mere mortals. Like any half-and-half heritage, these children grew up being a part of two worlds without belonging in either. But they had keen enough eyes and senses to serve interests operating out of the Alterum Mundum and not just the Conclave.

Most of them weren't any tougher than your average

human, which was a lucky break. But ones like my target made up for it by being twice as clever as your average spy. I was going to need an angle on this if I wanted to find him or her.

Someone was waiting for me in the parking lot when I rolled up. At first, I thought Lady McDeath had come back for another ass-chewing. Then I recognized the disheveled blonde hair and club outfit from earlier ... Kennedy.

Getting out of the car, I asked, "Lose your cameraman on the way here?"

Her answer was a slap to the face that stung my cheek like a whip crack.

I rubbed the tender flesh. "What was that for?"

"For not backing me up at Smoke & Mirrors," Kennedy snapped, the Texan accent bleeding into her usual news-broadcasting voice.

"And I was supposed to know you were there how again?" I queried. "Besides, I wasn't the one trespassing."

Her cute mouth scrunched into a hard pout of disapproval.

"Now that we've gotten the outrage out of the way," I said, "how did you know where I live?"

"You're not Harry Houdini," Kennedy retorted. "A little check through the phone records told me that this is where you hang your hat and run your business."

"Since I'm guessing that you're here because of business, let's get inside already," I suggested. What I didn't say was that I wanted to get her out of there as quickly as possible.

"Don't get any ideas," she snapped as she held up a finger.

"Last thing on my mind, trust me," I told her.

Normally, I'd have offered a drink to a visitor to my place. But since this was anything but normal, I just sat down on the couch and waited for Kennedy to do the same.

"So you want to tell me what you were doing in that club in the first place?" I asked, getting right to it.

The flirtatious smile came back. "I got a ... connection that told me Smoke & Mirrors was worth checking out. Didn't want to stand in line all night, though, so I snuck in through the side door when one of their boys came out for a smoke break. Hadn't been in the place for five minutes when that monster bitch grabbed me and picked me up." She shuddered at the memory. "Can you even call an iron freak like that a woman? I've known guys who work out who didn't have muscles that big. Can't imagine what kind of man would find that attractive."

"Well, seeing as that was the wife of Ramon De Soto who showed you the door, I'd say your imagination needs to open up a little bit," I informed her.

Kennedy's eyes widened. All she knew were allegations about how De Soto made his living. But I imagined what I had told her might change her mind about what kind of men found buffed-out women like Estella appealing.

"Now," I said, pressing on, "if we're done speculating about other people's love lives, how about you tell me—"

I never got to finish my question. A sudden screech of tires in the parking lot below cut it off. The hairs on the back of my neck told me that the vehicle making the noise didn't belong to kids looking for cheap thrills.

I got up and grabbed my Sig from the drawer where I

kept it in the kitchen, and then I moved to lock the front door. Kennedy was getting off the couch herself when we heard the sound of frantic footsteps coming up the stairs to our floor. I didn't recognize the voice as it approached my front door, but there was no mistaking the words: "Oh shit, oh shit, oh shit, oh shit ..."

This repetitive mantra ended in furious knocking at my door. Kennedy shot me an expression that meant, "What the hell, now?"

I took a quick glance out the peephole and distinguished a very disheveled Zian standing on the other side. What was he doing this far from the Indigo? I unlocked and opened the door, and my friend all but leapt inside.

While I was closing it behind him, he turned wild eyes in my direction. "They're after me!"

"Who?" I asked.

"I don't know, but they're maybe thirty seconds behind me!" Zian explained, looking around the apartment for somewhere to hide.

"Who's this?" inquired Kennedy, gesturing towards my favorite hacker.

"A friend who's in serious trouble, it would seem," I replied.

Zian looked like a deer caught in the headlights. I noticed that his eyes had started changing color, darkening to a deep, dark blue, and I cringed. As close as Kennedy was watching him right now, no way she could have missed that.

"How'd it happen, Z?" I asked, moving to block Kennedy's line of sight.

Zian ran a nervous hand through his bleach-blond hair.

"Came out of the club. I was just going on a food run when—"

Shots started banging against my door like a thunderous downpour against a windowpane. Every one of us hit the floor and scrambled behind the couch as the bullets kept coming. That was a lot faster than thirty seconds.

Peeking over the couch, I covered the door with the Sig. The sturdy wood was soaking the impact of the bullets from outside like a sponge, courtesy of Lady McDeath-powered protection over the apartment. I prayed that it would prove sufficient.

"What's going on?" Kennedy yelled over the noise. "Why are they shooting at us? *Who* is shooting at us?"

"No idea," I replied, and that was the goddamn truth.

I heard a thunk outside on the balcony and glanced over my shoulder. Almost at once, I spotted a metal hook, attached to what looked like a rope ladder. Kennedy, who was kneeling closer to the window, had a better view of what was going on out there. "Somebody's trying to scramble in that way," she warned.

"We're five stories up," I said, hoping she wouldn't do anything stupid to put us in danger. I focused my attention back on the front door. "Unless you see Spiderman coming over the balcony railing, I'd say we're safe."

"Tell them that," Kennedy said a moment later.

I glanced back at her and saw that she was pointing outside. Sure enough, there was a goon climbing up the rope ladder to get inside. I wasn't worried; Lady McDeath's protection covered every possible entrance into the flat. But when Kennedy ran over to the sliding glass doors, then I did start worrying.

"Don't!" Zian and I shouted together.

Kennedy's hand kept reaching for the handle. Of course, she had no way of knowing the mistake she was about to make.

"The glass is bulletproof!" I yelled.

She didn't hear a word I said, just pulled a gun out of her purse with one hand while she yanked the door open with the other. The goon was up to her knees when she gave him a couple of hard kicks to the head through the bars of the railing. He howled the whole way down until hitting the ground cut his scream short.

I gave the front door an apprehensive look. Just as I had feared, the stream of bullets was causing significant damage to it. Thanks to Kennedy wanting to play hero, the overall protection of the flat had been weakened to the point where the hit squad outside might get through any minute. At that moment, just to make things interesting, another goon vaulted over the balcony railing and grabbed Kennedy by the wrist. Give her credit for knowing something about self-defense ... she circled her wrist against her attacker's thumb before pointing the gun in her hand at his chest. Three shots center-mass, and he went over the railing, too.

Then, at the worst possible moment, she froze. If she had just come back inside and closed the door behind her, we'd have been all right. But instead, the enormity of what she had just done, shooting a man to death up close, got in the way of her survival instincts.

The shooting stopped. My guess was that they'd exhausted their clips. I heard heavy thuds against the door, like the barbells I sometimes heard my downstairs neighbors drop on the floor when they were done training. It would take longer than blasting their way with bullets, but the end result would be the same: it was just a matter of time before the door came down.

I had to get the flat's protection back up to full strength, or none of us would make it. "Kennedy, get back inside!" I yelled at the reporter.

She looked up at me with a dazed expression on her face.

"Get that hook loose and get back inside!" I repeated.

I was about to order Zian to get out there and help her, when she finally came to her senses and complied with my instructions. Weapon in hand, she bent down to wrench the hook free and then rushed back inside.

"Lock the door," I ordered.

I returned my attention to the front door, weapon ready to fire. The thuds kept coming, amidst loud cursing. Plaster dust, set loose around the hinges, fogged the air. If it were any other door, it would have given way a long time ago already. Mine held on as the seconds ticked by.

Then I heard a sound I never thought I'd be grateful to hear—sirens. Our assailants on the other side of the door appeared to hear them as well, and their pounding ceased abruptly. We heard feet take off down the hallway and hurry back down the stairs.

I checked Zian, who was looking intently at his smartphone. Tapping his shoulder, I pointed at the device.

"Emergency response signal," he explained. "I classed it as Priority One."

"Prowl cars aren't that thick in this part of town," I said.

"Must have been one close," Zian replied. "Gods, that was crazy."

His eyes were almost entirely black by now, and they

looked comically wide in his ashen face. I noticed that his hands had started shaking like he was chilled. He growled as he grabbed ahold of one of them to make it stop.

"Better they're shaking now than when the shit was hitting the fan," I said, giving his shoulder a good squeeze.

I went to check on Kennedy. Her eyes hadn't left the dark shadows that lay on the ground five stories below. She was shaking just as bad as Zian was, and she wore a stunned expression that I knew too well.

"It was you or them," I said. "And you didn't want it to be you."

Kennedy gave me a look and nodded.

I made tea for everyone, and we sat down to wait for the cops.

———

I didn't open the door again until I saw a badge through the peephole. As I had guessed from the pounding, the door had taken a hell of a beating. Some of my neighbors came out in the hallway, wondering aloud what was going on. The uniforms herded them back inside unless they had a statement to give. One of my neighbors across the hall had taken a round that had ricocheted off my door. It was a safe bet that everyone's sleep had been ruined for the night.

Morgan came in after a while, giving me the hard eye. "It's bad enough when you do this sort of thing out on the street, Vale, but this—"

"Hey, I've got no idea what this was about, for once," I protested, holding up my hands. "I'm minding my own business when my friend Zian runs up to my door telling me that there are some people who are after him. Next thing, they're knocking on my door with enough ammo to re-enact the St. Valentine's Day Massacre."

"That your name—Zian?" Morgan asked, giving the hacker a professional once-over.

"Yeah," Zian stuttered, still shaken by the ordeal. "It's actually Zianyon but ..." His voice failed.

Morgan grunted. "Who was chasing you?"

"I don't know, Detective," Zian responded. "I was just coming from the Indigo when I noticed this pair of cars behind me. I made a few moves on the road just to be sure it wasn't my imagination. It wasn't. That's when I came here. Bellamy's been ..." He had to stop for a moment to clear his throat. "Bellamy's been a good friend for a while."

Morgan raised an eyebrow. "If you say so ... okay, go over to the officer and give him your statement."

Zian nodded and did what he was told.

"Okay, that covers him," Morgan said.

He walked over to Kennedy, who had been sitting off to the side and staring at nothing.

"What business did you have with the likes of Bellamy Vale at this time of night, Ms. Kennedy?" Morgan demanded.

She blinked a couple of times before looking at him. Then she glanced at me and moistened her lips. "I was doing a follow-up interview ... on the Townsend kidnapping. Mr. Vale said that this time of night would be the best time to catch him. Since I work the late broadcast shift anyway ..."

I was impressed. Despite being disoriented and in shock, she had managed to feed Morgan a convincing lie about her presence in my flat. She then went on to describe the particulars of how she had killed the two men on the balcony. That made me uneasy for her. Admitting to murder one to a cop like Morgan was like waving a red flag in front of a bull. But then the detective lieutenant surprised me.

"All right, seems like a pretty open-and-shut case of self-defense," he told her. "Just the same, I'll need you to make a statement as soon as you're feeling up to it, okay?"

Kennedy nodded and went back to staring at nothing.

Morgan gestured at me to follow him. We retreated to my much-battered front door.

"I don't think that thing will be much good after all the target practice it's taken," he noted drily.

"I know a guy who can help me with that," I told him. "I'll give him a call in the morning."

"Funny thing," Morgan went on to say, "but from what I've seen of apartment construction, this door ought to be splinters by now. Why do you suppose that is?"

"I upped the security on it when I bought the place," I said, keeping reasonably close to the truth. "The line of work I'm in, I figured it couldn't hurt."

"Sure didn't hurt tonight," Morgan muttered, giving the door an appreciative knock.

"Guess I'll need to make a statement too?"

"You know it ... and you seem more up to it than your guests."

"Sure you don't want to take it yourself—"

Morgan raised a finger to stop me. "Unless you'd like to spend the rest of the night in the drunk tank ... don't push it."

He then pointed me to the officer I should talk to and went back to supervising the scene.

It was close to one in the morning by the time all of our statements were taken. The adrenaline was wearing off, and I was starting to feel sleepy. Still, given what had just happened, I'd have felt as safe sleeping there as I would have in the middle of a minefield. I didn't care if the cops were going to be camping around the place on the off-chance that our attackers had another go. When I brought this possibility up with Zian out in the hallway, he just shrugged.

"Yeah, well ...' he muttered. 'I'd say you could sleep it off at my place but, for all I know, those assholes could be over there waiting for another crack at me."

He gave me the ghost of a smile, and I felt bad for him. Now that the commotion was over, his eyes had regained their regular light blue color, but he was shaken.

"So how 'bout you guys sleep over at mine?" Kennedy offered, coming up to us. "I've got just enough room. Whoever was here ain't going to know about it, and nobody's tried knocking on the door with automatic fire lately." Then she seemed to have second thoughts about the offer. "You will be camping out in the living room, mind you. Either one of you gets the wrong idea ..."

Zian held up his hands and shook his head. I was seeing her show of bravado for what it was: she was trying to reassert control over her nerves. I could tell that having to shoot a fellow human being had really got to her.

Morgan came out of my place. "What's this I hear about you bunking somewhere else for the night?"

"My place," Kennedy said. "It's within the Cold City limits."

Morgan grunted. "All right, then ... have you all given statements?"

"And left the contact info," I answered.

Morgan tilted his head to the side. "Scram ... but don't go too far."

———

Before I followed Kennedy, I texted Mr. Townsend to let him know to expect me at about nine in the morning. That finally out of the way, I followed Kennedy's car, a little 1990s Nissan that had seen better days, back to her place. Zian was right behind me in his oh-so-eco-conscious Prius. Once we got past the second red light, my cell started ringing. The ringtone of "Do You Wanna Date My Avatar" by The Guild told me it was Zian.

The song wasn't my choice; it had popped up on my cell at the same time Zian's number had appeared, and both were now impossible to erase. I'd asked my hacker friend about it once and got a confused reply that left me wondering if Felicia Day may have come from Alterum Mundum. One thing that was sure, though, was that Zian had a serious crush on her.

I picked the phone up. "What's up?"

"Just wanted to tell you a few details I didn't pass on to the cops," Zian said. "Don't worry; this line is encrypted. Anybody trying to listen is going to get nothing but static and a headache."

"You shouldn't have," I said with reproach in my tone. "Lying to the cops is a—"

"My dad's gonna give me worse than the cops ever will,"

Zian countered. "Because really and truly, what happened tonight was all my fault."

"How do you figure that?" I asked as we got moving again.

"Right before I went on that food run," Zian explained, "I did a little more digging into those killings you were looking into. Well, not *those* killings, but I wanted to see if there was anything before those that tied in somehow."

"And you did this despite what your dad—"

"Look, I was doing you a favor," Zian snapped. "Given what we just went through tonight, the least you could do is act grateful."

I sighed. "I'm not *un*grateful, Z. I'm just ... I'm just ... worried. I don't want you getting hurt."

"Already got one dad, Bell," Zian said. "That's more than enough, trust me."

"So what did you find?"

It was Zian's turn to sigh. "The data's processing at a little offsite that I'm running a ways from the Indigo."

"Trying not to catch the eye of Big Daddy?"

"For all the good it's going to do me. Still ... had to try."

"How soon can you have that data crunched?" I asked as I followed Kennedy into a sharp turn left.

"Won't be before tomorrow night," Zian said. "Breaking down homicides into all the categories I have takes some work."

"Zian, I hate to ask, but I have to know. The files you gave me—how did you know about Thricin?"

There was a long pause at the other end of the line. "While I was on the system, I ... I noticed someone had done the same research you had me do. That ... someone had made the connection with Thricin and put her on the list. So I figured—"

"That someone would be your dad, right?"

"So ... what's the deal with Kennedy?" Zian asked, avoiding my question.

"She's a reporter," I told him reluctantly. "Maybe you've seen her on HDL?"

"Thought she looked familiar," Zian admitted. "She and I are working the same graveyard shifts, looks like."

"Something she wants to change," I said as we hit yet another red light. "We're kind of working together for a story that she's investigating."

"Seems more your type than Melanie Ramirez," Zian said.

"How did you know—"

"Hey, prince of information, remember? I like keeping tabs on my friends."

I tried hard not to get angry at what anyone else would view as a clear violation of privacy. But this was Zian, and I knew this was half curiosity and half making sure I was all right. I tapped my key fob in annoyance. That was when I noticed something on it that shouldn't have been there. I used the light of my smartphone to shine a peek at it.

"Sunnofa ..." I muttered.

There was a GPS tracker on the underside of the fob. My mind flashed back to Kennedy in my car the other night, twirling my keys in her fingers.

"Hey, Bell, you still there?" Zian asked. "Look, I'm sorry about crossing any lines on the Ramirez thing—honest."

The light had turned green, and Kennedy was already taking off. Moving to catch up, I said, "Yeah, it's okay. Forget it. Hey, listen, do you have any idea who was chasing you tonight?"

"That's definitely one thing I wouldn't keep from you or the cops," Zian answered. "Sorry, no ideas right now. I can break into the police database tomorrow, though, see what they've got."

Zian and I made some small talk for a few more minutes before ringing off. The whole time I was talking, the only thing I could think of was what Kennedy had said about her "connection" leading her to Smoke & Mirrors. I had a feeling the guy looked a lot like me.

———

The Mountain Shade Apartments block was neither the best nor the worst such complex in Cold City. On the one hand, it was no housing project. Plenty of taxpayers called this place home, and patrols in the area were brisk. On the other hand, even though it was the third-newest apartment complex in the city, it was already ten years old and showing serious signs of age. The parking lot needed repaving, the trees in the tiny front yards looked thirsty, and the collection of 1980s and 1990s vehicles spoke volumes about the relative age and economic bracket of the people who lived there.

As soon as I had pulled into a parking space next to Kennedy's car and killed the ignition, I pulled out my keys and placed them in my lap. Then I ripped off the tracker, tossed it on the floor and smashed it with my heel. I picked up the pieces, pocketed them and got out of the car, leaving the keys in the ignition.

Zian was already out and following Kennedy upstairs. I

was about to join them when another thought hit me. Earlier, I had parked the car a block from Smoke & Mirrors, and as always left the keys in the ignition in case I had to make a quick exit. So how had Kennedy known that I had gone in?

"Hey, Vale, you spacing out on us?" Kennedy asked.

I shook my head. "Just realized I left my cell in the car."

"I'm up in 1008," she told me. "We'll wait for you."

I nodded and went back to the car as Kennedy and Zian walked down the hall. I opened the driver's side door, then peeked back over my shoulder—all clear. Then I ran my hand carefully up the only piece of clothing I was wearing both tonight and the night I had my little chat with Kennedy, my jacket.

It was an M65 field jacket I'd gotten at the army surplus. It was made of a mix of sturdy dark-green cotton and polyester and had lots of pockets. I checked them all, and then I checked the collar and found another tracker under it. A tug and a bit more fancy footwork and Kennedy's "connection" was cut.

While I was more than a little steamed to find out that she'd been bugging me for inside info, I had to give her points for covering her bases. I didn't know if she knew my habit of leaving my car in out-of-the-way spots when I had to be somewhere, but she probably guessed that there were going to be some spots I would make on foot. I was going to need to keep a close eye on her.

Then another wave of exhaustion hit me. It was time to get some shut-eye before I wound up sleeping on the sidewalk.

14

PAYOFFS

When I woke up the next morning, I found Zian in the same chair he was in when I knocked off, hunched over his smartphone.

"You been up all night, Z?" I asked as I stretched my sore muscles. That couch was anything but comfortable to sleep on.

Zian nodded without looking at me. "Been checking the camera feeds on the Indigo, my offsite, and my place all night long. Also got a little info I've inserted into this morning's police reports from replaying last night's footage."

"And it took you all night to do that?" I asked, sounding doubtful.

Zian shook his head. "Just … wanted to be sure that they didn't try again."

"Did they?" I asked, getting up.

Zian shook his head again.

I was feeling grungy, having slept in yesterday's clothes, jacket included. A quick check of my smartphone told me that I wouldn't have time for a shower. I put in a text to the guy I'd mentioned to Morgan last night about the door situation at my place. Then I yawned and tried to get my hand through my hair, only for it to get stuck halfway in. The tousled mess my brown locks always ended up in was almost enough to make me miss my army days and the regulation short-cropped look.

"Kennedy still here?" I asked Zian. Neither one of us had been talking loudly, but I lowered my voice just the same.

"Yeah, and won't be going anywhere for a while, judging from the snoring." Zian nodded towards the bedroom. "She told me to wake her up at noon if she's not awake by then."

"Did you do that other thing for me?" I asked, putting my shoes on.

"Waited for Kennedy to get to sleep first," Zian said, finally putting down his smartphone. "Last night shook her up. I could relate, so ... we talked for a bit."

"Anything I need to know?" I asked, pausing as I did my best to straighten out my shirt.

"She asked about my eyes," Zian confessed, embarrassment showing on his face. "I fed her the usual, a strange variant on heterochromia that sparks when emotions run high."

"And she bought it?"

"Think so," Zian said, stifling a yawn. "You humans are all the same—throw in a big word or two, and you swallow the lot wholesale." He reached into his pocket. "Here. I got it done when she called it a night."

He held up a molding of her apartment key, encased in plastic. I grabbed it and slipped it into my pocket. Then my smartphone buzzed. It was my guy letting me know that he'd have the door taken care of by close of business today.

"You know, if you want to move in with the new girl-friend, there are easier ways to do it," Zian commented.

"Considering how things ended with my last girlfriend ..." I let that one hang in the air as I went out the door.

———

Argo Nautilus was one of the few local business success stories of the last eight years. The Great Recession had wreaked havoc on plenty of businesses large and small and AN, as the locals called it, was no exception. Up until '08, it had been a moderately successful maritime shipping company. Then the Lehman Brothers collapse removed the words "moderate" and "successful" from the company description.

AN's ledger bled red ink for three straight years before finally turning a profit in 2012. Now, having outlived and/or outmaneuvered all its previous competitors, AN was a key pillar of the business community. Half to three-quarters of Cold City's economic growth could be traced back to them pulling off the impossible. You've got to respect that.

Of course, their offices on the top floor of the Ditko Building was another reason I gave them that respect. They were nice and clean but unshowy. Even the executives were pretty low-key about their authority, sharing office space with the middle managers who made the company run.

There was one big exception to this rule: the office of founder and CEO Ian Townsend, whose door I had just been buzzed through by the secretary. Even so, it wasn't what I expected from one of this city's leading businessmen. In place of the usual motivational posters, there were Dali prints. Instead of coffee being brewed on the pot, my nose detected the distinctive smell of herbal tea. The only things that gave me an idea of my client's status were his desk, which was about the size of a Lincoln Continental, and the spectacular view of the bay from the window.

The man himself, a fortyish guy in a gray suit that matched the prematurely gray hair on his head, rose from his desk to give me a two-handed shake of the hand.

"Thank you for being so punctual, Mr. Vale," he said in a mellow baritone that was low but penetrating.

"I know that your time is valuable, Mr. Townsend," I said as we finished the handshake.

"Oh, please," my client said as he patted me on the shoulder. "You've more than earned the right to call me Ian."

"Just as long as you call me Bell," I replied with a shrug.

He looked puzzled for a moment. "Oh—yes, a shorter version of your first name, right?"

"And a lot easier to remember, not to mention pronounce."

Townsend chuckled as he walked back to his desk. "I'd offer you a cup of tea, Bell, but I've only got a few minutes to spare," he said as he pulled a piece of paper from an open desk drawer. "The rest of my day is going to be similarly tied up, or I'd invite you to lunch."

"Not necessary, Ian," I said, waving it off. "I'll just collect my pay, and we'll call it even."

Townsend grew more somber as he walked over to me with what I saw was a cashier's check. "Even," he said, lost in thought. "Heh ... even."

I took the check from him and noticed something unexpected. "Ian, this is more than what we agreed upon when I took the case."

That seemed to snap Townsend out of his reverie. "Time and a half. You've more than earned it."

"Not that I couldn't use it or that I'm not flattered," I said, feeling uncomfortable with the largesse being handed to me. "But are you sure?"

"I've rarely been this sure in my life," Townsend said, looking me in the eye. Then, looking off someplace else, he added, "When I think about ... Marion ... and where she was a few days ago ... and what could have happened ..."

The tears caught up with him. I saw a familiar pain in the man's eyes.

"You never get over losing a child," I said, putting my own hand on his shoulder. "I'm just glad that you didn't find out what that's like."

Townsend gave me a look. I could tell that he wanted to ask me what I meant by that. The secretary's desk buzzed him before the words could come out, however. He wiped the tears from his eyes and cleared his throat before pushing the button on the intercom. "Yes, Felice?"

"Mayor Galatas is here for her nine-ten appointment, Mr. Townsend," the secretary's voice said through the speaker.

"Give me just a few minutes," he said before letting the button go.

"Guess you really don't have time to spare," I remarked as I secured the check in my inside jacket pocket.

Townsend nodded. "But this was worth a few minutes of it ... thanks again, Bell. I mean that. If any of my acquaintances need your kind of services, I'll be sure to put a good word in."

"Word of mouth goes a long way in my line of work," I told him with a smile.

We said our goodbyes, and I returned to the outer office.

Her Honor Mayor Jacinta Galatas was sitting primly with a folder in her lap, perfect boarding-school posture. She had an olive complexion, dark eyes that matched her equally dark hair—the latter done up in a severe bun—and what looked like a decent figure under the tasteful but expensive pants suit she was wearing. But she was no youngster. Even if I hadn't noticed the laugh lines under her eyes and seen past the makeup to spot the occasional wrinkle, her eyes spoke of someone who'd been on this planet long enough to know how to be both polite and wary.

I got a hint of both as she spotted me leaving. "Mr. Bellamy Vale, isn't it?"

The fact that the mayor of Cold City even knew my name in the first place was enough to stop me ... well ... cold.

"Yes, ma'am," I replied, turning towards her. "If you don't mind my asking, your Honor, how do you—"

"Let's just say that a certain Detective Lieutenant Morgan has filed a number of complaints about you," the mayor explained as she stood up. "These complaints have made their way to the commissioner's desk and, in turn, my own."

"I'm assuming that these include my arrest photos?" I asked.

"Every last one of them," Her Honor assured me. "I wish I could say that they don't do you justice, but ..."

Being reminded of how I was doing a pretty good impersonation of a down-and-outer made me fidget a bit. "As you can imagine, I disagree with the lieutenant's characterizations of me in all the cases he's sent your way."

A half-grin tugged at the side of her mouth. "Given that no human being I've ever run across likes to be described as 'reckless', 'a menace to public safety,' and other related endearments, I would hope so."

I frowned a little. "Based on what you've read on me, Madam Mayor, what's your opinion?"

Galatas pulled a face as she gave the matter some careful thought. "It's difficult for me to say," she admitted. "On the one hand, given that what you do is borderline vigilantism, I can see where Detective Lieutenant Morgan has a point in his critiques. On the other hand, when I weigh that thought against the fact that Marion Townsend is now alive, well, and attending school instead of being buried, I find that his argument is much less black and white than he would like me to believe."

The intercom on the secretary's desk buzzed. "Send in the mayor now, Felice," Townsend's voice instructed.

"Right away, Mr. Townsend," the secretary replied.

"Well, it seems duty calls," Mayor Galatas said with a sigh. Sticking out her hand, she added, "It was a genuine pleasure to meet you in the flesh, Mr. Vale."

"Even with all that you know about me?" I queried as I shook her hand.

"Even with that," she assured me with a professional politician's smile.

As she turned to go in the office, I got a glance at what was written on the folder ... Orion.

———

By the time I got to the Tombs for breakfast, I hadn't figured out why Ian Townsend would be mixed up with the Orion project. Cinema Leone was twenty-one blocks away from AN's offices and didn't have any business-related buildings that weren't on the waterfront. Since I wasn't getting anywhere, I put the thought aside. One of the things I had figured out as a detective is that if you look at something too hard, it won't ever get around to telling you what it wants.

Tommy was waiting out front with a big grin on his mahogany face. That look always worried me. It meant he had just pulled a fast one on me or was about to.

"So ... you ready to pay up, son?" he asked by way of greeting.

"It's in my pocket right now," I said. I'd cashed the check at my local bank on the way over.

"Ah! We'll settle inside," Tommy said, leading me to the door. "Candice Kennedy's waiting at your booth for you."

I stopped dead in my tracks. "Why?"

Tommy shrugged. "She mentioned that you two were working together on a case."

"And you believed her?" I retorted in amazement and disgust.

Tommy's smile grew sly as he tilted his head to the side. "Maybe I did, maybe I didn't. But I figured that either way this was a prime opportunity for me to expand your dating pool a bit." He placed a fatherly arm around my shoulders. "Now come on. I know you haven't had any breakfast yet, and you're not leaving until you do."

I was too stunned to do anything but let him drag me in.

Kennedy was digging into her eggs Benedict as I sat down in the seat across from her, glowering.

"What?" she asked. "Isn't a girl entitled to a little breakfast?"

"Not when it's served up with a side of stalking and snooping," I answered, tossing what remained of the bug on my car keys onto the table.

Her eyes flicked over to the pieces for a second before focusing on me. "Oh, that's rich, coming from somebody who does it for a living."

"Why are you even here?" I asked. "Zian said you mentioned something about waking you at noon if you didn't—"

"I ... didn't have a good night's sleep," Kennedy explained. "After about nine or so, I got up. Zian told me where you'd be for breakfast. He's a really sweet guy, by the way. No idea why he hangs with a jerk like you."

I filed a mental note to read Zian the riot act later. "Didn't last night convince you that this story is way too dangerous to keep pursuing?"

She put down the orange juice she had just raised to her lips. "I had a journalism professor out in Houston ... tough, disagreeable cuss but knew his stuff, you know? He said something that I have never forgotten: the stories that scare you the most are the most important ones in your career."

"Nothing's more important than your life," I said. "You can always get another story. But you've only got one—"

Kennedy slammed her fist on the table to cut me off, making the cutlery jump from the impact. "Don't you talk to me about goddamn life, hoss! Where I come from, the only reason anybody keeps on living is so that you get the chance to get away." The Texas was coming back strong in her voice as she added, "I had a leg up on most with my pretty little face. But that's the thing about pretty ... put enough miles on the road, and it'll run out like all the oil did back home. Sure, it got me a foot in the door, but it'll never get me where I want to go."

"Out of the late-night ghetto?"

"Uh-huh," Kennedy confirmed. "That's going to happen when I reel me in a big fish of a story ... and these wolf killings look like being just that." Her piece said, she grabbed her fork and stabbed the eggs again. After taking a bite, she added, "My connection got me some basics, but I'm gonna need more info. That's where you come in, Vale." She saw the look on my face and leveled her fork at me. "Or maybe Morgan would like to know about you hanging with an alleged major crime figure in the shape of one *Señor* Ramon De Soto?"

"Nothing you could ever prove," I shot back.

"Don't need to," Kennedy said, with a vicious little smile. "That's his job. And seeing as he hates your guts like he does, I'd say he'd be highly motivated if I let that little tidbit slip."

I shook my head. If Kennedy told Morgan that story, she'd be handing him a license to throw me in jail any time he liked. Then there was the heat I might get from De Soto for stirring up the shit.

"This is blackmail," I told her.

"Sure," Kennedy admitted with a shrug. "It's also a straight offer. In exchange for me keeping my mouth shut, I help you solve this case. Win-win from where I'm sitting."

While she finished off her eggs, I thought it over. The math kept coming back the same way. I sighed. "Any other catches I should know about?"

Polishing off the last of her orange juice, Kennedy looked aside, like she was thinking. I knew better, given the triumphant expression on her face. Then she looked directly at me. "Well, apart from giving me exclusive rights to the story once we get to the bottom of it, you treating this like a partnership instead of a marriage, and you never, *ever* calling me 'Candy' or 'Sugar,' I can't think of anything." She got up from the table and grabbed her purse. "Thanks for breakfast, by the way."

"What do you mean 'thanks for breakfast'?"

She just gave me that smile again and walked out the door.

As she opened it, I became aware of somebody sitting at the counter just inside the door. She was wearing a coal-black power suit and had one of the nicest pairs of legs I had ever seen. Then I noticed the pin on her lapel … it was the same as what was branded on my shoulder.

My thoughts turned cold. The woman was staring daggers at the blissfully unaware Kennedy's back. She was in disguise, but there was no mistaking those solid black orbs … Lady McDeath.

I shook my head to be sure that I wasn't seeing things. Next thing I knew, the counter stool was deserted, and the door had shut behind Kennedy. Despite the always-perfect temperature inside the Tombs, I felt clammy. Why did Kennedy have to insist on getting herself involved?

Tommy came out from the back with a platter of scrambled eggs, whole grain waffles, and a glass of milk. If he noticed me looking freaked, he didn't let it show on his face.

"You know she didn't pay for her meal, right?" I said, pointing towards the door.

"Of course I do, Bell," Tommy said, setting the food down in front of me. "That's because you're paying for it."

"Hells, no!" I exclaimed, hating myself for the whine in my voice.

"Oh, cut the shit," Tommy said with a little irritation as he gathered up Kennedy's dirty dishes. "Seeing what else I could have charged you for info on Cinema Leone, you could at least *sound* grateful."

Hearing an echo of Zian's words the previous night irked me, but somehow, I managed to hold my tongue, and I didn't describe to Tommy how many different ways that aiding and abetting Kennedy here was a mistake of epic proportions. No, what I said instead was, "I'm guessing you found something interesting."

Tommy chuckled. "That's one way of putting it. Then again, seeing as how Cinema Leone is sitting on an intersection of three ley lines, it's kind of like saying that the A-bomb on Hiroshima made a big boom."

That got my attention. Two ley lines intersecting was enough to create a place of power that somebody on either side of the border could exploit. But three in one spot was the equivalent of the Hope Diamond or Russian plutonium for sale—not unheard of but so rare that it might as well be a myth.

"Figure Mr. Nicholls had any clue what his little place was sitting on?" I asked.

Tommy shrugged as he picked up the last of the dishes.

"I couldn't say. But it's kind of remarkable, don't you think, that an aging movie house can survive in a killer economy like ours?"

"Somebody had to have noticed that," I agreed.

"Heh, that's one way of putting it," Tommy agreed. "Seeing as I've heard about offers for that place stretching round the block 'bout three or four times, I'd say it was probably more than one somebody."

"Let's not push it, Tommy," I said, holding up a hand. "Most real estate brokers I know don't have a refined Geiger counter for ley lines."

"Yeah, but there's someone who did," Tommy said, putting the gathered dishes down on the table. He pulled a city map out from his apron. I noticed that Cinema Leone and the ley lines it was sitting on were already marked. Tapping his finger on the southernmost ley line, Tommy said, "That's where Old Man Nicholls checked out. A death like that would run up and down the ley line like an electric shock, pooling all that nice necromantic energy right at the intersection."

"So somebody had to die in that way and at that spot all along to give the line that kind of charge," I deduced. "That it was the theater's owner, who'd put a lot of decades and love into the place, doesn't strike me as a coincidence."

"That'd be my guess, too," Tommy agreed as he folded the map back up. "Either way, the angry son of a bitch who did it could sniff out where the lines were and make it happen in just the right spot."

He grabbed the dishes and let me eat my breakfast in peace. I don't know how that old man does it, but he always seems to know when I've finished, so I wasn't a bit surprised when he reappeared when I laid my knife and fork down, satisfied.

"Got any idea who owns the theater now?" I asked him.

Tommy grunted. "I look like the damn local registrar of deeds to you, son?"

"No, you look like a cigar store Indian on vacation," I deadpanned.

"That's 'cigar store Native American' to you, boy," Tommy retorted, getting a chuckle out of both of us.

Then he sighed. "If I had to guess, I'd figure the old man's heirs have got their hands on the deed. I give it a week before they say 'the hell with it' and unload it for as much as they can get out of it."

"Could be something that Kennedy could help me out with," I speculated. "At least that's safe to check out."

"She mentioned what went down at your place last night," Tommy told me. "Still a little shook up, but I reckon she can handle it, Bell."

"Handle what?" I asked in annoyance.

"Handle whatever and whoever this case of yours is going to throw at her. Last night was the ultimate sink or swim for her. How she told it, she swam it like a champ."

"The kind of waters I'm going to be swimming in, a hit squad like that would look like a birthday present."

"And?" Tommy asked, looking very unimpressed.

"And you think she's ready to take on any trouble that comes from across the border?" I asked him point-blank.

"Guess that's something you'll find out. Like it or not, she's all in regardless."

"Shit, like you need to remind me," I said, rubbing my forehead.

"Now I know you got something else on that overtaxed, undernourished mind of yours," Tommy concluded. "What is it?"

I stared hard at him. "You know anything about a changeling who's slinging dope that you're only supposed to get from Smoke & Mirrors?"

15

INFORMATION TRAIL

After I pulled the Stingray out of the Tombs, I aimed it towards Zian's offsite location. While I had been busy dealing with Kennedy, Zian had sent a Google map of the locale to my phone. I'd felt it buzz but had been too wrapped up with talking to Tommy to look at it until after breakfast.

I figured it was fair that I give Zian the heads-up that I was coming, so I hit the redial button on his secured line when I got to my first red light. The voice on the other end said, "We are sorry, but Zianyon cannot come to the phone right now. If you will please leave a message at the tone, I will make sure that he never gets back to you."

There was no mistaking the voice that was giving me that clever combo of snark and threat.

"Huh, hi ... Mr. Hermes."

"As much as I appreciate the show of respect, Mr. Vale," the King of the Internet said. "Let me assure you that 'Hermes' will suffice."

It made sense ... the Greek gods had never been big on

scraping and bowing like the denizens of some other pantheons. All they asked from us mortals was the same basic respect that we would give a human of higher station.

"Despite what my little greeting may lead you to believe," Hermes went on, "I am actually not upset with you this morning. My son, on the other hand ..."

"I take it that you found out what Zian was up to?" I asked as the light turned green.

"It is not as though he could ever hide it from me," Hermes said with a note of contempt. "I told him once already to let this matter drop ... and yet he insists on digging himself a deeper hole that may bury him yet."

"In fairness, sir, I didn't ask him to do that," I pointed out.

"No, but you're about to, Mr. Vale," Hermes countered. "That is what has me concerned. Last night you kept him safe. You may fail to be so lucky a second time."

"With all due respect, Hermes, it's too late for Zian to turn his back on this. Whatever he's found, someone else knows he's got it, and they are going to try again. Regardless of what he does from this point on, or how long they wait before making their move, it ... will ... happen. Unless we get to them first."

There was a long silence on the other end of the line. After stopping at another red light, I began to get a little nervous. Then I heard a long groan of irritation. "You have made your point, Mr. Vale. Very well ... if you will just hang up and dial this number a second time, you will get through to Zianyon."

"Thank you, sir," I said, suppressing a sigh of relief.

"But understand something," Hermes added in a stern

tone. "This is a temporary arrangement. I expect you to stay out of Zianyon's life when this is over."

The light turned green. While giving the gas a tap, I said, "No promises."

"And why are you choosing to tell me something so potentially bad for your health?" Hermes asked with a spike of hostility cutting through his calm façade.

"Rule number two: never lie to a client," I explained. "Besides, it seems to me as though Zian might have a few ideas of his own on the subject. He's not a child anymore, you know?"

Hermes grunted. "I respect the honesty of your answer, even if I have issues with it. Be that as it may, I think we should revisit this topic again at a later date."

The phone beeped, signifying the end of the call. By now, I was three blocks from the offsite. I hit the redial button again, and Zian picked up on the second ring.

"Hey, Vale!" my friend all but shouted into the phone, bursting with excitement. "How soon can you get here?"

"Two and a half blocks from you now, Z," I said with cautious optimism. "Everything okay?"

"Oh, yeah, better than okay," Zian assured me. "Just get here as soon as you can. I think you're going to like what I've found!"

About ten minutes later, my car was parked at a Rite-Aid on the corner, and I was walking up to a deserted factory that matched the place marked on the map. I never knew what the company's name was, but I recognized it as the less fortunate competition that AN had helped put out of business about three years before. The exterior walls were all aluminum siding, corroded from the sea air and neglect, and the near-roof-level windows stared at the surroundings with sociopath eyes.

I heard the front door unlock as I got close to it. A quick glance up enabled me to spot an unobtrusive spy cam sitting on the upper left corner of the door frame. The interior was a clean concrete slab that seemed roughly the length of a pair of football fields. Most of the trappings that had made this a major shipwright operation had long since been stripped out, right down to the lights.

An ancient loudspeaker emitted a high-pitched whistle before Zian's voice broke through. "Come on back to the manager's office, Bell."

That's when I spotted the faint fluorescent lights that were on in a room at the far end of this industrial grave. As I approached, Zian appeared at a window and waved me in, pointing to where the door was. I heard another automatic lock click open as I turned the knob and click back once I was through. By then, Zian was back at the ancient desk in the corner, typing away on a laptop of much more recent vintage.

"Not that I think you're being paranoid, Zian," I said, strolling across to the desk, "but did last night shake you up that bad?"

"Oh, I had this security in place before all that," he assured me, glancing up from the screen just long enough to give me a lopsided grin. "You can't be too careful."

His bleach-blond hair was its usual mess of rebellious strands, and he wore a black t-shirt that proclaimed, "Age of the geek, baby" and a pair of faded jeans.

"Give me another minute or so," he requested. "The factory's old Wi-Fi is good but it's not the Indigo's."

I pulled up a straight-backed office chair and sat opposite him. "While we're waiting, anything you can just go ahead and tell me?"

Zian's fingers stopped their keyboard dance. "Yeah. It turns out that there were four other deaths that tied in with the buildings around the Cinema Leone."

"How so?" I asked, leaning back in the chair as much as I could.

"Well, none of them fit the MO for the Berserker," Zian admitted. "But all of the victims were tenants of the buildings that got bought up by a shell corporation calling itself Fairwinds Inc. The day after the last death, the sales on all their buildings were finalized."

A red flag raised itself in my head. In my business, coincidences are a myth.

"What can you tell me about the victims?" I asked.

"Too much for me to repeat it without some data links," Zian said with a sigh of frustration. "That's why I'm—wait, here it comes!"

He gestured to me to come around to his side of the desk. I found myself looking at four different pictures on the screen. Having sat for pics like that myself, I made them for police mugshots.

"If these vics are what I think they are, I'm guessing nobody took a harder look at their untimely demises," I ventured.

"Sure," Zian agreed. "Why waste time on dead scumbags when you can be protecting tax-paying citizens?"

"How'd they go?"

"Different ways," Zian said, clicking on the first of the pictures. A police report popped up, complete with photos of a freshly shot corpse. "This first guy was a banger. Caught a bullet on a night when he wasn't looking for trouble, but trouble was sure looking for him."

Zian minimized the window and clicked on the second pic, pulling up a report that showed something that might have started off as human but was now mostly paste. "This second guy, a hardcore junkie, took a swan dive off the roof during his latest—and last—high."

Another minimize-and-click operation later, he brought up another report with a mangled corpse, although this one still looked human. "Number three was a street dealer, knocked down in a hit-and-run on his own corner."

The last picture brought up a report that looked like it could have belonged to a Homeland Security file on a terrorist. "Our final contestant was another banger who moonlighted as a thief. Too bad the last thing he stole was an antique music box packed with low-yield explosives. It blew up in his face the second he opened the lid."

"Nothing that links them together?" I asked, digesting the details I had skimmed through in Zian's presentation.

"Aside from where they lived and what happened to their place of residence after buying the farm?" Zian asked, raising an eyebrow at me.

I gave him a look.

"If there is some other link, the cops never found it," Zian told me, his fingers moving again. "Or if they did, they didn't bother looking closer. No sense wasting time on a stone whodunit when you can just attribute it to what passes for natural causes among the criminal class."

"Any other unusual deaths before or after that batch of kills?" I asked.

"As a matter of fact, yes, there was one," Zian responded. He brought up a folder marked Kurtzenberg on the desktop. "This case happened to be a solid citizen, so I have a few more details to work with."

Opening the folder, Zian tapped on a Word doc that was a mixture of words and pictures. The picture at the top showed a portrait shot of a man with a craggy face and flat-topped gray hair. He reminded me vaguely of James Cagney.

"Henry Kurtzenberg, age thirty-six," Zian told me. "Public works supervisor for Cold City of ten years' standing, no criminal record, and yet he winds up in another one of those buildings we're talking about, cut down in what the cop called 'a mob-style execution'."

"What do you call it?" I asked him.

"A murder case that went cold as of a week ago," Zian replied. "No motives, no suspects, no leads ... so no progress."

The precision of the hit as described in the report I was reading made me think of the De Sotos. Just the same, I decided to keep that suspicion to myself.

"Any buildings other than the Cinema Leone that Fairwinds don't have their hands on?"

Zian pulled up another screen, but the data was flashing too fast for me to keep up with it. It didn't seem to bother Zian. "A couple, but it's just a matter of time. Still, they've not been able to do any groundwork on what they have."

Time for me to raise my eyebrows. "And why is that?"

"Well, there's the move by Councilwoman Thricin to get the Cinema Leone historic landmark status. That slowed things down. And there's also been pushback from the city itself on the other buildings, a real shitstorm of lawsuits and injunctions that's slowed the Fairwinds' progress to a crawl."

"So," I reasoned aloud, "even if Fairwinds got the cinema tomorrow, all this would keep them from being able to do anything with it?"

"Bullseye," Zian said with a grin. "The most they'd be allowed to do is change the light bulbs."

I nodded, leaning against the desk. "Sounds like we've found the people behind the Orion project."

Zian snorted. "Did you *read* that last file I gave you? Orion's a project that the city *wants* to have happen. They farmed it out to an outfit called Arete."

"Hold it," I said, holding up a hand. "Since when does Cold City endorse the building of a luxury apartment complex at taxpayers' expense?"

"Since now, apparently," Zian said, with a shrug. "Arete's been the city's favorite no-bid contractor of choice for a while now."

"So maybe this is a kickback."

An old-fashioned telephone ring issued from my smartphone. It was my ringtone for anyone whose number I didn't have saved. I picked it up. "Vale Investigations."

"Hey, it's Kennedy," my caller said on the other end. "Got any new leads on our story?"

"Just got a major info dump from your new best friend from last night," I admitted. "Adds a few details to the picture."

"We should meet up," Kennedy said.

"Know Sundowner's Café on Canal Street?"

"Sure, I practically lived there when I first got here. Meet you there at noon?"

"Sounds good," I said, pushing myself off the desk. "See you there."

I rang off and turned to Zian, "I'm going to need—"

Zian was already holding a flash drive up in his hand. "Just plug it into a smartphone, and you'll see what I've seen."

I took the drive from him. "First time I dialed your number this morning, I ended up having a little chat with your dad."

Zian's face darkened.

"It's okay," I added quickly. "I squared it, at least for the time being. Saving your life last night probably had a lot to do with that. He should stay out of our way for the rest of the investigation."

"Yeah ... about that saving-my-life thing," Zian said, looking sheepish. "I called you on the carpet for being ungrateful last night, and I never got around to saying thank you myself."

"I don't know, Z, given what we're hunting, you may not be thanking me when this is over."

Zian grinned. "Well ... I'm thanking you anyway. You've more than earned that."

I returned the smile. But a part of me was still wondering if I wasn't making a huge mistake dragging my friend deeper into this mess.

16

MATCH MADE IN HELL

T he Sundowner's was hopping when Kennedy met me at the door. The lunch crowd was piling into the rather tight space, getting their quick fixes of coffee, tea, and other drinks that would have been at home on Tommy's menu in the Tombs. Once upon a time, the place had been a corner grocery store. You could still see a trace of that on the front window, where the only change over the years seemed to have been what was written on the glass, and the wearing off of the limestone tiles. But as long as I'd been living in this town, it was a coffee shop that gave the local Starbucks a run for their money.

I was downing my usual green tea (served up here with some all-natural lemon for flavor) while Kennedy was sipping a cappuccino blend. We were parked in the back left corner of the place, facing the door. I watched people going in and out of the narrow oak front door, passing by on the street, chatting away to each other at the tables and near the counter. Nobody looked like they wanted to plug me with a submachine gun, but why take a chance?

Kennedy's eyes were glued to her smartphone; the flash drive was plugged into it. She hadn't looked at anything else in the last ten minutes or so. Once she was finished, she looked up at me and asked, "Can I keep this?"

"Don't see why not," I said with a shrug. "If I need another copy of the info, Zian can hook me up."

"I have to say I don't recognize either company Zian was talking about," Kennedy admitted as she pulled the drive out of her phone. "But they've got names, so I've got a place to start."

"You might want to check on the current ownership status of the Cinema Leone, too," I added.

Kennedy snorted with contempt. "Like those kids aren't going to dump that place like a bad habit the second they get the right offer ..." Then she registered the look on my face and laughed. "All right, all right, I'll do my due diligence on that one, too." She took another pull of the coffee and shook her head. "Not sure I'm buying all of what you're selling me, by the way. For all I know, you're about to pull a double-cross on me that's gonna leave me looking mighty stupid."

"Why?" I asked. "What do I get out of humiliating you that won't cost me more?"

Kennedy pointed a finger at me. "Which is why I'm willing to trust that you're telling me the truth."

"Well, if you can't trust me, trust Zian," I said, gesturing with my tea mug. "He's where I got this info."

Kennedy sighed. "Yeah ... and you gotta figure that those guys were shooting at him for some reason, right?"

"Yeah," I said. "So ...?"

Kennedy shrugged. "So, okay ... but I got to ask. How did a sweet little computer geek like him ever hook up with a scoundrel like you?"

"It's a bit of a long story," I answered, hedging my bets. "But you and I aren't there yet on those kinds of stories. So ask me again later."

"Can't help it, I guess," Kennedy admitted as she drank more of her cappuccino. "Chalk 'er up to me being a reporter to the bone."

"You know, you sound a lot more Texas in real life than you do on the air."

She gave me another little laugh. "Yeah, I guess I do. When I've got a live camera on me, I'm doing everything I can to shove that hillbilly accent into the background. Kind of nice to let it out when the camera's off."

"I imagine that talking that way doesn't win you points for intelligence with some people," I deduced.

"God, don't get me started." She tossed her head in a way that sent her wavy blonde hair flying. "Add my kind of pretty to the way I talk, and most of my bosses think I'm the valedictorian of dumb blondes."

"Even without a Southern accent, they said the same thing about Marilyn Monroe," I told her. "But no matter what other mistakes she made, one thing she was never dumb about was business. She died hard, but she didn't die poor."

Kennedy grunted. "So she's why you don't assume every pretty girl comes standard with a single-digit IQ?"

"Partly," I admitted. "The other part is that making assumptions in my work can put you on the wrong track in a hurry."

I got to the bottom of my tea mug. "Before we go any further on this ... partnership, there's something I got to know upfront."

She gave me a "go on" gesture.

"How much of what we're going to do is going to be splashed across a news site, and how much is going to stay in the shadows?" I asked, looking her squarely in the eyes.

"Worried about the law, aka Detective Lieutenant Morgan, getting the better of you?" Kennedy inquired, smiling.

"Always," I said with a little chuckle. "But the bigger problem for me is that I've got to live in this city alongside everyone else in it, and there are certain ... people I've got to keep happy if I want to keep on living, period."

"You do walk a fine line, don't ya, hoss?"

I gave her a rueful nod.

"All right, just tell me what you need me to keep quiet, and it'll stay under wraps," she said.

"Mind doing some digging for me on an unrelated job?"

She pursed her lips. "What's in it for me?"

"Another story to tide you over while we're working on the big one."

"Well, why didn't you say so?" she responded brightly. "What's the skinny?"

"Tracking down a dealer for a client," I said, figuring that there wasn't any need for me to tell her which client that was. "They're selling stuff that you can only get from Smoke & Mirrors."

"Didn't peg you for DEA," Kennedy teased.

"Nah, I've got a problem with authority figures, or so I've

heard," I said. "No, this is just about money and a favor, like it usually is in my business."

The waitress came by to ask if I wanted a refill. Seeing as I had money to burn, I gave her the okay.

When she had gone, Kennedy picked up where we had left off. "It's got some possibilities ... got any info?"

"Still got to chase down some leads first," I admitted. "Mind running some background on them when I see how they pan out?"

"As long as I get first dibs on the story," Kennedy said, pointing at me with her mug.

The waitress came back with my refill. She was just going away again when I saw Ramirez walk through the door. I had just enough time to think "Oh, shit" before she spotted us in the corner ... *our* corner. Hells—how could I have forgotten that this was always our special spot back when we were dating?

Kennedy must have seen me looking over her shoulder because she turned around to get a good look at the absolutely furious Ramirez, who was staring daggers at the both of us. I've faced down my share of frightening characters and bad men in my time, but let me tell you ... Melanie Ramirez is scary when she is angry. She held our eyes for a couple more seconds then stormed right back out the door.

While I was remembering how to breathe again, Kennedy asked me, "Your ex?"

I didn't quite trust my own voice, so I nodded.

"Saw her at the scene of that second murder the other day," Kennedy went on. "She's a cop, right?"

"Batting a thousand so far," I told her.

"Better than what you're doing in the romance depart-

186 | CRISTELLE COMBY

ment," she observed. "I can't imagine why an upstanding, law-abiding citizen like you could lose a girl like that."

"I don't know," I replied with another shrug. "The same way that a perfectly ethical journalist like yourself can do a little B&E at the morgue the same night I did."

Kennedy laughed in my face. "What, you think that I was there just because of that video I mentioned?"

"That and the person I ran past on my way out was a blonde who just happened to be wearing the same lily scent you are today."

Kennedy grinned in appreciation. "Guess you do know how to do your job."

I nodded. "So ... while I can't imagine that you saw anything I didn't on the corpse, I'm thinking that what you did see told you that it wasn't an animal."

"Not even close. And the damn ME ought to have known that too," Kennedy said with a little disgust. "Back home, I was around all sorts of wildlife, not counting the men I dated. No animal I ever heard of made those cuts. You showing up at the same time told me that you were thinking the same thing. It's why I've been tailing you. You're the only guy on this case who's smart enough to see what I'm seeing."

I gave her a dumbfounded look as I sipped my tea.

"What, you're not used to a girl giving you a compliment?" Kennedy quizzed, clearly amused.

"Not used to being called smart," I admitted as I put the mug back down.

"Well, I gotta run," she said, standing up. "Even though the station said I could take an extra day, I'm not getting paid for the privilege."

"Hey, Kennedy," I muttered, a serious, concerned tone in

my voice. "Be careful about how far you push this. Last night may not be the worst thing that could happen."

She patted her purse in reply. "My friends Smith and Wesson might have something to say about that."

"Still ..." I let the word hang there.

Kennedy's face assumed an expression I couldn't decipher. Then she turned around and went out the door.

———

After I finished my tea, I spent the rest of the day putting my hard-earned cash to good use elsewhere. I paid off my utility bills and got in a month's supply of groceries, at long last. Once I had all the food put away, I asked Zian via text to send me a copy of the data I'd given to Kennedy. I stared at it for a couple of hours without coming to any new conclusions.

Dinner rolled around, and I decided a visit to the Tombs was in order. The early evening is when that little place is at its most packed. Customers had to park outside the apartment building next door. Every seat, be it booth or counter, was taken. Luckily, just as I came in, the couple installed in my corner booth settled their bill and left.

A cute college co-ed took my order. I figured the mention of my usual order would let Tommy know that I was there. If he had anything to share, he'd bring it with the meal.

I wasn't disappointed. Tommy brought the fresh, steaming burger and fries to me, navigating his way around the crowd to get to my booth. Once he was there, he leaned in close and stage-whispered, "Bran Connor ... don't know if that's a boy or a girl or even the right person you're looking for, but they got spotted trying to do some business in the Indigo the last couple of nights."

"Bad idea," I said. And it was. Drugs were forbidden at the Indigo for a wide variety of reasons, ranging from legal to ethical. But that didn't stop the occasional candy raver mistaking the place for a nightclub ... ditto some of their dealers.

"Sure is," Tommy agreed. "Somebody should tell Zian about it."

And that's what I did, the minute I finished up my meal.

17

WORDPLAY

From what I could see on the surveillance monitors, the Indigo was hopping just as much as the Tombs had been. A lot of people coming and going or staying there. Some of them were using the in-house computers, which ran better than almost anything you could get retail, or their own custom laptops. The laptops were tattooed with various stickers of brand names, slogans, and whatever struck the fancy of their owners. They were a good match for the people using them, who were just as colorfully decorated with fashion styles that ranged from neo-punk to post-goth.

Zian was pacing up and down the space behind me. He'd been doing that since he'd let me into the Indigo Below Security Department. He was wearing a black t-shirt with six yellow Pac-Man figures and the text "Six Pac" on it. Half of it was tucked into his dark jeans, while the other was hanging loosely around his bony hips. His business suit vest had long since been abandoned on the back of a desk chair.

Dealers are nothing but trouble, but Zian had a hatred of

them that I usually associated with family vendettas. His security people and the other operatives went about their business as usual, doing their best not to notice their boss's agitation.

"You know, you're going to wear that carpet or those shoes out if you keep doing that," I said, glancing over my shoulder.

"I don't care," Zian growled, his pacing just as furious as ever. "I want that little Arcadian freak out of my space after tonight ... no excuses, no exceptions."

I shrugged and went back to looking at the screen. Every face had a flash of pixel mesh go over it every few seconds, part of the Indigo's facial recognition software. It didn't matter how deep their records were buried, scrubbed, or hidden. If they were on a computer somewhere, the Indigo would pull it up in conjunction with whatever matches the system pulled on the faces.

"Hey, boss," said a rather plain Asian girl with glasses that did wonders for her face. "I think I got something."

Zian stopped pacing and walked over to her station. I was right behind him.

"No hit on the facial recognition," she went on to say, tapping her screen, "but I heard this customer call this other guy ... or girl ... 'Bran' on the mic."

I couldn't make much out of the figure Zian's girl was pointing out. It was almost like the shadows were swallowing it whole. But somebody was definitely handing something to a pasty kid with a shaved scalp, and I doubted it was aspirin.

"The buyer's name is Luc," Zian said. "Not a smart cookie, but he's a regular." He turned to another of his employees. "Text him. Tell him to meet me in the office.

We're going to need to talk." He registered the look I was throwing him and added for my benefit, "Not down here ... upstairs office." He jerked his head at the screen in front of us. "Think you can handle our other visitor?"

"It's why I'm here," I told him.

"I'll be keeping watch through the eye in the sky," Zian promised, holding up his smartphone. "As long as you stay in the Indigo, consider yourself covered. After that ... well, I'll see what I can do."

I gave his shoulder a squeeze before heading back upstairs.

———

It took me a bit of time to figure out where our mystery dealer was. Sure, he or she was in a dark nook somewhere, but there was no shortage of those, what with the mood lighting. I eventually found my quarry nestled in the shadows beside an ancient "Operation Wolf" arcade machine. The only things I could make out clearly were the hands, which were long, tapered, and adorned with a few silver rings. The fingernails, I noticed, were decorated with electric-blue nail polish. The fingers themselves were tapping the machine in time to the music coming over the speakers, a techno remix of the Stones' "Luxury."

As soon as I got close, the fingers stopped their tapping. Then the figure slipped out of the shadows with a prizefighter's roll and a slight swaying of the hips. The lean face with the laughing smile, the skinny jeans that clung like a second skin, the shoulders and chest that could have been that of a small man or a big woman—everything about this person was a walking contradiction of gender. But that was often the case with changelings. Gender tended to be more of a suggestion than the cold hard fact it is for most people.

"Bellamy Vale ..." The voice was as gender-neutral as the rest of her. I decided to make it a "her" just to keep things straight in my own head.

"Bran Connor," I answered.

The rest of the crowd around us was so wrapped up in their individual cyber-worlds that we might as well have not been there.

"Oh, and I so hoped to have you at a disadvantage," Bran demurred in mock disappointment with an effete wave of a hand.

"I'm a PI," I reminded her. "Details like names are things we tend to track down."

"Though not necessarily locations," Bran taunted, flapping a hand at the ceiling. "I mean, I have been waiting here for you to show up for two nights now."

I tried not to betray the surprise I felt. "Well, now that I'm here, I've got a lot of questions."

Bran shrugged before using her left hand to gesture for me to join her at a quiet corner table further towards the back.

As the original version of Bowie's "Jean Genie" began, I sat down on a stool in front of the small café table and waited while Bran settled herself on hers.

"Why don't we start with something obvious, like how you knew that I'd be here eventually?"

"Well, your connection to the crown prince of information is hardly a state secret," Bran said, cocking her head at me. "It seemed to me that you'd be coming here sooner or later for a hit of info that you can't get anywhere else."

"Which leads to Question Two: why did you want to meet?"

Bran smirked at me and hummed. "Guess I should come out and say something ... I was the one who gave you that warning about the Berserker hitting the Thricins." Her voice shifted to that of Melanie Ramirez. "You didn't hear this from me."

This time, there was no way I could conceal my startled expression.

Bran laughed in her normal voice. "Nice party trick, huh?"

"I doubt you threw me at that monster just for shit and giggles," I suggested, resolving to stay as still as possible to counter Bran's constant fidgeting.

"Far, far from it," Bran assured me. "But, hey, none of that was my idea. There's certain ... let's call them 'interested parties' ... who don't appreciate that damned Berserker making such a mess of things."

"Well, seeing as I'm hardly Conan the Barbarian material," I argued, "I'd say that you threw me in front of that thing as a delaying tactic. If you had an army on the spot, they'd have got the call instead, I suppose. But you had to make do with an anonymous tip to the cops."

"Oh, really?" Bran all but cooed in a deeper tone of voice that I would have expected. Then she gave me a "tsk, tsk, tsk" and wagged a finger at me. "For all you know, all those good, tax-paying citizens on that block may have made that same call a lot less anonymously."

"If they realized what they were hearing, sure," I granted

with a shrug. "But the whole plan hinged on Mrs. Thricin surviving the attack. The only way that was going to happen was you making the call to the cops right after you hung up with me."

Bran hummed again, looked up at the ceiling and chuckled before lowering her gaze. "I've got to admit you weren't supposed to survive that little encounter. I know you've got a knack for cheating death, but let's be serious ... there's death, and then there's death incarnate, right?"

I gave Bran a hard little smile of my own. She had no idea how true that statement was.

"Okay, look," Bran said, holding up her ring-festooned fingers. "I have to say that the parties I mentioned before were very impressed that you got the better of that Berserker. In fact, they're so impressed that they want to make you a job offer so that you can join our team."

"I kind of thought we already were on the same team," I countered. "Assuming I've guessed correctly and you work for Fairwinds."

"Affiliated teams," Bran corrected, laying her hands back on the tabletop. "You'd need to be on the same payroll as me to be part of this team."

I picked my next words carefully. "Just out of professional curiosity, did the people you're working for have anything to do with the intimidation or murder phase of things?"

"No, no, no ... far too direct and messy for them. They just reached out to certain ... local entrepreneurs early on to ensure our interests in that area. They proved to be a lot less resilient than we'd have hoped. Funny how they kept turning up dead once Vito started expressing an interest in doing business in that area ..."

I didn't see that one coming. "Okay, call me a poor, confused schmuck, but you lost me there."

"Hey, confusion is nothing to knock," Bran said, reaching across the table to give my shoulder a squeeze. There was surprising strength in the grip. "It gives you an incentive to do your job."

"Well, it's just that I heard this rumor that you and Vito were doing a little business with each other on certain ... recreational substances."

"Let's say, for the sake of argument, that Vitorini was indeed doing a side business with me. He's enough of a misogynist pig to think that's a good idea, what with Estella De Soto being one of his bosses and all."

I nodded at Bran with an expression intended to convey "Well?".

"Taking that theory a little further," Bran continued, "any involvement with Vito would have to pre-date my employment with my new superiors. A lot of our dead people had some involvement in that trade, though they were a bit, shall we say, antagonistic about Vito's interest in their business. I couldn't very well justify the conflicting interests in both that baby mobster's ambitions and my employers' desire to use the people they had selected, so ..."

"You're cutting Vito loose," I said. "And talking to me is your way of throwing him under the bus."

Bran gave me a triumphant pointing of the finger.

"So how does that explain the other part of the rumor, that Vito managed to get some of the substances he was after from you in the first place?" I asked.

"You've met Vitorini, right?" Bran inquired, leaning in a bit.

Wincing from the memory of our last little get-together, I nodded. "More than once."

"Then you know he's an arrogant, overconfident fool who thinks that somehow his dead father's genes make him a better criminal. So ... how hard is it to imagine that he thinks he's got enough product to get started in spite of his lack of prior experience?"

It made sense. It sounded like the same sort of tunnel vision that had made him grab Marion Townsend.

"So you're saying that he's been killing off these other guys to expand his—"

Bran made a face that stopped the thought cold. "Vito is stupid, sure, but not that stupid. If he's killing off people he could have recruited instead, he's doing it for a reason other than to help his little start-up business."

Bran leaned back and shook her head again. "Of course, while all this is going on, the other team hasn't been taking a break. Just ask their lawyers ..."

"So you're saying that this Berserker and Vito are both working for Arete?" I asked her, throwing the name out there to make sure Zian's info aligned with Bran's.

"You mean, considering that each of their attacks thus far have been a direct assault on Fairwinds' interests? I would say that is a safe bet, yes."

"Let's get back to that offer you mentioned at the top," I said. "If I say yes, what do you want me to do?"

"Oh, something you are impeccably qualified for," Bran told me, flashing me a bright smile that looked like it could cut flesh. "Track the Berserker back to his lair."

"Track him but not kill him," I said, noticing the gap.

"Who was it who said that you're not exactly Conan the Barbarian material, hmm?" Bran's smile widened. "No, a quick report on its location will more than suffice. I'll have back-up I can call in after that."

"And the pay?" I asked, leaning forward like I was interested.

"Negotiable," Bran answered, with an offhand gesture. "I wouldn't insult you by naming a figure that might be too slight for such a hazardous task."

It sounded good ... if I was a guy who believed that these Arcadian types always played it straight. But none that I had ever heard of would ever fail to use a loophole that would leave me without my promised money—or my life.

"I'm going to have to think about it," I said. "Money's only a good incentive if you're alive to spend it."

"True, very true," Bran agreed, producing a business card from what looked like thin air but was more likely just her sleeve. "When you do make that final decision, give me a call."

She got up from her seat. "Now, as delightful as this conversation has been, I am afraid that I have things to do, people to see. Briefest goodbyes are the best ... *adieu.*"

She moved away so quickly and so quietly, I could have sworn she was a ghost. I got up and walked out of that nook myself. I felt a buzz in my pocket from my cell. Zian had sent me a text: "Just finished looking at Luc's stash. Positive match for Smoke & Mirrors supply."

I ducked behind an oversized Star Wars arcade machine that was surrounded by a noisy crowd and leaned against the empty seat of a racing game next to it. Then I texted back, "What about Luc?"

About thirty seconds later, I got Zian's reply. "Gave him a choice: lifetime ban from the Indigo AND being turned over to the cops or tracking Bran back to that fae's lair."

"U sure that's safe?!" I texted back.

"Do it myself, but I'm not in your class," was Zian's response.

I was in the middle of a reply when he sent another text: "Like to be, though."

I deleted my reply and sent something else instead: "You rule the Internet. That not enough?"

I heard a cry of delight from the crowd around the Star Wars machine as I read his reply. "Not anymore. Last night changed my mind."

"On what?" I texted, feeling a sense of alarm.

"On lots of things," Zian replied. "Funny how a few real-world bullets can do that."

I texted back quickly. "Your dad's already pissed at u AND me. Why push it?"

It was about a minute and a half before I got the reply to that. "I need more."

A chorus of dismay from the crowd at my elbow matched my feelings, and I leaned my head back against the machine. One thing that Zian did not need was to be more dead. A part of me was happy that he wanted to get more involved with the real world, but the rest of me was plain terrified that he'd chosen the absolute worst moment to do it.

"You still there, Bell?" Zian texted.

"Sure," I replied. "Just thinking over what u told me."

After a few more seconds of thinking it over, I added, "This shit's dangerous."

"I know. I got shot at, remember?" came the caustic reply.

"And u still ...?" I texted back.

"Crap! Got a problem!" Zian texted me in a hurry.

"What?" I asked.

"Office, behind the above-ground server. NOW."

I realized that I was standing just opposite the location he was referring to, so I walked straight to it. One click of the door lock later, I found Zian sitting in front of another desk and staring at a custom laptop with positive dread. He was wearing a mic headset but had a pair of mini-speakers attached to the audio output jack.

"Luc, I've got a friend of mine with me now," Zian said into the mic. "Tell him what you just told me."

"Yeah, hey ..." The half-broken voice of a panicked teenager sounded over the speakers. "They made me. Now, somebody's after me."

"Who?" I asked into the mic on Zian's head.

I could hear the sound of running on the line, and Luc was panting as he replied. "If I knew who, I'd have said, don't you think?"

"Where are you right now?" I asked.

"Corner of Sprang and Broome. I lost sight of that Bran bitch about a minute ago before ... oh, God! They're right behind me!"

"What is it?" Zian asked. "What are you seeing?"

The only answer we got was a scream of horror and agony, and the call was cut off.

"Jesus! What were you thinking, Z?" I demanded, slapping the desk for emphasis.

"Luc was just supposed to follow Bran back to her hideout," Zian snapped back at me, tearing off his headset. "Then he was supposed to send an anonymous tip that would put the cops onto her faerie ass for dealing illegal substances. No confrontation, no stupid hero moves ... just the same sort of snitching Luc's been doing for years!"

"Well, not anymore," I said, feeling my voice get louder. "Now he's probably dead ... and that could have been you if you'd gone after her!"

We stared at each other for a minute. Then Zian looked away, guilt coloring his pale face. He sank into his seat, defeated.

I should have left the argument at that, but fear got the better of me. "That's the thing about the real world, Z. Everything ends when you die. You can't insert a coin and get a do-over."

Zian's head whipped my way, and his voice rose a level. "Don't patronize me, Vale! I'm not a child. Despite what you may think, I know how life works—or have you forgotten how we met?"

I raised both hands, palms up, "I know, Z. That's not what I meant. I'm just ..." I passed a weary hand over my tired face, contemplating how to finish that sentence. Angry? Scared? Bone-achingly tired? "Worried," was all I said.

Glancing at the security camera displays on the wall of the small office, I noted that the world continued to move forward at its usual frantic pace, oblivious of what had just happened. The kids below were dancing, drinking, or tapping away at their computers with an abandonment I envied.

"All right, what's done is done," I said, turning back to face Zian. "Any way we can find out what happened to Luc?"

He nodded and returned his attention to the computer, attacking the keyboard like a rainstorm attacks a roof. He stopped a few minutes later and waved me over to the screen. He had pulled up a live Internet feed of the Headliner News. Kennedy was in front of the camera at the corner of Sprang and Broome. Once he was sure I was watching, Zian turned the sound on.

"... shocking attack occurred moments ago," Kennedy was saying. "Initial details are sketchy, but it seems the victim died of multiple stab—"

Zian shut the sound off again. "How in Tartarus did she get out there so quick?"

"I don't know," I said. "Was she coming by here to talk to you?"

Zian shook his head. "No, she doesn't know this place exists. That's the whole point of the offsite. We were supposed to be comparing notes there tomorrow afternoon."

I noticed something on the screen that got my attention—Bran being taken into custody. "Hey, kick the sound up again."

Zian took it off mute just as Kennedy said, "... a reputed drug dealer, who was a mere two blocks away from the scene, was apprehended during a preliminary check of the neighborhood. No evidence has yet been presented to link the dealer with this heinous crime, but police officials are confident that—"

Zian killed the sound again. "Go and find out if Bran had something to do with this."

The idea of putting myself in Morgan's crosshairs made my gut clench in dread. But the only way I was going to know everything there was to know about Luc's death was to get there without delay.

Another buzz came through my phone as I made a beeline for the front door.

The text I found was self-explanatory: "If my son dies the next time he tries to help you, there will be a VERY stiff penalty. And trust me when I tell you that no one, not even my dearest uncle, will be able to protect you from my wrath."

18

THE BAD SLEEP WELL

There was no sense using the Stingray to get to the crime scene. Not only would it have drawn the wrong kind of attention, but it only took me about five minutes to get there on foot. Prowl cars were swarming the area, gumball lights flashing as the cops did their usual. The body had been covered up with a tarp, but I spotted Luc's pale right arm sticking out from under it like the proverbial sore thumb. I could make out some sort of tribal tattoo on the inside forearm but no defensive wounds. Maybe they were on his other arm.

One person's presence at this grim scene surprised me. Mayor Galatas was standing in front of a swarm of cameramen and reporters, giving an impromptu press conference with a face and body posture that said "social crusader" to me. I had to admit, even though she looked like she'd just rolled out of bed with an expert makeup job, Her Honor cut an impressive figure. I was enough of a cynic to wonder how many votes Luc's death had just bought her.

"Guess I shouldn't even be surprised that you're here," Ramirez said as she crossed over from the police business side of the tape.

"Just happened to be close by when I heard the news," I said with a shrug.

"Indigo?" she asked, arching an eyebrow at me.

When I nodded, she said, "We found a cell in the vic's hand. His last call was to a number that we couldn't seem to trace ... sounds like your hacker friend's signature."

"Wouldn't know anything about that," I said. I endeavored to change the subject. "What's the mayor doing in this part of town, let alone a crime scene?"

"That's the beauty, if you want to call it that, of an election year," Ramirez replied. "The department doesn't mind Her Honor getting a little screen time just as long as we get credit for doing our jobs right on the campaign trail."

"So this is a PR kickback?"

Ramirez grunted something that didn't pretend to be a laugh. "Good way to put it."

"How's Morgan handling having a politician all over his crime scene?" I asked, looking around for the detective lieutenant, who was sure to be around if Ramirez was.

"Why don't you ask your new girlfriend, *pendejo*?" Mel snapped, cocking a thumb in the opposite direction of where I was looking.

Sure enough, Kennedy was right in front of Morgan, with a cameraman in tow, firing off a series of questions that my least-favorite cop did not want to hear. From what I could make out, he was sticking to officialese and curt answers, the smartest play he could have employed with the mayor on site.

"Mel," I said, turning my attention back to my ex, "I'm telling you that she's not—"

"And she just happened to be with you at our old spot at Sundowner's, right?" she shot back, reminding me once again of a wronged housewife.

"Business, Ramirez," I said, out of patience. "That's all it was. You've got city taxes to pay your salary. I have to go out and earn mine any way I can. Sometimes I even get a chance to make the world a better place."

Ramirez sighed and shook her head. "This isn't another of your crusades, is it, Bell?"

Something about that hurt tone made me feel a little ashamed of myself for a second, but she didn't wait for me to figure out what to say.

"What am I talking about? Of course it is. They're about the only things that ever matter to you."

I wanted to tell her that she was wrong and that I was sorry. I wanted to tell her that every time she walked out, my heart broke a little more. I wanted to say a lot of things that my tongue wasn't letting me get out.

"Why do we keep doing this?" she asked in exasperation. "As long I've known you, it's always been the same. We get together, and you get a case, you start to ignore me, we fight, we break up, rinse and repeat."

I looked down at my shoes. By now, I was past wanting to get my mouth to work and looking for a graceful way to get out of there.

"Want to hear something funny?" Ramirez asked.

I didn't, but I had a feeling that it might give the opening I was looking for, so I nodded.

"Those cases are the only times that I'm sure there's a

good man in there somewhere," she said, her voice getting wistful. "I just wish he'd stay around me for longer than a couple of weeks at a time."

I looked back at her. Something about that statement made me come to a conclusion. "You're saying that you want to try this again?" I asked, finding my voice.

Ramirez gave a quick shake of her head, looking irritated. "I don't know. Ask me again some other night when I'm not mad at you." Going back across the tape, she added, "I'll go earn those city taxes you were talking about."

I let out a long, uneasy breath as she walked off. It wasn't painless, but it could have been a lot worse. I noticed that Kennedy was just wrapping up her non-interview with Morgan and splitting from her cameraman to walk in my direction.

"Now, why am I not surprised to see you out here?" she asked as soon as she was near enough.

"Not as surprised as I am to see you," I said, an accusation behind the statement.

"Hey, if you're implying that I knew about this ahead of time, you're a lot less smart than what I told you at the café," she retorted. "As far as the rest of the world knows, this is just another late-breaking story on my usual night shift. Until I spotted you, that's all I thought too."

"Might be connected to that dealer I was telling you about this afternoon," I told her. "But I'll need to know more to say for sure. Morgan let anything slip?"

"Yeah, that there's a dead body in the street that shouldn't be there," Kennedy said with annoyance. "How about we talk about something that could get us somewhere, like all those victims on our main story?"

I took a quick peek around to make sure no flatfoot was hanging around. The coast was clear. "Okay, give it to me quick."

"All our first batch of victims had been 'requested' to move on out," Kennedy said. "Every last one of them told the landlords where they could stick that request. Sure, they had a rap sheet that included plenty of jail time, but that's never been grounds for an eviction that I ever heard."

"Then they get dead," I added. "Thanks to those rap sheets you mentioned, the cops don't look too hard at the murders."

"And no living relatives to speak up for the departed," Kennedy concluded. "Just another 'price of doing criminal business' moment here in Cold City."

"What about Kurtzenberg?" I asked. "You know, the guy that the CCPD *did* care about."

"Here's where it gets weird," Kennedy said. "Just before his very untimely demise, Mr. Kurtzenberg was having his crew look at two of the properties for 'health and safety reasons,' one particular spot in each building. Looked like he was on that kind of inspection on a third building the night he died."

"What was so bad about the spots he was looking at?" I asked, knowing there was more.

"That's just it," Kennedy answered. "Nothing. I've been over property records and blueprints until I felt like my eyes were going to start crying blood. I keep coming back to a big zero every time."

I spotted a uniform coming our way. "Might be a good idea to split for a few minutes," I told her. "Don't want word to get back to Morgan that we've been spotted here together."

Kennedy didn't miss a beat, just walked away as casually as if I were a fire hydrant.

I took the opportunity to shoot my favorite hacker a quick text to give him a heads-up that the cops might be coming his way. Once I was done sending it, Kennedy was in front of me again.

"Let's blow this popsicle stand," she said, grabbing my hand by the ring and little fingers.

As soon as we were a block away from the lights, she turned on me. "Could you do an interview with me on this?"

I opened my mouth to object, but Kennedy cut me off. "Off the record ... consider yourself a protected source which will never be quoted directly."

"Just remember what we talked about before about info dispersal," I reminded her.

"You're keeping your word, so I'm keeping mine. But I need a few blanks filled in. I can do the rest after that."

I shrugged. "Where do you want to do it?"

"Just give me a lift home, and we'll talk on the way."

It's a funny thing. I'm usually good about remembering details. I can tell you things about someone's clothes that they would never have thought of, recall conversations good enough to pass muster, and tell a decent narrative from beginning to end. But for the life of me, I can't remember that interview I had with Kennedy while I was driving her home. Then again, there's a good reason for my memory problems on this. I was listening to one of Kennedy's questions when a big guy suddenly appeared in my headlights. The oscillation between a psycho football player and a demented goalie told me immediately who it was ... the Berserker.

19
___

DIRTY DEEDS

B efore I could slam on the brakes, the Berserker gave a
bone-chilling war cry two seconds before he put his fist
through the hood. I bounced around in the seat while the
shriek of shredding metal accompanied the destruction of
everything from the grill to just past the engine block. The
airbag slammed in my face while my seatbelt tore into my
shoulder. It was better than flying out of the windshield, but
not much.

I punched my thumb onto the seatbelt buckle and
pushed the door open to get out. Funny how that was one of
the few things on the car that was still in one piece. I looked
back to see Kennedy doing the same thing on her side.

I heard a heavy growl and turned my attention to the
front of the car. I don't know if it was because of the collision
with the car or the shit quality of the Glitter, but the
Berserker was now standing there in his full psycho glory,
the white skull gleaming like a death's head. Another low

growl came from the bottom of his throat before turning into yet another war cry as he charged me.

I got out of the way just in time. A quick glance around told me that we were in Derby, the worst area in Cold City if you were counting on police response to save your ass. I had just enough time to realize that that was precisely why we had been ambushed there before the man-monster snarled, "Pay!"

By some miracle, the wall behind me had soaked up the impact of that wrecking ball on legs hitting it. I wasn't so sure if I was going to survive taking that kind of a hit, Lady McDeath or not. The Berserker ran at me again but at a slower pace this time, the better to swipe at me with his steel-clawed fist.

I ducked and rolled out of the way, grabbing my knife from my ankle holster on the way. By the time I was on my feet, the beast was disoriented, giving me a chance to stab between the metal plates in his side. That's when my luck ran out.

The second the knife sank in, the Berserker whirled—too fast for me to keep a grip on the blade. His studded knuckles crashed into my side like a sledgehammer. I went flying, hitting the asphalt as hard as the man-beast had hit me. I cried out with pain and found myself wishing that I'd thought to bring my Sig with me.

As if in answer to my silent prayer for a firearm, shots started ringing out. They bounced off the Berserker's armor just like mine had done the other night, but at least they distracted his attention from me. Kennedy was crouched behind the wrecked car, delivering shot after shot from her .40 S&W. Another inarticulate roar came from the thing's mouth as it started running down Kennedy's position.

"Get out of the way!" I yelled, pushing past my pain to get the words out.

Kennedy didn't need to be told twice. She did a quick sidestep half a second before the Berserker did more damage to my car by flipping it into the air. The poor, abused Stingray crashed into the wall, taking out a window, before landing back on the ground with a loud crunch.

Kennedy, meanwhile, was running over to me and taking hold of my arm to haul me up.

"We've got to spread out," I said between coughs.

"Shut up and get on your feet, hoss," Kennedy snapped back as she helped me do just that.

My legs were barely under me when the Berserker started uttering sounds I could understand. Not that the words were any comfort: "Die! Human!"

I got a glimpse of my knife in his back before he turned around again. Kennedy held me under the shoulder with one arm while aiming her .40 with the other. Even she had to know it wasn't going to be enough.

I heard a familiar sound I couldn't place as the Berserker made a run at us. In fact, I didn't place it until its source crashed into that bastard full tilt boogie ... a Prius. The car knocked the creature down like it'd been hit with a giant fist out of some cartoon. It didn't do the car much good, mind you ... the hood was smashed in from the impact along with every window in it. Kennedy, for her part, emptied the rest of her clip into the now prone serial killer.

This bought us a few seconds of respite, but the fight was far from over. As soon as the Berserker got back on his feet, he would kill every last one of us. I took a few steps backward and felt my foot tap against something metallic ... a can of hair spray. Judging from its undamaged condition, I guessed it must have escaped from Kennedy's purse. I reached down to grab it just as her handgun clicked empty.

Kennedy gave me a look that seemed apologetic. "I got to get a clip out of my back pocket."

"I'll buy you some time," I assured her with a nod.

She let go of my arm, and I willed myself to keep standing. Once I was sure that I could, I started walking towards the thing, which I knew had killed four people already.

"Gotta admit, I'm surprised," I yelled. "I mean, I knew you were good at murdering old men, women, and children who didn't stand a chance. But I wondered how you'd do against someone who could fight back."

The growl as he rose was what I was going for. Sure, this divinely empowered thug had no qualms about snuffing out any mortal life. But pointing out what exactly he was stung him in that abomination he called "honor."

"You see, I wonder if that's the reason why you didn't finish me off last time," I went on, wrapping my free hand around the Zippo I always kept in one of my jacket pockets. "You'd have to work at your kill, and you're just too lazy to want to bother."

"Maggot," the Berserker sneered while I used my thumb to pry the top off the spray can.

"Wow, the way you speak English, I'm surprised the word is even in your vocabulary."

By then, I knew I had to be in Kennedy's line of fire. That was deliberate on my part. I stood a better chance of surviving what was coming next than she did. The monster was on his feet now, pulling my knife from its back and brandishing it like it was a sword. I slipped the Zippo out of my pocket and opened it.

"Well, what are you waiting for, you pussy?!" I shouted. "Do what you came to do!"

The Berserker aimed the knife at my belly as he ran at me, but I was ready. I brought my hands up and lit up the Zippo. The stream from the can hit the flame, turning the haircare product into an instant fireball. My would-be killer screamed in agony as the flames hit him square in the face, making him drop the knife as he tore off the bear skull. Another myth about the Berserkers busted.

Then he started swinging blind, catching me in the chest with one of his swipes. It sent me flying the way the Prius had him, knocking me to the opposite side of the street, where I hit something hard and metallic.

I could hear Kennedy's gun doing its business as I shook my head clear. It turned out that a dumpster with two doors on top had broken my flight. Somehow I still had a hold of both the spray can and the Zippo. Using the dumpster's side to brace me, I got back on my feet. The side I was on had an open door where all sorts of foul things were producing a distinctive aroma. A glimpse of some moldy newspaper inside gave me an idea.

Climbing up the side a little, I sparked off the spray can again with the Zippo. This time, my makeshift flamethrower began burning the trash inside. Once the spray was lit up, I threw open the door on the other side of the dumpster to make sure the fire was getting enough air. In no time, I had a bonfire going so intense that I had to get out of the way to avoid getting burned. I could feel the heat coming through the metal as I slid down the side.

I heard a roar from the Berserker and then the sound of its heavy feet running off into the night. Then another set of feet, much lighter, came closer ... Kennedy.

"Mind explaining to me how you knew a dumpster fire would make him run when getting hit by two cars back to back had no effect whatsoever?" she asked as she helped me to my feet.

"Publicity," I wheezed as we staggered back to the wrecked cars. "He didn't have any qualms about killing anything he could get his hands on. But that ..."—I nodded my head towards the burning trash—"... that is way more attention than he wanted. Whoever is holding his leash must have given him precise instructions to keep a low profile."

The driver of the Prius was groaning from the pain of his self-created wreck. A flash of messy bleach-blond hair told us both who it was.

"Zian!" Kennedy said. "How did you find us?"

"Is he ... is he gone?" Zian asked, his voice croaking with strain.

"Yeah, Z," I said, pulling the door open, the metal yawning in protest. "You did good."

At first glance, it looked like nothing short of the Jaws of Life would get Zian out. But the Prius' safety features made the job a lot easier than I expected. We were soon able to get him out and lay him on the ground. My own injuries were screaming at me the entire time I was engaged in this mission of mercy.

"Are you okay, Zian? Did the crash do something to your eyes?" Kennedy asked.

She was bent over him, a tissue in hand as she dabbed at a wound on my friend's scalp. Even in the dim light of the streetlamps, it was obvious that the dark color of his eyes was eating too much at the whites to pass for human.

"It's heterochromia," I explained, backing up Zian's previous explanation. I leaned against the totaled Prius, my strength spent. "His eyes change like that when he's under intense stress."

Zian nodded, and as I watched, his eyes started to return to their normal, lighter hue.

"I thought heterochromia was a permanent difference between both eyes," Kennedy objected. "I looked it up earlier."

"It's a rare condition," Zian said as he got up. "Runs in the family."

He propped himself up against the Prius next to me, affording me a good look at his injuries. He had a cut to the side of his head, but it had stopped bleeding. His Pac-Man shirt was torn in two places, but the wounds beneath seemed superficial.

I locked gazes with him. "You okay?" I asked.

He waved my concern aside and glanced at his totaled Prius. "I loved that car."

"Yeah, I kinda liked mine too," I said with a mirthless chuckle. "Now, about how you found us ...?"

"I was heading to your place," he explained as he started patting his pockets. "I thought we could figure out what happened to Luc together. Then I saw that ... thing, and I just improvised."

"The fire department's going to be here pretty soon,"

Kennedy interrupted, indicating the blazing dumpster. "I'll get us a cab out of here."

Zian had picked up my knife while I wasn't looking. After he had handed it back to me, he pulled out his own phone, the screen intact despite the crash.

"I'll send an SOS to my favorite towing company to get the cars out of here," he said, his fingers working the phone's screen. "I know some mechanics who can work miracles."

"I'll pay you back," I offered while sheathing the knife.

"The Tartarus you will," Zian retorted. "Everything from the tow to the repairs is going to be on the house. Just got to find some mundane office-related supplies my father won't look at twice to file it under." He winced. "If he saw how bashed up I was, he'd finish the job the Prius started."

I remembered his father's last text message to me and shivered.

20

GOOD RUN OF BAD LUCK

I groaned in pain when the smartphone woke me up with the upbeat "Do You Want to Date My Avatar." A glance at my watch told me it was close to ten-thirty.

It took a couple of seconds for me to remember what had happened before I went to sleep. After our near-fatal encounter with the Berserker, we'd caught the cab Kennedy ordered a couple of blocks away from the dumpster fire. I was barely holding on by then. I hadn't even taken off my jacket before I collapsed on my bed and was out in seconds. Now every inch of me felt heavy, bruised, and every bit as filthy as the trash I'd burned last night.

But one thing at a time ... I picked up the phone.

"Yeah," I grunted.

"Hey, Bell, it's Zian," my savior of the previous night said at the other end. "Just checking in to see how you're feeling."

"Like I was the one who got hit by two cars instead of that Berserker," I admitted. "But I'll live. You?"

"A little sore and a few bruises," Zian admitted. "I need

to see you right away. Some of the work I was doing at the offsite may have just paid off for us."

"How?" I asked, straightening up a little more and doing my best to ignore the soreness.

"Better if I tell you in person," Zian assured me.

"Umm, I don't mean to be critical, but wouldn't me seeing you in person require one of us to have a functioning car?" I asked, moving myself into a sitting position.

"Just heard from my guys—both of our cars are ready for pickup."

"That was amazingly fast, considering what kind of shape both of them wound up in. They must have worked all night!"

"Family connections go a long way."

I rose to my feet. "So ... any chance you might bring my Stingray over?"

"Absolutely," Zian assured me. "Give me half an hour."

"The way I'm feeling, I'll be glad to give you two," I assured him.

We rang off, and I headed to the shower to clean up the filth and dried blood off my skin. I had just finished putting on fresh clothes when I heard a knock at my newly refurbished front door. I suspected that the people who'd been trying to kill me for the last couple of days wouldn't be that polite, but it didn't stop me from retrieving my Sig before I went to the peephole. The fisheye showed me it was Kennedy.

The look on her face when I opened the door was ... well, overwhelmed might be the best way to describe it. She came in without a greeting, and I shut the door behind her. She saw me peek back through the peephole to check she was alone.

"Nobody's after me, Vale. At least, I don't think so."

"Morning to you too, sunshine," I said, turning to her. "What's going on?"

She licked her lips before taking a seat on my couch. "I can't get last night out of my head," she admitted. "That ... thing ... looked like a man, but what kind of man shrugs off bullets like they're raindrops and survives not one but two cars plowing into him?"

I was glad that she hadn't realized that it was the Berserker who had plowed into my Stingray, not the reverse. "C'mon, Kennedy," I remonstrated with her, "you've been a reporter long enough to know that there's plenty of reasonable explanations for why he was able to take and dish out that kind of damage ... steroids, PCP, body armor—"

The shocked expression on her face was replaced by an angry stare in my direction. "Sarah Connor didn't buy that speech in *Terminator,* and I'm not buying it now. I know you know more than you're telling."

I took a deep breath. "All I can say is that there's a very good reason I've not been letting you know more."

"Well, how about confirming the very solid suspicion I have that whoever or whatever we were tangling with is behind those wolf killings?" Kennedy asked, not letting me off the hook.

After the previous night, the truth on this one was the least I could give her. "Yeah ... and I doubt you would have believed me before last night if I'd told you what that SOB could do."

Kennedy's face softened a little. "Well, it's not like you

didn't tell me that this could be dangerous ..." Then she sighed a little huff of frustration. "But that's not all that's bothering me this morning."

I sat down next to her. "What is it?"

"Ever since I woke up this morning, nothing's been going right," she explained. She held up her right hand. Her otherwise flawless manicure had a couple of chipped nails. "That happened first thing this morning," she said, putting her hand down. "On the way to work—"

"Wait, don't you work the late shift?" I queried.

"Sure, but the head of the station doesn't," she answered. "I was going to see him about putting our little story on an exclusive basis."

I nodded.

"Anyway, on the way over to the station, my car got an ugly scrape from a passing bike," she went on. "It left a scar that's going to take more money than I've got to buff out. Then I get an offer of coffee while I'm waiting for the big cheese, and things get even worse—not only was it the vilest version of bean juice ever brewed, I wound up spilling it on my hand while my taste buds were kicking me for doing that to them."

"Maybe you're just having a bad morning," I said with a shrug. "After the night you've had, and lack of sleep."

"And I want to believe that, hoss," Kennedy replied, looking at me with an eagerness that was two steps short of desperation. "I really, really do, more than I want to believe what you just tried to sell me about that man-mountain we ran into last night. But my guts keep screaming at me that this is something else ... something bad."

I was starting to get a little uneasy. I didn't want to think that what was happening to her was what I suspected it was. But, like I said, I don't believe in coincidence as a rule.

"Got any coffee that might taste better than that swill at work?" she asked, changing the subject.

"Can't stand the stuff myself," I admitted. "How about some green tea?"

"Sure. Just my luck today to come to the only guy in this city who doesn't have any coffee in his kitchen."

She eyed me as I got up. "You're sure you're okay? You look like crap, and you're taking beating after beating this week."

"I'll be fine, just need some sleep and rest," I said, grabbing the box of tea bags from the cupboard.

That made me take my first real look at Kennedy. Despite the obvious short night, she looked fresh as a rose. She was wearing a peach blouse and a black pencil skirt over ankle-high black boots.

She looked suddenly apologetic. "Ahh, hell, I didn't wake you up, did—"

"Nah, nah," I told her as I poured water into my electric kettle up to the two-cup mark. "Zian already did that by calling me up just before you got here. Wanted to see if I was okay."

"How 'bout him?" Kennedy asked as I fetched a pair of cups from the cupboard.

"Sore, but he's good," I assured her. "He's coming by in a bit. Got time to stay and compare notes?"

Kennedy cast an appreciative glance around my place. "Right now, I think this is the safest place in Cold City for me."

The water reached a full boil. As soon as it clicked off, I

set about making the tea. "So how'd the meeting go with Mr. Station Chief?"

"About as bad as everything else today," Kennedy said with a shake of her head. "Somehow, my dipshit cameraman managed to lose the recording we made of that murder last night. I got blamed for that."

"Why?" I asked, making a face.

"Hell if I know, Vale," she scoffed. "Not the first time that I got shot down. But this one hurt. Not only was I not given the exclusive on this story, but I—and I quote—'needed to stop pretending that I was Lois Lane.'"

"Damn prick," I muttered. More than one CO I'd served under in the Navy came to mind ... ticket-punchers who took a sadistic delight in making their subordinates miserable. God help you if you happened to be a woman under their command.

"Hope this doesn't make you think that I'm bad luck to you," I quipped, only half-jokingly.

"Ahh, it's nothing," Kennedy said, pulling a notepad and pen from her purse. "Just jitters from last night mixed with a lot of disappointments this morning. I mean, c'mon, I was shooting at a human tank last night, and this morning, I'm freaked out about a cup of coffee?"

The tea had steeped by then. I pulled out the bags and tossed them in the trash. "How much sugar do you want?"

"Just one scoop, thanks. Damn it, I swear this pen was full the last time I used it."

I felt my gut clench a little at that last sentence. This many small things going wrong in succession was beginning to look like more than coincidence. So many coincidences in a row, in the circles I swim in, are usually anything but ...

Still, I did my best to keep the unease off my face as I handed Kennedy her tea.

No sooner had I handed the cup to her than the handle broke off, and the mug fell to the table, shattering. Tea spilled everywhere, including on Kennedy's bare legs. Thank God I'd let it cool down some before I brought it over.

We gave each other a look. It was a look based on a mutual acknowledgment of what was happening—coupled with absolute fear over what could be causing it.

———

I'd just finished cleaning up the mess when I got another knock at the door. Zian was waiting on the other side this time. He looked a little surprised to see Kennedy when he came in.

"Umm, I didn't come at a bad time, did I?" he asked.

"Now why would you say something as foolish as that?" Kennedy challenged him. She had taken her shoes off and was half sitting and half lying on the couch as she finished drying her legs with a towel.

"Well, I mean, if you and Vale need a little more private time, I can always—"

"Stop digging, Z," I warned, putting an arm around his shoulders. "You're already in a deep enough hole."

"Oh ... oh," Zian stammered. "I-I'm so sorry I ever thought—"

Kennedy shot me a look of gratitude then cleared her throat. "Let's talk about something else, what do you say?"

Zian nodded, and I let him go. He sat down next to her on the couch while I remained standing.

"You all right?" Kennedy asked Zian with honest concern as she slipped her shoes back on. "You took a hell of a hit last night."

"Just a little sore," he answered. "And glad everybody got out of that one alive."

"So what do you have for us, Zian?" I asked, getting the conversation back on track.

"Everybody's smartphone still work?" he asked, pulling out a trio of flash drives.

After handing us each one of them, he plugged the remaining one into his phone. Once he was sure we'd done the same with ours, he said, "Scroll down to page three."

Kennedy nodded when she saw what was coming up on her screen. "I've been digging into these murder victims you told Vale about," she told him. "All of them had rap sheets with gang and drug-related crimes plastered all over them. I couldn't find any connection between them, but if they got in Ramon De Soto's way, there wouldn't be anything to find."

"I don't buy that for a second," I countered. "Everything I heard, De Soto's only that kind of brutal when all the better options are off the table."

"What if he wants to send a message?" Kennedy argued.

"Then he does it with one guy, not four in a row," I told her, knowing I sounded more defensive than I needed to.

As we continued scrolling, I spotted a pattern emerging. "Looks like every one of them had some kind of ultra-violent charge on their record."

"I'd peg them for local muscle," said Kennedy.

"My money's on Arete being behind these killings," I said at last. "Blood is a very big expense, but if they've got deep enough pockets to take on the city ..."

"That matches up with the work logs of the late Mr. Kurtzenberg," Zian remarked. "Check page nine. He had a lot of contact with Arete in the course of his work, helping them coordinate the Orion project."

"That wasn't all he was doing," Kennedy added. "Like I told Vale last night, he was also doing some solo work on a couple of buildings."

"In each one, he concentrated on one particular point," I put in. "Anything unusual happen around the time of Kurtzenberg's death that might tell us something?"

Zian thought for a moment. "Page fifteen."

A look at the page in question showed how the legal wrangling between Fairwinds and Arete had heated up considerably around that time.

"When they weren't taking on Arete, it looks like Fairwinds was going toe-to-toe with the city," Kennedy noted. "That leaves us with the two more recent murders and the one that Vale here prevented. Also, the first signs of Arete popped up around the time that the first batch of killings got started."

"Yeah, it's in the file," said Zian. "If you look at page twenty-three—"

"Do any of these records show that Arete was incorporated about a year and a half ago?" Kennedy demanded.

Zian did some quick flicking through his reams of data and then shook his head.

"All hard copy," I surmised. "The incorporation paperwork was never put on a computer system. But it's there for anybody else who wants proof that the outfit is for real."

"It's a classic shelf corporation," Kennedy concluded.

"Umm, shouldn't that be 'shell corporation'?" Zian asked.

"No, no," Kennedy replied, shaking her head. "I meant what I said. How it works is that the corporation is formed on paper, all the i's dotted, all the t's crossed. After that, nothing happens for a while except regular maintenance of the taxes and whatnot needed to keep it operating. Then, when it's time to use it for what you needed it for, you take it off the shelf and get to work."

"Like, say, when it's time for a big gentrification project like Orion that you couldn't justify in a city council meeting," I speculated, tapping my chin. "Which means this ties in with somebody at City Hall."

"I haven't seen that hard copy you mentioned yet," Kennedy admitted, "but I got a source I'm trying to develop ... might hand it over to me in the next day or two."

"So when did Fairwinds come into the picture?" I asked both of them.

"Page thirty-two," Zian told us.

One quick scroll later, I saw that the official incorporation had taken place a full year before the first killing spree.

"Don't bother looking up the corporate officers on those papers," Kennedy advised us. "I checked them out and—"

"They were all bogus cut-out IDs, untraceable," Zian finished, sounding embarrassed. "I sort of found that out the hard way."

Scrolling down a little further, I came upon the various property purchases Fairwinds had made. "These addresses are all in the same area as the Cinema Leone, right?"

"Yeah," Zian confirmed. "Almost everything that Arete and/or the city didn't gobble up first."

Further down, I found a long trail of correspondence between Fairwinds and Mr. Nicholls. The amounts being offered would have enabled him to buy a multiplex and self-finance it for a full year. But Nicholls kept sending back the same letter over and over. If you had to boil the verbiage into a single sentence, it'd be "no thanks."

"I'm pretty sure it's buried on this drive somewhere, Z," I pondered aloud, "but just out of curiosity, how much—"

"—is Cinema Leone worth?" Zian finished with a smirk as he leaned back on the couch. "The figure I saw on the property value was something like half of what the city offered to take it off Mr. Nicholls' hands."

"How's it stack with this figure?" Kennedy asked, holding her open notepad up to Zian.

Zian read what was written there and whistled. "That's about three times the city's offer if you wrote that down right."

"That's what Fairwinds is offering Nicholls' heirs per my sources. I doubt they were exaggerating."

"Okay, what's so damn valuable about an old-time movie theater?" I asked, trying to conceal the fact that I already knew the answer to the question. "I loved that old place as much as the next regular, but from a real estate standpoint, it's worthless."

"When it comes to land, nearly all of it's worth something to somebody," Kennedy countered, picking up her phone. "Back in Texas, my grandma and grandpa had this little tar shack house they lived in for fifty years or so. They made all the improvements that you'd expect, installing air conditioning and water heaters and so on, but that poor place was a health and safety inspector's worst nightmare. I loved the place because it was their home, but nobody would have shed any tears if it had burned to the ground. Just the same, they kept getting uninvited visitors ... the corporate kind."

I put it together. "There was oil on the land where the house was?"

"You got it, Vale. One of the last untapped fields in all of Texas and, once the oil companies figured that out, Grandma and Grandpa couldn't get any peace. They kept offering them small fortunes to sell, but they wouldn't hear of it. The fools had to wait until both Grandma and Grandpa had passed before they could grab it."

"So the real question is, what's so valuable about the ground under the theater and everything else around it?" Zian deduced.

Kennedy gave him a kiss on the cheek for getting it. My friend's face turned fire-engine red.

Kennedy looked at her phone again and frowned.

"See something else we need to look at?" I asked.

"No, just noticed the time," she answered, pulling the drive out of the phone. "Okay if I keep this?"

"I made sure there were three drives for a reason," Zian told her with a smile and a nod.

"So you're working the day shift today?" I asked her.

"Just so I can catch up on what I missed the day I was out," Kennedy explained as she got up. "It's hard to do that when you're chasing stories all over town all night long. This was my lunch break. Gotta be back in fifteen."

"Okay if ... if I walk you down?" Zian asked, looking about as shy as a high-school freshman asking the prettiest cheerleader out on a date.

She shot him a smile that lit up the room. "Love you to."

I watched the two of them from the door as they headed for the stairway. No reason why I should, except that my instincts were telling me that I needed to keep a close eye on them.

When it came, it was quick, eye-blink quick. Something like a shadow flashed past behind the two of them. Without warning, Kennedy's left heel snapped, sending her down the stairs. Poor Zian tried to catch her, but all he managed to do was get dragged down with her. As I heard both of them yelp and hit the bottom, I ran out after them to check they were all right.

Kennedy had landed right on top of Zian, who was groaning from the fresh jolt he had just given the previous night's injuries. Given how many stairs there were between the top and the bottom, I knew for a fact that my little hacker pal had just saved our favorite reporter's life. Kennedy's breathing was ragged—the kind you hear when a person is terrified at what is happening to them, what keeps happening to them. Zian gave me a look over her shoulder. I nodded. Coincidence is overrated as a working concept.

21

GRAVE MARKERS

Z ian wasn't happy about it, but Kennedy and I insisted on looking him over. A peek under his shirt revealed bandages around his chest. His ribs had gotten cracked in the crash the previous night, and we learned that his doctor had advised him to avoid any further hard collisions like that for the next couple of weeks.

"And here I go and set your recovery back by who knows how long," Kennedy murmured.

"Isn't your lunch break almost up?" I asked her as Zian put his shirt back on.

"It was up about three minutes ago," Kennedy said. "Whatever's going on with me today seems to enjoy putting me in these lose-lose situations. This keeps up, I might even be fired when I get back."

She gave Zian another peck on the cheek and an apology for hurting him. He bore it as best he could but let us help him out of the building.

Once outside, Kennedy waved goodbye to both of us and climbed into her Nissan. As she sped off, Zian turned to me.

"Your new girlfriend's in serious trouble, Bell."

"What is it going to take to convince everybody—" I began irritably.

"Her coming out as a lesbian and you marrying Ramirez in a public ceremony," Zian interrupted without missing a beat. "Now if you're done being offended, you mind having me elaborate on the trouble that I was talking about?"

"You saw that shadow-shape thing too, just before she fell?" I asked.

Zian looked surprised that I'd seen it.

"She's had escalating bad luck for the entire morning, Zian," I explained. "The last instance before the heel-snapping happened right before you got to my place. My tea mug broke in her hands."

"But nothing else happened while she was in your place, right? Nothing like what we witnessed just now?"

"No. Might have been because of the protection I've got on the place. It wasn't until she got back outside that her first near-fatal bit of bad luck kicked in."

"Sounds like we're dealing with a Yattery Brown," Zian muttered.

I raised an eyebrow. He hastened to explain.

"It's an old story about a fairy that a farmer saves. It pays him back by doing all the chores, but fairly incompetently. The farmer then does the one thing he's not supposed to do —he thanks Yattery Brown aloud—and his troubles go from bad to worse. Eventually, the bad luck kills him."

"No offense, Z, but that's hardly what's going on here," I pointed out.

"Didn't say it was, but it's the usual shorthand around my family for this kind of curse. Things will just keep getting worse for Kennedy unless we figure out how to break it."

"The girl gives you a couple of pecks on the cheek, and you're all in when it comes to saving her?" I asked. The situation was serious, but picking at Zian helped keep my nerves steady.

"Hey, if you blow it with her, I want her to know that I'm an available option," he retorted.

I tried to hold back a chuckle.

"But seriously," Zian went on, "who'd want to do that to her? And who'd have the chops to pull it off?"

"The only fae creature I've been in contact with is that changeling dealer, Bran Connor," I told him. "But all Connor's dealings have been with me. Why would she bother with Kennedy? Or know enough about her to curse her in the first place?"

Zian stroked his chin. "Well, Connor would have seen Kennedy the night she got arrested ... I think maybe this has something to do with this investigation the three of us are involved in."

I felt a frown tug the corner of my mouth. "Makes sense up to a point. Lady McDeath won't let anybody kill me but her. Your dad probably spends half his time protecting you. With Kennedy not having any protection and not knowing anything about Alterum Mundum, she's the weak link in the chain."

"But then we're back to how they knew about her being involved," Zian pointed out. "Guess it doesn't matter in the short term. Until we can figure this out, I'd prescribe a good luck charm for Kennedy."

"Assuming you brought my car with you, I know just the place to get one," I told him.

Zian waved me towards the far end of the parking lot. "Surely you're not going to Mad Mao for this?"

"What if I am? That old Taoist wizard might be touched in the head, but his charms are worth their weight in gold."

"Well ... it's just that I've heard stories," Zian ventured.

"In other words, you've never actually been to see the man yourself?"

"Hades, damn it, is this another one of your 'I need to get out more' lectures?" Zian asked with irritation. "I love you, Vale, but I think you try too hard to be my dad sometimes."

"Can't help it," I said, which was the truth. "You're a sweet guy whose actual dad has been sheltering him a little too much."

Zian didn't say anything after that. We arrived at the Stingray. You'd have sworn that it had just rolled off the factory assembly line. Every detail was showroom perfect.

"The keys are in the ignition," said Zian.

"Don't know what to say, Z," I told him. "Except 'thank you'—and that hardly seems to cover it."

A wan smile returned to my friend's face. "Look, Bell, you were right when you said that I've never stopped long enough to be curious about real life. It's just ... before you came into my life, I never thought about it. Now I can't think about anything else."

"Hasn't been so great so far," I said.

"Hey, banging up the Prius was my choice, and I'd do it again." He pulled out his smartphone and tapped something briefly into it. "There's something about real-world contact with people that no VR or online forum has yet to match."

"Hope you never get around to regretting it," I said. If his father thought staying away from me would cure Zian of this hunger, he was deluding himself. He'd gotten a taste of real life all right, and there was no going back.

We spent a couple of minutes checking the Stingray for any tiny traces of the damage done the previous night, but there was nothing. Then a cab pulled up, and I figured that's what the texting had been about.

"As soon as you find anything on Kennedy's problem, give me a shout," he said as he walked away.

"That phone line runs both ways," I called after him.

He gave me a nod and a wave in acknowledgment. Then he got into the cab, and I got in my car.

———

It took seven times for me to get through to Kennedy's cell while dialing from the driver's seat of my Stingray. On the first six attempts, the call went straight to voicemail on the third ring. In between attempts three and four, I thought about whether or not to go ahead and spill the beans to the De Sotos on who their would-be competition was. I was going to have to do this eventually, and their taking Connor out might break the curse into the bargain. But too many faerie curses were designed to outlive the death of their creators.

All this was going through my head when Kennedy picked up. "Hey, Vale. What's going on?"

"Did you know that I tried to call you about six times before this?" I asked.

"Really?" She sounded surprised. "I never got them. The bloody phone's been acting up all morning."

"That figures ..." I muttered.

"What's that?" Kennedy asked. "Reception's not good."

"Listen, I'm going to pick something up for you, something that might help with that problem you talked about this morning. Where's a good place and when?"

"I've got an interview with Ian Townsend in about an hour," she told me. "Know the CVS at the corner of Mitchell and Scarborough?"

"That's on the way between your station and AN, right?"

"You're good, hoss," she said. "If you can be there in about half an hour, I'll be glad to take whatever you can give me."

"All right, will do. Meantime ... be careful, will you?"

She must have heard the concern in my voice because she took it seriously. "As much as I can, Vale. It's all I've been doing since ... you know."

"Yeah," I said. "See you soon."

She said goodbye, and I turned the key in the ignition.

———

Bad luck struck again as the Headliner van carrying Kennedy rolled up to the CVS parking lot. Its passenger side rear tire popped with a crack, and the tire was already three-quarters flat by the time it came to a halt. The driver, a young guy who looked like he'd just graduated high school the previous week, jumped from the vehicle and all but moaned, "Ah, man! Of all the times ..."

"You got a spare for that?" I asked, walking up to take a look.

"Nah," he answered. "The only way we're going anywhere is to fix this one."

"It'll take less time if two guys do it," I assured him. "I got a jack in my car if you need some additional support on that beast."

The driver gave a little laugh. "I know I'd feel a lot safer if you'd bring that jack over."

"Look at it this way, Dave," Kennedy said as she emerged through the passenger door. "This could have been a lot worse."

"Just the same, Candice, we're kind of on a tight schedule," Dave said, tapping his wristwatch. "So ..."

"So you get your stuff out, and I'll get that jack," I told him.

"You got an air pump too, mister?" Kennedy asked, making like she didn't know me. "If we could put one of those together with a little tire sealant, we might get back to the station in one piece."

"Think I might, miss," I said. "Want to help me check?"

Kennedy gave me another one of her lamplighter smiles and followed behind me as we went towards my car.

Once I was sure we were out of earshot, I asked, "What's with the charade?"

"Well, there's a rumor going around that I'm married," Kennedy said as we got close to the Stingray. "I should know. I started it."

"You know, a ring might go a long way towards making that theory more convincing," I said, popping the trunk open.

Kennedy gave me a girlish giggle. "Oh, it's more fun having them guess who the lucky guy, or girl, is. I keep a rotating number of pictures in my purse that I pull out when I want to stir the pot."

I pulled back the floor of the trunk. "You're unbelievable, Kennedy."

"So's been the last couple of days," she said. "Now ... what have you got for me?"

"Keep an open mind," I said, reaching into my pocket. I pulled out a silver chain. Suspended on it was a Chinese bronze coin that was strung through the tiny hole in its center.

Kennedy wrinkled her nose. "Where'd you get this, the antique store that sold the Gremlins?"

"Hey," I said, handing it to her. "I'll have you know that this is a specially made Taoist good luck charm."

"So what's all this writing mean?" Kennedy asked, looking the coin over.

While I got out the jack, I explained. "The crowded side is a mix of regular Chinese conji and what Taoists call 'magic writing.' It's a prayer to the god of thunder to protect the wearer from the demons of bad luck."

"And the neater side with all the Morse Code?"

"That's the bagua," I said, looking for the air pump. "Comes from the same system as the I-Ching. That's referencing the power of the universe to cut you some slack."

I found the air pump tucked behind my own spare tire, so I pulled it out and shut the trunk. Kennedy was holding the necklace like it was poisoned wine.

"Look, Kennedy," I said patiently. "Ask yourself a question ... what do you have to lose by wearing it?"

She frowned at me but put it on. "My daddy would kill me if he knew I was using what he'd call 'heathen prayers.' But since Jesus doesn't seem to be too interested in saving my ass ..."

"There's a BP station down the street that'll sell you that sealant," I said. "I'll go help Dave."

We parted ways. Dave was grateful beyond belief that I had managed to get both the jack and the air pump I'd mentioned. We had the tire off by the time Kennedy got back with the sealant. A few more minutes and the van was ready to go. Dave took down my info so he could return the air pump when they'd done with it. We all said our goodbyes, and I went back to my car.

Once I had closed the driver's side door behind me, I gave the number Bran had left me a call. She picked up on the second ring.

"Bellamy Vale," she said just a little brightly. "I'm so glad you decided to call me back."

"Shouldn't you be stuck in a jail cell right about now?" I asked, on the defensive. "I saw you got hauled in by the cops for dealing and murder one last night."

"Well, it's fortunate for me that I was able to establish a solid enough alibi to be taken off the murder suspect list," Bran said. "As to that whole misunderstanding on the drug charges ... my employers retain very capable lawyers."

"You know, it's a funny thing," I said, doing my best to act as casual as Lt. Columbo ever had. "You get arrested, and the reporter on the scene suddenly has this incredible streak of bad luck happen to him right after that."

"You don't say?" Bran responded. "You're well-informed

on this matter. This reporter wouldn't happen to be a new client of yours, would sh-he?"

I caught the slip but didn't let on that I had. "I take my clients' confidentiality very seriously, Bran. You know I can't talk about that."

"Of course, of course," Bran replied. "That is part of the reason why they hire someone like you in the first place."

"Let's say that something ... out of the ordinary is causing this to happen to our reporter," I suggested. "Any idea where I should start looking?"

Bran sighed. "Sorry, no can do. Have you come to a decision regarding my offer?"

"Not really," I admitted. "The more I look at it, the more unsure I am about what the right thing to do is. I have to imagine that this offer has a time limit on it."

"Let's say forty-eight hours," Bran proposed. "If you don't get back in touch by then, I'll just assume the answer is 'no' ... fair?"

"More than fair," I agreed. "I'll be in touch."

We rang off, and I started up the car. I didn't turn towards home, I was betting that a look over Kennedy's apartment might help me find where the curse originated from.

———

There was an apartment complex just across the street from Mountain Shade, so I stashed the Stingray there. Once the busy four lanes of traffic gave me a break, I went across.

Most of Kennedy's neighbors were gone for the day to whatever job paid their rent here. The duplicate key Zian had made slid in just as easy as if it had been the original. I walked in and started searching.

One common feature of most curses is a personal possession. The cursing party gives the person they're cursing something that acts as an active link to the spell. Touch it once, and you're done for. It could be nearly anything, depending on the tradition. While it was possible that Kennedy was carrying that item on her right then, something about that mention of chipped nails was telling me that it was here.

In the twenty minutes I was looking the place over, I found out a little bit more about Kennedy. Like a lot of kids who'd clawed their way out of hardscrabble backgrounds, she'd been an academic dynamo — valedictorian of her high school graduating class, an AA in some community college I'd never heard of, a magna cum laude BA in Communications from UC Berkley ... she had a solid enough record to show that she'd never gotten by on just her looks.

I found a lifetime membership card in the NRA on her bookshelf, but I also found plenty of Democratic memorabilia from various campaigns of the last twenty years in a hope chest at the foot of her bed. That collection ranged from paraphernalia from President Obama's two successful campaigns to a folded-up old picket sign that read "Remember Ann Richards."

Oh, and about that bookshelf ... plenty of hardboiled fiction populated that space. She seemed to have every book Mickey Spillane ever published in his lifetime and complete collections of the work of Robert E. Howard, forgotten Texas son and creator of Conan the Barbarian. Scattered here and there were some books by another Texan writer, Joe R. Lansdale, and one of my personal favorites, Max Allan Collins.

Well, while it would be interesting to know all this if I was going to be dating her—not that I was thinking about that ... much—I was no closer to finding anything that would help me figure out what was attacking her. I knew it would come to this, but I'd been putting it off by trying to find what I was looking for in more conventional ways. But there was no other option, so ... I turned on my sixth sense.

Even though I was bracing myself for the usual unpleasantness, I got knocked off my heels a bit. There was a force in this apartment that was magical, active, and ready to deal out death. That last part was what I had been counting on. I forced myself to keep my psychic sight on. While it was good for finding evidence that vanilla eyes would miss, it was not the best of tools to track magical links. The way it feels—it's as if magic has its own protection around it, which also acts as a repellent. The stronger the magic, the harder it pushes back.

Fighting my reluctance to go closer to the source of the necrotic energies, I followed its trail to the kitchen counter. At that point, however, it became too much, and I shut off my sixth sense.

I spent another minute or two convincing my stomach that it could hang onto its breakfast. That's when I noticed that the only thing in front of me was a pharmacy receipt. I looked it over, turned it over, and found nothing remarkable on it that the naked eye could ever make out, which meant that there was only one thing left to do.

Apologizing to my stomach in advance, I turned my sixth sense back on. Fighting to keep my concentration up, I spotted a sigil scratched on the front side of the paper. It was barely there, and I knew it would become invisible the instant my body made me shut off my extended sight. Pulling out a pen, I did my best to trace it. I'd just finished the last mark when my sixth sense decided time was up.

I collapsed on the counter from the strain. It took several deep breaths to get a modicum of control back, reminding me that this was important. Once I felt steady enough, I pocketed the receipt and the pen, and I left.

I spent the next two hours after getting back to my apartment poring over my books for a match for the sigil. While several of them were close, none of them were an exact enough match to be helpful.

I switched over to the Internet for information, typing up "Celtic runes" in Zian's private search engine out of the Indigo. If this curse was fae in nature, investigating the Celtic angle seemed a natural place to start. It sent me to the Ogham alphabet, sometimes mistakenly called "Celtic runes." Certain letters in that alphabet were a near-perfect match for the lines on the sigil and, when put together, were all about turning the Wheel of Fate against the affected party. With this new information, I went back to my reference books.

Now, I'm no magician by any means. Any knowledge I've got of the art comes second to third-hand at best. Still, I had managed the occasional ritual to help me out in specific situations like this. An hour later, I'd managed to come up with a counter-ritual to break the curse. But whether it would work or not was anyone's guess.

After lighting candles at the four cardinal points of the compass, I started off the ritual with a classic: cutting myself at the juncture of my thumb so that it would bleed on the sigil. Once the drips started to hit the paper, I recited Celtic phrases I'd culled from my books, calling upon the Morrigan to cleanse the accursed of their bad luck. Maybe the Morrigan answered my call. Maybe something else did. All I know is that I felt ... something ... rise from the sigil after I'd repeated the summons enough times.

Bracing myself for a headache or worse, I took a peek at the paper with my sixth sense. The levels of death energy had been intense before, but now they were starting to spike, driving a psychic ice pick into my skull as I looked at it. It took all I had to keep the sight switched on. Digging into my last reserve, or possibly reserves that weren't even mine, I kept reciting the Celtic summons, the mark on my shoulder itching under my skin.

Though there were no flames, the paper burned in my hands. I could feel the heat pouring out through my fingers. The summons wasn't enough to break the link: I was losing the battle. As a last resort, I pulled the bident Lady McDeath had given me from my pocket. I had just enough time to muse that this would be the first time I had used this on a living target when it happened.

I got a feverish rush of images, as I usually do when using the bident. A lot of them were almost too fast to follow, possibly because this was a living being I was tapping into. But some images and impressions bled through with perfect clarity—Kennedy checking out at a drugstore while a kid manned the cash register, and the kid drawing the sigil on the receipt while Kennedy was looking at some cosmetics on display.

Then I got a final, definite image: my friend running for her life through an open office layout with her .40 S&W in hand. I followed her around the corner of a desk, which she ducked behind, only to get a bullet to the face. Then the picture cut off.

That gunshot snapped me out of my reverie with a start. It left me flat on my back, breath erratic. Both the bident and receipt had fallen out of my trembling grasp. I knew I wasn't moving, but the world sure did spin a dance around me.

I hated how long it took me to get my bearings back, grab my Sig, and be out the door. Praying I wouldn't be too late, I ran out to the Stingray in order to get where I'd seen Kennedy in that vision ... the offices of AN.

22

DOMINO EFFECT

Maybe it was some of Mad Mao's magic rubbing off on me from the charm. Maybe it was Lady McDeath's protection on the Stingray. Maybe it was the fact that I'd spent so much time on the streets of this city, I could navigate the quickest route from Point A to Point B blind-folded. The end result was the same. Despite keeping way over the speed limit all the way, I got from my place to the Ditko Building without trouble.

The parking lot was nearly full when I rolled up, typical of an office building during a workday. Looking up, I noticed broken windows on AN's floor. I found Ramirez standing by her car and talking into her cellphone. There were no other cops around her, not even her partner ... I gathered she must have been off-duty when she spotted the first sign of trouble.

I slid into a parking slot a couple of spaces down from her. She had closed her phone and was wearing her contempt face as I clambered out of the car. As she opened her mouth, I held up my hand.

"Before you say anything that you'll regret later, Mel," I said, "the only reason I'm here is that I got a tip, the same way as with the Thricins the other night. I'm just here to help; it's your show."

She closed her mouth and looked at me a little stunned. Just then another window broke upstairs. Someone, presumably the idiot who was doing the breaking, started shouting. "My magnificent mongoose screams beige dreams in Skylar!"

I had just enough time to think, "What the hells?" when a dozen people burst out the front door, running like the Reaper was right on their tails.

"So what's the situation?" I asked Ramirez as I waved the escapees over to us.

"*Mal* ... and getting worse by the minute," Ramirez said, looking up at the windows. "I was on my lunch break when I saw the first of the windows shatter."

"Wait, you're here because of a broken window?" I asked, arching an eyebrow at her.

"Five broken windows," she countered, her voice sounding like an old-fashioned teletype. "Different points at once, way too many to be an accident. When I got close, I started hearing the screams from upstairs. That's when I put in the call for back-up."

Our fleeing office workers had gotten close enough to stop us talking.

"What's going on?" Ramirez asked, flashing her badge.

"These ... these people," a guy in his fifties in casual office wear stammered. "They just ... just started ... shooting, beating, punching—"

"Easy, Phil," a woman in her mid-thirties, dressed in a

sensible office dress, said, putting her hand on the man's shoulder. "Your heart ..."

"Did any of you see how many of them there were?" I asked, feeling my nerves go coma calm.

"Once the guns started going off, we didn't care," a young black guy in his mid-twenties told us. "After that, it was just put as much space 'tween us and the bullets."

"I've called for help," Ramirez said. "Why don't you all get to the far side of the parking lot, just in case? We'll send people as soon as we can."

Our refugees were in no mood or shape to argue, especially when two or three of the attackers started spouting more word salad at the top of their lungs. I pointed the shaken-up workers in the general direction they needed to go, and they went along without any complaints.

As more windows were broken upstairs, I turned to Ramirez. "How long since you put in the call for back-up?"

"Just finished it when you rolled up," she said. "ETA fifteen minutes."

More people started coming out of the door in a panicked hurry. It went from a trickle to a flood tide in seconds. A couple of shots went off above our heads, and Ramirez ran to the crowd to help steer them. I was about to join her when my smartphone rang. Recognizing the ringtone, I yelled, "Not a good time, Zian."

"Yeah, I know," my friend said on the other end, the tip-tap of his fingers on some keyboard just audible. "Ditko Building's under siege, and it's not your usual terrorists either."

"How do you even know about this?" I asked, waving stragglers from the crowd towards the evac area.

"Got a 911 text from Kennedy," Zian explained, his calm voice a counterpart to the frightened cries of the people around me. "Just hacked into the building's security cams ... looks like you've got between five and seven assailants inside. What I see on the cams tells me that this isn't as random as it looks, Bell. All those people I hear in the background are being herded outside."

"Why would they want everybody out of the building?" I asked.

"Not everybody," Zian corrected me. "There's still a couple of people that our mystery assailants are chasing deeper into the Argo Nautilus offices: Kennedy and ... some other guy."

"Describe him," I said, already knowing who it was. A few quick words later confirmed my suspicions: Ian Townsend.

By then Ramirez had noticed I was on the phone. I hung up as she came over.

"Who was that?" she demanded.

"Kennedy," I lied. "She's inside with Ian Townsend right now, cornered by our local terrorists."

"But why would—"

"I don't know and neither does she," I said, using the truth to cover for me. "She had to hang up before I could get any more out of her. How much longer on that back-up?"

Ramirez checked her phone. "Not soon enough. Sounds like at least a few of those *cabrones* are armed." She pulled out her nine. "Going to back me up?"

"All the way," I affirmed as I pulled out my Sig.

Ramirez stuck up a finger. "Just remember who's in charge."

"Hey, didn't I say it was your show?"

———

One or two stragglers came out as we went in. Ramirez told them to join the others, and we continued on our way. The whole place was as dead as a Russian civil rights meeting—nothing but deserted desks and empty spaces that echoed back our footsteps as we headed towards the stairs. I covered the door to the stairway while Ramirez opened it. All clear, except for some crashing noises higher up. She swept the corners, waving her pistol like a spotlight, then gave me the nod, and we started going up the stairs. It was a spacious stairway, broad enough for two people to go up at the same time. We kept looking and aiming as we climbed the flights up to the fifth floor.

We were just passing the third-floor exit when the door from the stairs slammed open behind us. A guy in a three-piece suit, who looked like he was in the middle of a PCP high, ran at us screaming, "Thus forever for peasants who break!"

As Ramirez and I swung our guns over to him, somebody dropped down on us from above, yelling similar insane nonsense.

This second assailant landed smack on top of me, damn near causing me to crack my head on the stairs. I felt my bones protest as I slammed into the concrete. While I was thus dazed, my attacker—who I now saw was a woman in what had once been a classy pantsuit before it got a landfill makeover—jumped off me and went to help her partner fasten Ramirez in a squeeze play.

Ramirez smashed her elbow into the crazed woman's face a second before shooting the rep from the Barmy Business Bureau in the foot. The man howled as the nine mil hit home, and Ramirez capped it off with a knee to his groin. Meanwhile, Psycho Sister had landed right next to me, and I still had a hold of my gun. At that close a range, it was a simple business putting two bullets through her kneecaps.

"Nice covering me," Ramirez grumbled as she helped me up. As soon as I was on my feet, I put one more bullet through the uninjured foot of the male assailant.

"The hell, Bell!" Ramirez exclaimed. "He was already down!"

"And now he'll stay down," I told her.

Ramirez gave me a disgusted sigh but went back to taking point on the stairs. I didn't take my eyes off the fourth-floor entrance until we had gone up the next-to-last flight of stairs.

I opened the door to the fifth floor very carefully. I could hear a lot of things being broken, along with the occasional insight like "Furry mocha is time to die!" But the only thing there to greet us was a corpse.

Ramirez stepped inside to examine the dead guy while I swept my Sig around the office spaces. I spotted a couple of the attackers turning the place over, but nobody had noticed us yet.

"Vale," Ramirez whispered. Her tone told me that she wanted my eyes on the deceased. She took over standing guard while I looked him over.

I pegged him as between forty and forty-five, and his clothes were in the same disarray as our attackers on the stairwell. From the state of his clothes, he looked like he'd gone swimming in some toxic swamp. The cause of death was easy enough to spot. The blood that had spread over his gut was fresh and very red. It'd been a slow death.

Then I saw two things that gave me pause. First, I found a duplicate for the Ogham sigil on Kennedy's receipt drawn in ink on his forearm. Second, I found the necklace I'd given Kennedy clutched in his hand by the chain.

"So ... mean anything to you?" Ramirez hissed, her eyes and her gun waiting for the bad guys to figure out that we were there.

"Kennedy was wearing this necklace the last time I saw her," I said, pulling the chain free of the death grip.

"Which was ...?"

"This morning."

Before Ramirez could respond, we heard a flurry of gunshots, evidently an exchange of gunfire. They sounded like cannon booms, but that was probably just the acoustics of the place. The noise was coming from one of the managers' offices on the right.

"How did these idiots get weapons into this building?" Ramirez asked as she started running towards the sound, with me right behind her.

We heard a yelp as one of the shots got a little too close to a nearby desk. The pitch of the voice told me it was Ian Townsend, who was apparently trapped in his office. I looked to see where the shot had come from and made out three assailants firing handguns from behind desks at the far end of the office space. Closer to Townsend's office, someone was firing back at them with a handgun from behind another desk. A flash of blonde hair told me it was Kennedy.

Ramirez and I ducked behind a desk of our own.

"Never figured your new girlfriend for the Sarah Connor type," she muttered at me.

"Will you let that go already?" I snapped.

"Mr. Townsend's pinned down," my ex observed, ignoring me. "Not much we can do unless we get an opening."

It came two seconds later. Kennedy managed to drop one of the attackers, but then I heard an ominous click from her S&W. The two remaining shooters turned their attention to my new favorite reporter.

Ramirez and I exchanged glances and made our move. I laid down some covering fire while she ran to the next desk. She then returned the favor as I went the opposite way. It took us a lot more time than I would have liked, but Ramirez eventually made it to Townsend while I found my way safely to Kennedy.

She was working the slide of her .40 as I ducked down next to her.

"Gun's jammed!" she hissed. "Can't get it—"

"Forgot your jewelry," I said, holding up the necklace.

"Can't you see that—"

"By all hells! Just wear the damn thing, already!" I demanded, hearing Ramirez's firing from Townsend's office.

"This is so stupid," Kennedy muttered. But then she wrapped the charm around her gun hand. Once she'd done that, the next pull of the slide cleared the S&W's chamber.

That was when I realized Ramirez was trying to shout something to me over the shots. The acoustics were so screwy that I couldn't hear a word she said. I got what she meant a second later, when one of the shooters rushed forward towards us.

"Die, you die!" the man screamed as he took perfect aim at my head. His eyes were burning bright orange, as he pressed the trigger. I held my breath for the shot ... which never came.

The slick floor swept him off his feet, making him crash chin-first on the tiles. Kennedy didn't hesitate. She steadied her gun on my arm and put one in his head. I winced and raised my hand, feeling the heat from the muzzle flash. But it could have been a lot worse. In the background, I heard what seemed to be three guns firing it out at regular intervals.

As I watched, something smoky and foul started coming out of the dead's man mouth.

"What the hell?" Kennedy breathed.

The black cloud assumed the shape of a man from the waist up. Tiny lights flickered on and off inside it, like fireflies. Other than that, it was as undefined as a mannequin in a mall.

It started rushing at Kennedy, who emptied her clip at it. Do I even need to say that all the shots passed right through it? Earlier, I'd caught sight of a letter opener sitting on a nearby desktop, pure silver by the looks of it. Having nothing to lose, I made a grab for it and used it to stab the shadow in the arm.

The thing gave an unearthly howl as the point hit home. I lost my grip on the letter opener as the living fog whirled around and used its other arm to pin me to the desk leg. I felt its smoky fingers start to crush my larynx. My attempts to get a hold on it were working out about as well as Kennedy's attempts to shoot it. In the background, meanwhile, Ramirez was keeping up a steady rate of fire, though the guns returning fire seemed to be faltering.

I reached out my hand in search of the lost letter opener. Once I found it, I brought it up, swinging and cutting the fog arm in two. I had just long enough to get a gulp of fresh air before the arm reattached itself, the black particles of fog coming together again seamlessly. I swear I saw the thing smile at me, lights twinkling inside the black cloud.

I tried again with the letter opener, but I wasn't fast enough. An ethereal hand immobilized mine, and the vice grip on my throat returned. Somehow, I had my doubts that even my impressive death insurance would be powerful enough to repel this thick concentrate of bad luck. As I felt myself losing consciousness, I croaked, "The charm, the charm!"

Almost at once, the creature's head was knocked aside, and the hand came off my throat. Taking in a deep breath of fresh air, I realized Kennedy was using the charm as a knuckleduster. She was punching the crap out of the vaporous monster while it continued to scream. I grabbed the letter opener and used it to stab the smog cloud in the chest. On the third swing, it caught the center hole of the charm on the way, embedding it with the point. One final scream that felt like it was going to rip out my eardrums and the lights inside the creature started to grow brighter. They wound up burning the thing from the inside out in a flash-bulb burst, leaving behind nothing but a bad swamp gas smell.

The guns behind us had stopped firing. Then I started hearing ... wailing. It wasn't the unearthly kind of wailing I'd just heard up close, but human grief and agony. I made out "Oh, God, oh, God, oh, God ..." and "I didn't ... I didn't mean ..." among the cries. It looked like what we'd just overcome had possessed more than just the guy Kennedy had put down near the office entrance.

"You all right, Mel?" I called out over the desk as I picked up the letter opener and handed Kennedy her good luck charm.

"Yeah," she called back. "So is Mr. Townsend. What about you two?"

"We're good," Kennedy piped up, her face looking like she was anything but good. Then she turned to whisper to me. "All right, what the hell just happened, hoss?"

"Not now," I said, glad that the explanation was going to have to wait. "I promise I'll tell you later ... but not now."

The steady cadence of the Tac Team's boots heralded their busting through the stairs door. Ramirez got up and showed them her badge. Kennedy and I did the same, minus the badge part. Our poor attackers weren't in any kind of shape to do more than cry and moan.

———

"Looks like I owe you again, Bell," Ian Townsend told me as we exited the building.

"This was a team effort, Ian," I reminded him. "Kennedy kept you safe while Ramirez and I made our way up—"

The sight of Morgan fixing me with one of his usual scowls stopped the words cold. Townsend noticed. "Do you want me to—"

"Just go make your statement, Ian," I told him. "I'll be fine."

I wasn't sure if I would be, but it made no sense dragging him into whatever mess Morgan was going to create for me.

The detective lieutenant shook his head as I approached. "There are easier ways to commit suicide, Vale."

"Can we just get this over with, Morgan?" I asked in irritation. "I promise that my suicide attempt quota has been filled for the day."

"What the hell were you even doing here?" he demanded.

I fed him the same line I had Ramirez about Kennedy calling me.

"You getting cozy with that reporter?" he asked. "That's just my luck."

"None of your damn business," I said. "She was in trouble; I helped out. Now, if you're going to charge me—"

"Oh, I'd love to," he rumbled. "Right now, I'd bust you for taking a penny off the sidewalk if I could get away with it."

I heard the frustration behind the bluster. "But ...?"

"But, seeing as you assisted Sergeant Ramirez and helped save a prominent citizen of the community, my hands are officially tied."

"Guess you'll need yet another statement from me," I said, sighing with relief.

"Talk to one of the junior officers," Morgan rasped, and started to walk away. Then he came to a dead stop. "Know what, Vale?" he said, not looking back at me. "One of these days, you're going to push that economy-sized luck of yours too far. That's when you, or somebody close to you, is going to pay for it. When that happens ... you'd better pray that you can look yourself in the eye afterwards."

Something about the way he said that ... it sounded

almost sad. But before I could ask him about it, he walked off.

———

I'd just wrapped up my statement when Mrs. Townsend showed up on the scene. She wasted no time giving her hubby a tight hug. My heart went out to her. In a little under a week, she'd nearly lost two members of her family.

I walked over to the happily reunited couple and noticed that Kennedy was coming towards them from the opposite direction. Mrs. Townsend spotted me over her husband's shoulder and gave me the same big hug she had just given him.

"I can't thank you enough, Mr. Vale," she whispered in a voice edged with tears.

"I was just a side player this time, Mrs. Townsend," I demurred. "Ms. Kennedy behind you here is the real hero."

Kennedy's eyes widened at my words of praise, but before she could say anything, Mrs. Townsend had enveloped her in another of her hugs. I couldn't make out what she was saying to her reporter-savior, but the gist was probably the same as what she'd told me. Kennedy returned the hug and murmured assurances in her ear, then gave me a look over the grateful woman's shoulder.

"Soon," I mouthed as I walked off.

As soon as I was a good ten feet away from them all, I made a decision. I pulled out my smartphone and dialed up Smoke & Mirrors. "Yeah?" said a voice at the other end.

"This is Bellamy Vale," I said. "I have a message for Mr. De Soto."

"*Si?* What is it?"

"Bran Connor."

"Huh?"

"Bran. Connor." I said the name as distinctly as I could, separating the first and last name for complete clarity. "He'll understand."

"Whatever, man," the drone on the other end said and hung up. That was another one that Estella De Soto was going to have to teach some manners. But Bran Connor was going to find out the hard way that crimes don't go unpunished in this city.

23

PUZZLE PIECES

The mug of green tea in Kennedy's hand had gotten cold. Not that it mattered—I wasn't even sure she remembered it was there. This was not surprising, given that Zian and I had just told her what we all had fought the other night, what the Cinema Leone was sitting on top of, and why she'd been having such a bad day.

It was a little past sundown, and we were back at Zian's offsite. After a heated argument on the phone that had gone on for half an hour, Zian had agreed to back my play on bringing Kennedy up to speed. He did want us to stick to details that she had already observed, which was fine with me. The less she knew about Alterum Mundum, the safer she was.

"I ..." Kennedy said, trying to get her mouth to work, but the rest of the words wouldn't come.

Zian took the green tea from her hand. While he was putting it in a microwave that sat on a cabinet behind the desk, I took her hand in mine.

"I've been where you are. I know it's a lot to take in. But I swear on whatever you'd consider holy that it's the truth."

She nodded, but still no words.

"Look," I added, "I know that you're going to need to write something close to the truth about all this when we're done. But it's important that all the crazier stuff never—"

Kennedy withdrew her hands angrily from mine. "I'm overwhelmed and exhausted, not stupid!" she snapped, her Texan accent harshening the words.

I gave her a few moments to simmer down. She took a deep breath.

"Besides," she resumed, "how could I prove even half of what you're saying in the first place?"

"You'd be amazed by the numbers who have tried," I told her. "But, for safety reasons, I'd advise against it."

"Why did you do it?" she asked, giving me a stare I couldn't read. The question had a sinister tone to it.

She saw that I didn't understand and tried again. "Why did you save my life from that curse you were telling me about? You could have just left me to die from all that bad luck to make your life easier."

"No ... I couldn't have," I assured her, hearing my voice turn somber.

The microwave beeped, and Zian placed the reheated mug of green tea back in Kennedy's hand.

"A really long time ago," I continued, "I found out what the value of human life is. It cost me dearly. So, keeping my secret versus your still being among the living—it was no choice at all."

Zian looked a little ashamed of himself. He needn't have

been. His argument for secrecy had been a good one. I just didn't consider it good enough.

Kennedy's expression changed again. It seemed that what I had said had gotten past her usual defenses. There was a rare softness in her voice when she replied.

"Well, I'd have voted for me staying alive too if I'd have been asked."

"How did you wind up being at AN in the first place?" Zian asked as he took his own seat behind the desk.

"Just doing my job," Kennedy explained. "I was there for a follow-up interview with Mr. Townsend to talk about the aftermath of his daughter's kidnapping. I was just getting the recorder set up when, all of a sudden, bang! Here come all these filthy-looking gunmen talking like they're on an acid trip and looking like they'd spent the night in a dumpster. I barely managed to get Mr. Townsend into an office before they started shooting at me."

"Which is when Ramirez and I came in," I added.

"Just in time to watch the Smog Cloud of Doom give up the ghost ... literally," Kennedy concluded. "I mean, goddamn, what was that thing?"

"I think I can tell you that, Candice," said Zian.

Oh, so now he was buttering her up by using her first name, was he? Why that should have mattered to me, I didn't bother to ask myself.

"I'd say you two were up against a will o' the wisp," he explained. "They tend to hang around swamps and use their pretty lights to lure humans into them. They're living honey traps for Arcadia so—"

"Wait now, what's Arcadia?" Kennedy asked, holding up a hand.

"Fairyland," I said.

"They use humans as foot soldiers," Zian told her. "The human brain doesn't cope well with possession, however—hence all the mumbo jumbo they kept spouting off. Anyone who survives the experience is cracked afterwards. At best, they've got years of shrinks, medications, and nuthouses ahead of them. At worst, they commit suicide."

"Any links between the people who pulled off the attack?" I asked him.

"I ran the files twelve times through twenty-six different filters," he said, shaking his head. "Always got the same result: no connection prior to the attack. And before you ask, no terrorist background on any of them either."

"But if I was already under a curse that was doing its job, then why would they go there to kill me?" Kennedy asked.

"I'd say they didn't," Zian speculated as he turned on his laptop. "Wrong place plus right time equals bad luck ... courtesy of the curse itself."

"The target was Ian Townsend," I said. "He's got some kind of connection to the Orion project, but I don't—"

"And I do," Zian interrupted me, turning the laptop around. "Check this out."

Onscreen was a final draft of terms for the sale of a building in the same neighborhood as the Cinema Leone, dated the day before. The seller was Ian Townsend, while the purchaser was none other than Arete.

"I thought all Ian's properties were on the docks," I said.

"He told me something as I was getting set up," Kennedy broke in. "That building was his bankroll back when he was first starting out. He used the collected rent money to finance his first factory after about five years or so."

"But the building's getting harder and harder to maintain," Zian said, turning the laptop back towards him. "The last health and safety inspection report was the final straw for him. He started looking around for buyers the very next day."

"That was one of the two buildings that hadn't been bought up last time we checked, right?" I asked.

Zian nodded. "The other one just became the newest acquisition of Fairwinds Inc. about thirty-six hours ago. All the territory beside the cinema's been seized by one side or the other now."

"I still wonder if it's De Soto who's behind these killings," said Kennedy. "If he's as in charge as my sources have been saying, his income's gonna take a hit."

"We've been over that already," I countered, impatient that we were covering the same ground again. "I *know* it's not De Soto. If I had my suspicions on who could have done those people, I'd point the finger at Vitorini. It's more his style."

"Be nice if we could get some kind of confirmation on that," Kennedy said.

For just a second, I wondered if I should tell her. Then I realized that I'd just revealed the existence of a Berserker, the power of ley lines, and the involvement of the Fae in city politics and decided that this was small potatoes by comparison.

"Actually ... tomorrow night, I'm going to meet someone to get that confirmed for sure," I told her.

"Who?" Kennedy asked.

"Confidential source," I said, speaking her language.

She gave me a smile. Well, it was better than telling her I was going to meet both De Soto *and* Vito.

"There's more bad news, I'm afraid," Zian said. "I've been looking over the plans for Orion. Something's been bothering me about them since I first got a copy. I finally figured out what that is."

That got both mine and Kennedy's attention.

"There's a text by Pythagoras, dealing with sacred architecture," he explained. "It's about harnessing energy in certain ... special spots in the world to get the most use out of it, like ley line intersections."

"You mean like Feng Shui?" Kennedy asked.

"Similar, but it's like comparing a house to a power plant," Zian went on. "I should mention that this text isn't something you can order off Amazon. In fact, as far as the outside world knows, it went up in flames with the Library of Alexandria over a millennium ago."

"But you recognize it, which tells me that there's at least one copy out there that made it," I said.

"At least two copies," Zian corrected me. "The one that I have and the one that Arete is using to help build Orion."

"Well, what about those things that Kurtzenberg was working on just before he died?" Kennedy asked. "What were they?"

"That's something I wish I knew myself," Zian admitted with a sigh. "But what they were doing inside these buildings was kept off the record."

"Looks like we've got the makings of a hell of an exclusive," Kennedy said, leaning forward like it was a meal she'd been waiting for all day. "I'll just need to prune the details a bit."

"If you need any help with the pruning or some proof that isn't quite the truth, just let me know," Zian volunteered with a goofy grin.

If I had said that to Kennedy, I'd have probably gotten a scowl, but she just shook her head. "You, my friend, need to get out more."

Go figure.

24

EXIT INTERVIEW

The back of any business building always has the same look. No matter how slick or glitzy the front is, the back end has the feel of a warehouse gone shabby: plain concrete or brick walls, at least one dumpster, and a nondescript door giving access to the inside. The back of Smoke & Mirrors was just like that, with washed-out gray concrete walls and the additional detail of a pair of De Soto's Super-Secret Service standing by the door.

As I walked up, the no-neck white guy with the crew cut on the left greeted me. "Good evening, Mr. Vale. You're expected."

"You boys always stand watch at the back door?" I asked, remembering how Kennedy had slipped in unnoticed the last time I was here.

"Only when *los jefes* are expecting trouble," said the bald black guy on the right. His Spanish pronunciation made me think he was from somewhere in South America.

"Well, last I checked, I hadn't given them any," I joked.

"Just the same, I'm afraid you'll need to stand for a frisk, sir," Crew Cut said, stepping forward a little to let me know that this wasn't a request.

I raised my arms and let the pair of them pat me down. I'd left the Sig in the car. If I wasn't safe from the likes of Vito while either of the De Sotos was in the same room, then I was in a lot more danger than I thought.

Two minutes later, the black guard tapped the door twice. Estella was standing on the other side with a welcoming smile on her face. Tonight, she was wearing a strapless black dress that hugged most of her curves like a second skin. The only exception was at the legs, where the skirt ended at mid-thigh to show off her stupendous muscles. She beckoned me through the door, and it shut behind us with a clang.

"It's good to see that you are okay, Bell," she said, leading the way inside. "It is fine that I follow Ramon's practice of calling you by your first name, *si?*"

"I've been called much worse," I told her.

"I can well imagine," Mrs. De Soto said with a slight grin. "By the way, I insist that you call me Estella from this night forward."

I wondered if the tone she gave that request in was the same one she used when she had to issue orders to her men that had to be obeyed at all costs.

"Ramon is waiting in the office," she said, waving one of her thick-veined arms towards the right.

What little I could make of the dimly lit surroundings showed the place to be a bit posher than the back entrance, but more low-key than the club out front. The carpet was so deep that it nearly swallowed my shoes with each step. Lighting came from Art Deco style fittings on the walls.

Two more guards stood at attention outside the office door. They gave Estella a respectful nod as she opened the oak door. Ramon De Soto was standing inside, a tumbler of a drink in hand. He had been looking out at the club floor below through a window that took up the upper half of the wall on my left. On my right, the room was dominated by a desk the size of a Barcalounger, with a pair of plain, straight-backed chairs drawn up in front of it.

A practiced smile appeared on De Soto's lips at the sight of me. He walked over to shake my hand.

"You never fail to impress, Bell," he said by way of greeting. "Thanks to your assistance, the matter of Bran Connor has been ... resolved to our satisfaction."

"You're welcome," I replied, not wanting to be told the specifics of how that had been achieved.

"I am certain that Bell would also appreciate what you promised him, Ramon," Mrs. De Soto suggested.

"Ah, of course," her husband agreed with a slight chuckle. "Forgive me, *mi amigo*, but my wife is quite correct when she reminds me that you did not do this for free."

He walked to his oversized desk, and we followed. Opening up the nearest drawer, he pulled out a bound stack of twenty-dollar bills and handed them to me.

"I trust that cash is acceptable?" he asked.

I eyed the stack. "This looks like a little more than—"

"—the agreed five hundred? *Si*, you did us two additional favors that warranted the extra money."

"Would I be out of line if I asked what favors?" I inquired.

"Ramon"—Mrs. De Soto, who'd been standing near the window, interrupted us—"he is here."

There was no need to ask who she meant ... it had to be Vito.

De Soto nodded and beckoned me towards a chair. I noticed that he had never gotten around to answering my question and decided not to push it.

Vito arrived in the doorway half a minute later. He was wearing a three-piece suit, all in black, right down to the tie, and his brogues gleamed. His eyes latched onto me with burning hatred, but before he could open his mouth, he noticed Mrs. De Soto standing by the window and seemed to shrivel a bit.

"Still dressing as sharp as ever, Vito," I said, leaning back in my chair.

"Still pushing your luck further than you should, Vale," he retorted, heading for the empty chair.

It felt surreal to be sitting this close to Vito. I could feel anger ebbing off him in waves. Hells, I was certain my own dislike of the man was easy enough to spot on my face, too. Yet, we kept our cool, as if this was nothing more than a casual meeting between business partners.

De Soto sat down, looking like a high-school principal ready to give two bullying children a lecture.

"Mr. Vale has several questions for you, Alonzo. He has paid us very handsomely for that privilege. I know that you and he have had your differences, but for tonight, these are to be set aside in the interest of satisfying his curiosity. *Tu comprendes?*"

"*Si, El Jefe,*" Vito answered, turning his attention to me.

To my ear, it felt as though it burnt his Italian tongue to have to speak in Spanish.

I got right to it. "Did you kill Henry Kurtzenberg?"

"Who?"

"Public works supervisor for the city," I said. "Got killed Mafia-style near the Cinema Leone. Ring any bells?"

"Not even alarm bells," Vito said, folding his arms.

A manicured hand landed on his shoulder and gave it a hard squeeze.

"Alonzo, you have two choices," Mrs. Do Soto said as Vito's face started to register pain. "You can answer Mr. Vale now, or you can answer me later. Which one do you prefer?"

Just as suddenly as it had landed, the hand was removed.

"Okay, okay," Vito said, rubbing his shoulder. "It wasn't me."

"Of course not," I responded, unimpressed.

"No—really!" Vito protested, mindful of Mrs. Soto just behind him. "What's some old jerk who works for the city to me? He wasn't part of our thing, so I had no reason to waste him. But somebody went out of their way to make it look like I had."

"Like, say, a former business associate who cut ties with you when they got a better offer?" I asked. There was no need to bring Bran's name into this conversation, but I wanted to do something to make the two-cent kingpin squirm.

"Maybe," Vito said carefully. "I don't know ... and I've got no idea why they would, all right? Bangers getting dropped around there is just part of the day to day. But whacking a citizen is just asking for trouble nobody needs."

"So you know the area, done business there?" I asked.

Vito started squirming in his chair like a worm on a hook. "Not exactly."

"Either you have, or you have not," De Soto pointed out. "Which of the two is correct?"

Vito writhed some more. "*Jefe* ... I swear on my mother's grave that I did no business that would be at odds with our—"

"That was not Mr. Vale's question," De Soto insisted gently, sounding like a father handing his son a mild rebuke.

Vito nodded and found the right words at last. "I was doing some work for an outfit called Arete. They had me doing a little ... pest control so that guys like Henry could do their job."

I wondered how much money Vito's "pest control" had cost the man at the desk. "So you knew Kurtzenberg?"

"Enough to say hello to, not enough to ask out for a drink, if you get my drift," Vito said. "He was all right but boring, you know? Not anybody I'd ever figure rating a slap, let alone a hit."

"Before he died he was building something special at a couple of places," I said, playing a hunch. "Any idea what they could have been?"

"Near as I can tell?" Vito said. "Pyramids."

The disbelief on the two De Soto faces matched my own.

"I know, I know," Vito protested, holding up his hands. "I don't get it either. But I swear to God, that's what he was making. They were all in this weird blue stone and came up about three feet from the floor." He was drawing figurative pyramid shapes with his hands to illustrate his meaning. "Never did get why he built those things himself when he had a whole crew that could have made them in about an hour. But he always came in after hours, did the work himself."

"So the crew he was supervising wasn't involved at all?" I asked.

"Just in cleaning up the area," Vito said. "And even then, he only wanted certain spots to be ... well, spotless. He was just as careful about where those pyramids went too, did everything short of line up their exact coordinates with a GPS. You'd think he was painting the Mona Lisa or something."

"He ever mention any more of those that he needed to do?"

"I told you before, Vale," Vito spat back with irritation. "We weren't tight. All I can tell you is that if he had any more to do, he didn't get to them before he died." Then he barked out a short laugh and added, "Hell, he didn't even get to finish that pyramid he was working on before he died."

"So that one never got done?" I persisted.

"Oh, it got done," Vito countered. "After Henry got killed, some other golden boy took over and finished it. Main difference was that Choice Number Two was guarded like the president."

"Where was the unfinished pyramid at?" I prompted.

"That was the other weird thing," Vito admitted with a shrug. "It was in a building that Arete didn't even own yet. Must have gotten some kind of clearance with the owner, or maybe he didn't know that it was going on."

"Who was the owner?" I asked.

"Ian Townsend ... yeah, *that* Ian Townsend. Mr. High And Mighty Savior of Cold City was getting an offer from

Arete. But word was he was getting another, better one from somebody else."

"Who?"

"Does it matter? All Arete cared about was that it wasn't them. So they had me grab his kid as leverage for a deal."

I felt the blood in my veins starting to boil but did my best to ignore it. "It's a bit of a leap to go from grabbing a little girl to help out your boss to sending her father a ransom demand if he ever wants to see her again."

"Hey, we all know how loaded Townsend is," Vito said. "All Arete cared about was getting him to sell. I figured, why not make some money on top of it? To me, it was win-win. Arete gets their building, Townsend gets his kid, I get a little extra dough on top. Everybody's happy."

"Then I crash the party and turn it into lose-lose," I said, letting an edge in my voice show.

"Yeah, why did you have to go and mess up a good deal, huh?" Vito asked, his eyes throwing daggers at me.

"Is it my fault that Marion's father and mother were a little concerned that you'd have given their little girl back to them in less than pristine condition?" I asked.

"Whatever," Vito snapped, the irritation back. "All I know is, thanks to you butting in, my extra-curriculars got found out by *El Jefe* here."

"Self-flattery will get you nowhere here," Mrs. De Soto growled. "I knew you were working for some other organization from the very start."

"And because she knew, I knew," her husband added, giving Vito a pointed stare. "The only thing we were waiting for was definitive proof, which was provided for us by Mr. Vale."

I perked up at that. Could it be one of the things I had been paid extra for? If it was, I couldn't have been happier that it'd been at Vito's expense.

"Okay, last question," I said. "Who was in charge of the people you were working for?"

Vito barked out another harsh laugh that made him sound like a braying donkey. "If you think they are the kind of people who just hand out that info, you're dumber than I thought, Vale."

"And if you didn't check these people out to make sure you weren't being stung by the cops, you're a sloppier crook than even *I* thought," I shot back.

Vito grunted and sighed in the same breath. "Okay, okay ... Arete is a shell corporation for somebody else ... I'll give you that much."

"Not good enough," I pressed. "Who's this somebody else?"

Vito sneered at me. "You've got no clue, do you? Some PI ... you got to come to *me* to find out that the people you're talking about go straight to the top of the local food chain? Give me a break."

"A name, Alonzo," De Soto said, and it sounded as though he was as interested in the answer as I was.

"Galatas," he replied, teeth clenched.

I had to work hard not to let the shock register on my face.

"Anything else?" De Soto asked.

"There was another name that they kept tossing around a lot ... might be the guy who was in charge of all the weird work like Henry was doing."

I made a "go on" gesture.

"Horace," Vito said. "That was the name. Horace."

"Horace what?"

"Like I'd know," Vito said, some of the arrogance coming back.

I leaned back and sighed in satisfaction, nodding to De Soto to let him know I had what I'd come for.

"Now if you're done with your questions," Vito said as he got up, "I've got other things to do tonight."

"Before you go, Alonzo, there are some matters we need to discuss privately," De Soto said, his hand slipping just below the lip of the desk.

Vito sat back down as a couple of men came through the office door, more casual than the steroid brigade I'd come to think of as the Do Sotos' security. They were both wearing club clothes and holding a knife. I recognized the blades as being obsidian by the dull sheen.

Though I hated him, I couldn't stand by and do nothing. I had to give Vito a chance, some kind of warning at least.

"Why so sore, Vito?" I asked, doing my best to walk the tightrope. "It's not like I tied you to a chair and threatened to kill you if you didn't tell me."

I was hoping that somewhere in that very addled brain of his, he would take the hint I was tossing him.

"You're not always gonna have my boss's mini-skirt to hide behind," he sneered, crossing his arms over his chest and making sure to look straight ahead. It was his way of giving me the cold shoulder, but it was also preventing him from seeing the real danger coming in from behind him. "So why don't you get your sneaking, scheming ass out of here before I do something we're both going to regret?"

Way too late for that, I thought.

Mrs. De Soto had walked around to where I stood. "I shall see you to the door, *si?*"

It took everything I had not to scream at Vito as she led me away from the desk. Out of the corner of my eye, I saw the two knifemen move as the office door shut behind us. A couple of seconds later, I thought I heard a scream. I kept walking.

After Estella De Soto had given me a quick *"Vaya con dios,"* she closed the back door behind me. Bald Guy gave me a funny look. "Is something the matter, Mr. Vale?"

Guess it must have shown on my face. "Nothing a good night's sleep can't take care of."

He and Crew Cut looked unconvinced, but both gave me a nod. As I walked away, I knew that sleep was the last thing that was going to help me with what I'd just seen. Could I have just witnessed the end of the Vitorini Empire?

25

FINAL COUNTDOWN

T he sound of keystrokes greeted me as I stepped into the offsite's office. I expected it to be Zian hammering away at his laptop like a woodpecker on a redwood, so I was a little surprised to see Kennedy working on a duplicate of his laptop at the other end of the desk. Zian had both hands sitting in his lap as he read from his screen.

"So who's winning the latest Overwatch match?" I quipped.

"Compared to what we're looking at, hoss, Overwatch is about as exciting as checkers," Kennedy said.

"We've been crunching data ever since noon," Zian chimed in, his eyes glued to his screen. "Kennedy called in sick, and I got her set up just as soon as she got here."

"All of which means you've got something to tell me that we didn't know before, right?" I asked, grabbing my own chair.

"Oh, yes," Zian assured me. "Check this out ... Fairwinds Inc. is a front for some old friends of ours."

"Define 'old friends,'" I said.

"The kind that are usually too lazy to lift a finger to help, but who appear to have made an exception this time around," Zian clarified, giving me a look that said, "work it out on your own, so I don't have to spell it out."

My mind connected the dots ... the Conclave. Whatever was going on, they'd been trying to stop it a long time before I got involved. That's what Bran had meant by "affiliated teams." Lady McDeath may have been one of them, but if it was anything like your average corporate boardroom, there were plenty of factions within the structure.

"Got to give them credit for discretion," Zian went on. "They've been doing everything they can to stop Orion from happening in every legal, under-the-radar way that they could. Figure the Berserker getting involved changed that equation in a hurry."

"I've got news, too. I have a name for the person behind Arete ..." I paused for effect. "Jacinta Galatas."

"As in Mayor Galatas?" Kennedy echoed, blue eyes wide open.

I nodded. "My source mentioned another key player too," I put in. "Just a first name ... Horace."

Zian's typing went from a thousand words a second to a million. Kennedy started working on hers as well, albeit at a slower pace. A few minutes later, both came away disappointed.

"Strikeout for me," Kennedy said. "How 'bout you, Zian?"

"Same," Zian said. "Even ran it through the stuff I had on Fairwinds and came up a goose egg. Sure you heard the name right, Bell?"

"My source was sure that this Horace was connected to Orion," I said. "But he could have heard it wrong."

Something about the way I said that made Zian get this distant look.

"What'd I say, Z?" I asked, hoping that I'd just given him the connection he needed.

"Not Horace, Bell," Zian said slowly. "Horus ... the Avenging Son of Osiris and Isis and the old Egyptian name for the constellation of Orion."

Kennedy and I came around to his side of the desk as he attacked the keyboard with renewed vengeance. In about ten seconds, he'd pulled up an overhead map of the area that Fairwinds and Arete were contesting. A pair of blue dots marked a pair of locations.

"Okay, these are the work sites that I couldn't get info on," Zian said, pointing them out. "Now, if we overlay this map with Orion's belt ..."

He did just that with a few keystrokes. The locations were an exact match for the right and left stars. Then I noticed where the middle star was sitting.

"The Cinema Leone," I said, pointing to the spot. "Per my source, they were building blue mini-pyramids at each site."

"Hang on a second," Kennedy said, tapping her temple with her index and middle fingers. "I heard about something like this."

Zian and I both looked at her in surprise.

"Oh, not exactly like this," she said. "When I first got hired at the station, they gave me this shitty job. I had to go through the crank file, full of all these letters and emails on how 2012 was going to be the end of the world. One of them talked about the pyramids at Giza and how the layout of them matched up with some constellation and how that was cosmically bad news."

"Okay, but what's the point?" I asked.

"Well, obviously, they're going to be using those ley lines you keep going on about for something," Kennedy offered.

"The sheer raw power and versatility of the juice those lines carry make the possibilities damn near infinite," Zian added.

"But you've got it narrowed down," I said, making a half-question out of the sentence.

"Almost wish I hadn't," Zian said, tapping the map window. This time, he put an overlay of the local ley lines on top of the map. That was followed with a ghost of the blueprints for the Orion complex in light blue to make sure they didn't get lost in the mess. "The way the structure of Orion is laid out, it'll act as an energy sink for any raw spiritual juice coming into the intersection at the movie house. But when you add in the very violent death of the Cinema Leone's previous owner here"—he made a red dot pop up at the approximate spot, right on the lowest of the ley lines feeding into the intersection—"you taint the whole spot with death energy that narrows down your practical uses of it. With juice that bad, it can only be used for one thing, Bell. I think they're going to open a gate to the Underworld."

I felt the air get sucked out of my lungs at those words.

"You mean like—Hell?" Kennedy asked, looking startled.

Zian grunted. "Trust me; there are spots down there that make Hell look like Disneyland."

"So what happens when the gate opens?" Kennedy pressed.

"All sorts of nasty things come through," Zian said. "First, they'll take the city. Then they get the country."

"Then the entire planet," I finished. "It'll be like a global 9/11."

"Why would Galatas want to do a damn fool thing like that?" Kennedy all but shouted, her Texan accent cutting through her words.

"Don't know, don't care," I told her. "What matters now is figuring out how to stop her."

"Which leads me to point number two," Zian said, bringing up the second window. This one showed a map of the stars above the Earth. Cold City was marked at the bottom center.

"Even with all the power that intersection takes in," Zian explained, "it wouldn't be enough to open up a gate. It'd need a celestial kickstart ... like, say, the project's namesake coming over the area at some time in the near future. And when I say 'near future,' I mean two days from now."

The stars started moving. Orion was labeled as it slid into view from the right. As soon as it got over Cold City, the movement stopped. Three lines were drawn from each star on the belt to three sets of coordinates on the ground.

"Those the coordinates for the work sites and the Cinema Leone?" I asked.

"You know it," Zian affirmed. "It's going to take another three thousand years before we see this configuration again."

"Hell of a deadline," I observed, "... and pretty good incentive to step things up with a Berserker to help clear the way."

"But the plans for Orion never went ahead, thanks to all

288 | CRISTELLE COMBY

the legal wrangling," Kennedy pointed out. "So what good's this going to do them now?"

"It all goes back to those pyramids Bell found out about," Zian said. "The rest of this is largely window dressing for the public. But if you can get all three pyramids ready to go and the right angles carved into the buildings proper, they'll have everything they need to swing that gate wide open."

"But neither side owns all of the territory," Kennedy argued. "So how are they—"

"Trust me, Kennedy, the moment that thing becomes active, there won't be enough people left alive to care who owns the buildings," I informed her. "My guess is, Galatas and Arete stopped playing fair, right around the time they got a freaking Berserker to do their dirty work. Red tape or not, those charges are in place ... trust me."

"So, when's it gonna go boom?" Kennedy asked.

Zian's lips tightened. "Any time between now and forty-seven hours from now, when Orion passes over us."

I took a look at my watch. It was two in the morning. Unless we did something, the end of the world would kick off at one in the morning two nights from now.

"We need to come up with a plan," I said. "Fast."

That was when we all heard a loud bang, and the walls shook.

26

MEETING THE MOTHER

I had just enough time to say, "What the hells?" before the next bang hit the old factory's front door. It sounded like a cross between a ship's guns going off and the heartbeat of some Lovecraftian monstrosity.

Zian dialed up the front door camera feed. A group of eight armed men in trench coats over tactical armor were standing outside. They were all watching what looked like a giant scorpion punching its way through the door with its tail.

"Want to make a bet those are the assholes that tried shooting us up the other night?" Kennedy conjectured as she grabbed her S&W from her purse.

"Never bet against sure things," I said, feeling grateful that I'd taken the time to grab my Sig before coming on over. "Though the seven-foot-tall scorpion is a novelty," I added, hating myself for not bringing some extra clips ...

The scorpion hit the door again. If what I was seeing on

the camera was any sign, it only had two to three hits to go before we were breached.

"Can you guys hold them off for a few minutes?" Zian asked. "I've got an idea that might get us out of this, but I need time."

I glanced at Kennedy, who nodded.

"Just have it ready to go before we run out of ammo," I said, as Kennedy and I walked quickly towards the office door.

We took position behind the nearest girders, each of us at opposite ends of the factory. I wasn't optimistic about our chances. Two of us with handguns against a crack crew with automatic weapons and a pet tank ... I'd rather have been fighting the Berserker with a penknife.

It took four more hits for the door to give way with a crash. The scorpion bent the doorframe further out of shape by squeezing through it. The armored thugs following right behind it looked like a living wall of Kevlar.

I thumbed back the hammer on my Sig and waited for the right moment. As soon as they started spreading out, I popped around the side and squeezed off a shot. I ducked back in time before the return fire hit my position like a storm of lead raindrops. It was good to know those old steel girders would repel anything short of a mortar round.

Kennedy popped out from cover and fired off a few shots. That attracted its share of return fire and gave me an opportunity to make another contribution. Our assailants responded by relying on the scorpion for cover. The creature itself seemed to be impervious to our nine mils and .40 slugs, which were doing rubber ball bounces off its armor. But there was only so much protection to go around, and I managed to catch one of the attackers in the leg, making him pitch forward on the floor.

I did a quick mental shot count. I was down to five shots, so I needed to make every one of them count. I was getting glimpses through the scorpion's feet of our attackers' legs, so I knelt down and poured my last five shots in their direction. I only managed to knock down one more for my trouble.

The scorpion had advanced further inside the open space, its eight legs making strange clickety sounds on the bare floor. Its tail was enormous, and the venomous stinger seemed to swing in search of a soft target.

It went after me, pincers opening and closing. I had just enough time to duck and roll out of the way when the stinger hit the girder.

"You know, people in Asia eat things like you," I muttered, getting back to my feet.

It mustn't have liked the joke, for the stinger came swinging dangerously close to my torso again.

"Where in the hells are you, Zian?" I whispered to myself. I knew he had said a few minutes, but what was taking him so long—

The thought was interrupted by a strange gurgle-cum-howl from the office door. It was so unsettling that everybody froze and turned to see what was making the racket, even the scorpion. Then Zian stumbled into view, still making that weird noise again as he slumped against the wall. He looked ... puffier is the word I'd use.

He made the sound twice more and then gave a great howl as he was suddenly enveloped in a blinding golden light. I think my eyes could have handled staring at the sun for an hour better. When the light faded, an imperious, six-foot woman stood where Zian had been. She wore the serpent crown and accoutrements I recognized as belonging to Old Kingdom Egyptian rulers. She also had olive skin, black hair, kohl-darkened eyes, and a figure that could only be described as perfect. She turned those dark eyes on the intruders.

Our attackers opened fire, but the bullets hissed and turned into steam within a foot of this vision. Then, in some ancient tongue that I suspected was spoken before the first pharaoh had even been born, the woman pointed at the scorpion and said something. The beast immediately turned away from me and grabbed the nearest of our armor-clad assailants with its right pincer. A sharp crack later, he was just a crushed sack of meat and bones.

A wave of panic passed through the other men, and they opened fire on their former protector. Even at that close range, it worked out about as well as it had for Kennedy and me. One of them caught one of his own bullets through a ricochet off the scorpion's plates. To their credit, the other three continued firing while backing away. The tail impaled one of them in the center of his chest, while the pincers quickly dispatched the other two.

The woman gave the scorpion fresh orders. In response, the creature flicked its tail to remove the corpse stuck on it and began to pile the bodies up in a stack. While it was doing that, Kennedy and I ventured from behind our cover. I had a hundred questions on my lips, but right then, I couldn't get any of them to come out of my mouth. A quick look at Kennedy told me she was having the same problem.

The woman spoke once more to the scorpion, which promptly retreated and faded to nothing.

"Thanks," I told her, finally finding my voice.

She looked at me with an unreadable expression. There was so much contempt in her stare that I wondered if I should be kneeling in front of her or something.

Then, as suddenly as she'd appeared, the woman doubled over in pain and collapsed to her knees, making the weird howls again. A flash of light later, Zian was standing in her place.

"Who the hell was that?" Kennedy asked in a bewildered voice as she approached to check on Zian.

"And why do I get the feeling that you just did something else your dad would kill you for?" I added as I helped him to his feet.

"That ... that was Isis, mother of Horus," Zian gasped as he tried to find his legs. "I summoned her up with a shapeshifting spell that I got out of my dad's Hermetic database."

"How does that work again?" Kennedy asked while checking him over the way a concerned mom would her kid.

"Dad has a real long-winded explanation involving the collective unconscious and quantum physics," Zian answered, managing to give her a grin. "But simply put, you tap into the universal connection to all living beings to make the god, or goddess, in this case, within you come forth."

"You were aware of what she did?" I asked as we made our way unsteadily towards the violated entrance to our compromised safe haven.

"Every bit of it," Zian confirmed. "But it's like I was a passenger in my own body. Tartarus, I'm feeling weird now."

"Nobody summons a divine being lightly," I said, giving him a dark stare. "Be glad she went away again that easily."

It would have been just wonderful to have to deal with a possessed Zian on top of all the other crap we had to juggle already.

"No worries. That kind of spell never lasts long," Zian explained. "And it takes a special kind of juice to get it on in the first place."

I nodded. The way he'd said it let me understand that had he not been the son of Hermes, it wouldn't have worked. Nice to know.

The door was a total loss. Short of substantial reconstruction, which would take time we didn't have, there was no way we would be able to reblock the entryway against further intrusions.

"The way you talk about it, it sounds like that stunt was anything but safe," Kennedy commented, with more than a trace of reproach in her voice.

Not to mention a big violation of the agreement the Conclave had struck, I thought.

"I wouldn't have done it at all if we weren't in such dire straits," Zian admitted. "There's a reason Dad keeps that spell locked up. But one thing all the old stories of ancient Egypt agree on—nobody plays with Isis. And she has a way with scorpions."

"My guess is that Mayor Galatas was the one behind those thugs," Kennedy told us.

"Yeah," Zian agreed. "Guess my snooping into Arete's files left a bigger data trail than I thought."

"Then we're moving this op to my place," I said, leaving no room for discussion in my voice. "The protection on the apartment should keep out any more unwelcome guests.

Whatever you need to do to ensure quality Internet over there, Z, now's the time to get it together."

Zian nodded. "Might be able to tap into your protection to beef up my Internet security if I handle it right too."

"While he's moving in, we should try hunting down Her Honor before she figures out her not-so-merry men failed to close the deal," Kennedy suggested.

"Once I get moved in, I could try to see if Fairwinds can give us some backup," Zian added.

"Hurry it up. There's no time to lose," I said, as I checked my watch for a countdown update.

27

DESPERATE TIMES

I hadn't realized how hungry I was until I dove into my first slice of supreme pizza. It came from a little place called Andolini's, a small pizzeria that managed to do enough business to stay afloat but not so much as to attract the attention of the big chains. Kennedy was enjoying the eats just as much as I was, but she looked concerned.

"I have to tell you, hoss," she said after polishing off her second slice, "this is probably the first thing that's gone right all day."

"No argument," I agreed, getting my own second slice from the box. "Everything since the attack at the factory has been a complete bust. The fact that we can't find Her Honor has got me to thinking ... what if the attack was a diversion?"

"Her way of keeping us busy while she finalizes her plans," Kennedy mused.

"Any luck getting Fairwinds to help?" I asked Zian.

"None whatsoever," he admitted. "Fairwinds Inc. has ceased to exist."

"They folded the corporation?"

"Weren't you listening to me, Bell?" he snapped. "I said they *ceased to exist*. I tried accessing their databases only to find the server disconnected. All traces of their corporate website have been scrubbed. Every record of their business dealings just went down a black hole so deep even I couldn't find them. On top of that, every bit of paperwork I found on their official incorporation is gone like it'd never been there."

I growled my frustration. The damn Conclave had apparently just decided to go from Plan A to Plan V. That is, they'd just bailed and left me alone to deal with their mess.

"So much for backup," I spat.

"You were expecting something else?"

"Yeah, at least somebody to point us in the right direction to solve our mutual problem," I admitted, letting my frustration show.

"We know where they are going to be," Kennedy pointed out. "We even have a rough idea of when. The only real fly in the ointment I'm seeing is that the spot's going to be under constant surveillance from now until—"

Her phone rang before she could finish the thought. She looked as annoyed as I felt as she picked it up.

"Kennedy," she answered.

Her face went from annoyed to concerned as she listened to what her caller had to say.

"Yeah, I'm near a TV," she said, snapping her fingers at me. "Hang on."

I got the remote and turned my TV on. It was already tuned to Headliner News. What greeted me was something I hadn't seen since that horrible day in September so many years ago. A thick cloud of dust was billowing out of the area surrounding the Cinema Leone. What little I could discern through the cloud showed nothing but ruins and rubble as far as the camera could see. The caption at the bottom read "Series of Explosions In Downtown Area."

"My God," I breathed.

Zian said a prayer under his breath in Ancient Greek.

"Yeah, yeah, I'm still here," Kennedy said to whoever was on the other end. "Give me a bit, and I'll come in. Yeah, you be careful too."

She hung up. "That bitch just made her move."

I shook my head. "Why'd you agree to go in?"

"Whatever's going on, we're going to need a set of eyes on the ground to figure out what's changed," Kennedy explained.

"I can do that with my drones once I get them prepped from the Indigo," Zian protested.

"Yeah, well, can your damn drones figure out how many cops, feds, Homeland Security guys, and who knows what else is going to be watching that site?"

Kennedy winced as she finished. It had probably come out a little harsher than she intended.

"No reason we can't do it both ways," I said, smoothing the waters. "Zian, before you get those drones in the air, pull every schematic of the area that's on file. Streets, buildings, sewers, gas mains ... if it was part of the permanent structure, I want to know about it."

Zian tapped the laptop he'd just finished setting up in my living room. "Give me a few minutes, and you can have it all."

"Can you send me a mapping program with that?" I asked, reaching for my own laptop and powering it on.

"Easy peasy," Zian confirmed while his fingers did their usual dance.

Kennedy was picking up her purse when Zian stopped her. "Before you go, Candice, I want you to have something." He handed her an earbud. "It's tuned into a comm program on our laptops. Whatever you can't say on camera that's important, just say when no one's looking."

Kennedy pulled back her hair to stick the bud in her right ear. "Soon as I'm sure I've learned everything I can, I'll make a break for here ASAP."

None of us had anything to say after that. Kennedy gave my shoulder a quick squeeze before going out the door. Zian stayed glued to his laptop.

———

I kept the TV going while we worked. Just like every other great disaster ever broadcast, early reports were contradictory at best. Fifty people were dead. A hundred people were hurt. The buildings were empty. The damage to property was massive, but how much was still standing was obscured by thick clouds of dust. The clouds themselves were full of every harmful substance humankind had used to build cities in the last two centuries: lead, asbestos, other things best forgotten. The worst part was that these clouds were so large that they were spreading over huge chunks of the city.

With the mayor absent, the vice-mayor was left to declare a state of emergency. Martial law was in effect, with a curfew imposed on citizens after ten in the evening. The cops themselves were unable to go in due to the heavy, harmful debris cloud. The best they could do was set up a perimeter and keep fellow citizens out of harm's way. The FBI, CDC, and Homeland Security had been notified, and every possible measure had been taken to prevent another potential terrorist attack. On camera, their estimated ETA was within the next twenty-four hours. Off camera, Kennedy told a different story.

"The feds won't be out here until the day after tomorrow at the soonest," Kennedy whispered through her earbud. "Until then, City Hall is on its own."

"Along with the rest of us," I said as I ruled out yet another initially promising approach into the zone on my laptop. "More than enough time for Her Honor to finish what she started today."

"Don't the cops have any drones of their own to look things over?" Zian wanted to know.

"They were supposed to have been provided by Home-land Security about six months ago," Kennedy told him. "Through what they labeled 'a bureaucratic error,' the requi-sition request managed to get lost in the city machinery."

"Somehow I doubt that was an accident," I muttered. "How's the search for survivors going?"

Kennedy sighed. "Better than it would have been without Zian's drones doing recon ... but it's a long way from great."

I felt sick inside. Between the infrared scanners on Zian's drones and some discreet info dump of our findings into the PD's systems, we'd managed to save some people. But not all of them. That madwoman of a mayor had just snuffed out, at the last count, somewhere in the neighbor-hood of three hundred lives. I wanted to pay back the favor (with interest).

"I think I've done all I can to help search and rescue," Zian reported. "How soon can you get back?"

"Should be going off shift in about an hour," Kennedy replied. "Hope you've got a plan by then, Bell."

"When we do, you'll be the second to know," I promised. "Talk soon."

I shut off the comm and went back to the map. I was looking for something, anything that could get us into the zone in its current state. The streets that led to the Orion Project area—Bloch, Hammett and Cooke—had all been turned into gaping chasms that not even Michael Jordan could have jumped across. Several key buildings around the zone had been leveled by the blasts to form makeshift but effective barriers nobody was climbing over or pushing through. Even the sewers had been affected, according to Zian's drones. Every access tunnel that was on record had been collapsed by the explosions.

"Bingo," I said at last. "119 Wolfman Lane, just off of Cooke, a private house that just got demolished about a week ago after the last resident in it died."

"And a vacant lot helps us how again?" Zian asked.

"By what's under it," I told him. "There's a 1950s bomb shelter in the ground. The main entrance is on Wolfman, but it's also got an auxiliary exit tunnel that'll take us right next to the Leone."

"Assuming the exit itself didn't collapse in the blast," Zian pointed out.

"The tunnel runs right under the sewer line," I said, warming up to the idea. "Might have a little leakage, but everything built down there was meant to withstand A-bombs. I'd guess it's managed to hold up under this."

Zian frowned. "What are the coordinates for the exit on that tunnel?"

I gave them to him. He sent one of his drones through the cloud to find it. One infrared scan later, he'd found a manhole cover that was clear of heavy rubble. More importantly, it looked like nobody was around watching it.

Zian peered closer at the readouts. "Looks like every building inside the Orion Project zone has been leveled ... with three exceptions."

There was no prize for guessing which three ... the pyramid locations. I reopened the comm channel to Kennedy. Once I confirmed she was alone in her Nissan, I told her about my discovery.

"Are you kidding me?" Kennedy asked. "We're supposed to trust a seventy-year-old fallout shelter to be clear enough for us to make a grand entrance?" She sighed. "It's up to us, ain't it? And *just* us."

"No backup, no reinforcements, no second chances if we get it wrong," I confirmed. "That's why we're going to get it right the first time."

"I'll swing by my place to grab some clips for my Smith and Wesson," Kennedy said.

A drone landed on the balcony. Its upper compartment opened to reveal a brown-paper package. I looked at Zian.

"Some party favors to help us take care of those pyramids," Zian explained as he got up to retrieve the package.

———

We drove to the disaster area in Zian's Prius. Thanks to its modified engine, it could run silently when on battery power, which is handy when you're trying to evade authorities on patrol. We had to run without headlights, but Zian compensated by using night-vision goggles. The cloud of debris muted the usual glare of the street lights. Before we left, another of his drones brought over some World War I-era gas masks to keep the shit in the air out of our lungs. We'd use showers to get the soup off our skins when this was over.

The fallout shelter entrance had a little dirt and grass covering it up, but it was easy enough to find. The dusty, broken-down interior of the bunker was little better than an abandoned cave, all exposed metal rebar and decaying stone. We moved, tapped, and banged just about everything in sight to find the hatch to the tunnel.

It turned out to be in the floor in the far right corner of the pantry. It was an old-fashioned submarine-style hatch with a few traces of rust, hidden under an upside-down, half-rotted wicker basket. It took all three of us pulling at that thing for it to spring open. The body heat we kicked up in the process slightly fogged up the lenses on my mask. It reminded me of my time in the Navy and the summer I served on a submarine.

We stared down into the black mouth of the now open tunnel and heard a dull roaring sound that was loud even through the masks.

"Sounds like a river," Kennedy said, her voice coming in clearly through my earbud. "A pretty good-sized one."

"Acoustics play all kinds of tricks in tunnels like this," I told her, taking the lead down the hatch. "Probably nothing but a stream singing into the mic."

I can be such a freaking optimist. At the bottom of the

ladder, a veritable cascade of water was shooting across the tunnel. I guessed the blasts had cracked open the sewer line above us more than I thought.

"That what you call 'some leakage', Bell?" Zian asked me.

"Oh, shut up, Zian," I retorted. "At least the current's flowing in the right direction, or we really would be in trouble."

"Seeing as the only way we're getting where we need to go is by shooting these rapids without a boat," Kennedy pointed out, "I'd say that we're *still* in deep trouble."

I took a minute to think about it. "The tunnel's a straight shot to where we need to go. The trick will be all of us grabbing the exit ladder at the right time."

"Might want to form a human chain to make sure none of us get swept away," Kennedy suggested.

Zian was the last of us to come down. He got low enough to grab Kennedy's hand on the ladder. I grabbed Kennedy's lower hand and readied myself to let go. "On three ... one, two, three!"

The water hit me as hard as I imagine Zian's Prius had hit the Berserker the other night. I tightened my grip on Kennedy's wrist as the water carried us along. It was a bitch keeping my head above water—those antique gas masks made for poor aqua-lungs. I began to realize that I had just made a big mistake. The water was going too fast. I'd have an easier time catching a bullet with my hand than I would the bottom rungs of the ladder at this pace.

Then, thankfully, the current slowed down as the tunnel angled upwards. It still had enough force to push us along but nowhere near the initial hard jolt that had gotten us started. A quick look behind me confirmed that Kennedy had as firm a grip on Zian as I did on her. I was able to catch the exit ladder with no trouble at all.

Soon we had climbed up to the exit, and I was pushing open the manhole cover. A quick three hundred and sixty-degree peek showed the coast to be clear of humans, if not the nastiest smog cloud this city had ever seen. We all clambered out and spent a few minutes checking over our gear. Zian had had the foresight to put everything in waterproof packs, and all our stuff, from mine and Kennedy's guns to the low-yield explosive "party favors," was as dry as they'd been at my place.

I couldn't say the same for our clothes, though. Everything, from my army jacket to my combat boots, was soaked.

Zian checked out his smartphone. "We've got a new problem."

I groaned. "The old ones weren't bad enough? What's this one?"

"I don't know how," Zian said, "but we just managed to lose a little over an entire day in about twenty-six seconds."

It took a moment or two to take it in. Kennedy was the first to get it on board.

"That's why the water was so fast when we got started," she suggested. "Time was speeding up."

"Probably due to the ley lines being tapped for Galatas' grand opening," I deduced. "Nothing we can do about it. How much time we got left?"

While I couldn't see Zian's face through the gas mask, his body posture spoke volumes. "Fifteen minutes and eleven seconds."

I felt my nerves go into a coma at his words. They did

that every time a real crisis was on, giving me space to think my way out of the jam.

"We got three pyramids to take out, and there's three of us," I said.

"Fair division of labor," Kennedy responded. "How 'bout one of those explosives?"

Zian handed her one. "It's rigged to a timer. Make sure you set it to give you enough time to get clear."

"I'll take the one in the Cinema Leone," I volunteered. "You two grab the outer pyramids. Keep in touch through the earbuds."

Zian handed me another explosive package, and we went our separate ways.

28

DESPERATE MEASURES

I had to rely on my smartphone's Google maps app to steer me towards the cinema. The fog from the debris was at its thickest there, and it seemed like my way was blocked by some ruin or pile of rubble every few seconds. The way the particles clung in the air, I almost wondered if whatever had sped up time in the tunnel was now keeping the dust from settling.

"How close is everybody?" I asked through the mic.

"If my app's working right, should be just about there," said Kennedy.

"I think I'm close, too," Zian chimed in.

I took a quick check of the timer—eleven minutes and counting.

"Any opposition that you can make out?" I asked, thinking I saw a structure that was standing ahead of me.

"Nothing here but me and the ruins, far as I can tell," Kennedy reported.

"Pretty clear at my end," Zian said. "Well, clear isn't the proper word for it maybe, but nobody else around so far."

"Sounds like I might be the one who ends up entertaining guests," I said. "Stay safe."

I hadn't been hallucinating. The distinctive red carpet that Mr. Nicholls had never gotten around to replacing told me I had arrived at the cinema. I approached the intact front door with caution, but there was nobody there. Why would there have been? The street outside the entrance had been bombed out, and anybody dropping in by air was going to be just as lost as I would have been without my smartphone.

Just the same, I stepped to the side of the door before giving it a slow, careful push. Nobody inside. I went in.

By that point, it was getting too hard to see my way around with the mask on. The interior was clear of the dust, so I took a chance and pulled it off before depositing it under the cash register at the ancient concession stand.

Then I heard chanting coming from inside the auditorium. According to the layout of the movie house that Zian had made for my phone, that was also where my pyramid should be. I crept up to the side of the double doors to the theater, listening for any sign of trouble.

"Just got to my pyramid," Zian said in my earbud. "Coast is ... well, that is—"

"Get your drift, Zian," I whispered. "What about you, Kennedy?"

"See mine just around the corner," Kennedy replied. "Got a similar lack of human life around me. That whispering because you've found our hostess?"

"Maybe," I acknowledged. "Whoever it is, sounds like they're getting the party prepped. Initiating radio silence."

The double door on the far side had been mangled a bit, but by sliding across its intact twin, I got a look into the auditorium—and saw Her Honor as I doubt any of her constituents had ever seen her before.

Prowling the stage in a shift that went down to her ankles and hugged her curves, she was wearing a complete set of ancient Egyptian regalia. In her right hand, she held what looked like a clay boomerang, which I recognized at once as an Egyptian magic wand. She was pointing it at an electric- blue pyramid that was standing in front of her in the middle of the stage, right in front of the cinema screen, surrounded by a circle of burning candles in tall holders. As I watched, she continued chanting in a language that sounded a close match to the stuff that Zian had said earlier during his manifestation as the goddess Isis.

I took a quick look at my phone and saw that the doomsday clock was down to eleven minutes. But I had made a fatal error of judgment, for when I looked up again, a couple of burly men in Viking costumes were standing immediately in front of me. Before I could pull out my Sig, the nearest one of them had landed a hard punch in my solar plexus while the other one knocked me over the head. My cry of pain provoked immediate responses over the earbud.

"Vale, what's going on?" Kennedy asked in alarm.

"Bell? You all right?" Zian asked with even greater panic. "Bell!"

I was too battered and out of breath to say anything. As the guards grabbed me and dragged me to the stage, I was thankful that the earbud had stayed in and that neither of the doormen had noticed it. Ten more similar Northern assholes were approaching the stage right behind my captors and me.

312 | CRISTELLE COMBY

Jacinta Galatas looked down at me with a combination of amusement and contempt as her lackeys dumped me at her feet.

"So glad you could join us, Mr. Vale," she said with a sneer as one of the goons patted me down for weapons. "I was hoping that you could make it."

I did my best not to betray my despair as the Sig and the explosives pack were taken from me. "I aim to please," I struggled out.

"Yourself, most of all," Galatas replied. "Just like nearly everyone else in this restless wreck of a city ... it's far past time for it to be leveled."

"Why destroy a place that you're already the mayor of?" I demanded. "What did it ever do to you?"

"To me, nothing," Galatas told me as her goons hauled me to my feet. "To everyone who has ever come here looking for safety and stability, everything. The balance of this place has marked it as beyond redemption. Today, the balance will be corrected by He Who Rules Below."

I filed the name away for later reference. "That little title could apply to a lot of the Underworld's resident landlords. Who did you have in mind?"

Galatas gave me a mirthless grin. "Why tell you when you can meet him yourself in the next few minutes?"

She had a point.

"Your persistence in interfering with my business has been remarkable," she said. "Even that curse placed upon your new girlfriend barely slowed you down."

Why did everybody automatically assume that Kennedy and I were seeing each other?

"That was you?" I said, playing for time I didn't have. "You were the one who put the curse on Kennedy?"

The costumed mayor pulled her head back, plainly impressed. "Very good, Mr. Vale. I admit that, compared to the writing of my ancestors, the Ogham alphabet is child's play. So was slipping a clerk a piddling bribe to draw the necessary sigil in invisible ink on her pharmacy receipt."

"And the will o' the wisp?"

"A holdover from Connor's incompetent attempts to stop me," Galatas said with scorn in her voice. "It followed its masters' wishes long after they stopped being their wishes."

"Bell, if you can hear me, we're down to a little over nine minutes," I heard Zian say into the earbud. "If we want to cock up Her Honor's bridge between worlds, we need you to take out your pyramid too."

"Give me some more time," I said.

"Oh, but you are out of time," Galatas said, not sensing that I wasn't talking to her. "I have an old friend of yours who would like to illustrate that point."

Two of the Viking boys got out of the way as the Berserker entered the circle with one of his trademark growls.

"Not your typical muscle for hire," she mused, "but he served his purpose well. Watching him chew you up is a bonus."

I stood, empty-handed, and swallowed as I wished they'd at least left me a weapon.

"My charge is all set," Kennedy said as the Berserker crossed the stage. "I hit the switch; she's gonna be pebbles three seconds later."

"Bell, whatever you're going to do—" urged Zian.

"Hold off," I whispered, hoping they heard me. "Got an idea."

The bear skull-covered head turned to me and rumbled, "Human."

"Murderer!" I answered back with contempt.

That got me another punch to the solar plexus from one of the Viking goons. I fell to my knees once more, but defiance raged in my heart.

"What?" I snapped at the Berserker after taking a ragged breath. "Need one of your groupies to hand out your beatings? Need that junkyard armor to feel like a man?"

I knew I was hitting a nerve when a bear roar bellowed out of his throat.

I pulled the knife from my boot as I got to my feet. "You and me ... no backup, no protection. Just steel in the hand and blood on the floor."

The Berserker growled his acquiescence, while Galatas snorted and then gave a shrug. As far as she was concerned, me dying wouldn't get in the way of what was about to happen.

"What the hell you doing?" Kennedy all but yelled in my ear as the stress made her Texan accent thicken to the level of the fog outside.

"When I give the word, blow the pyramids," I whispered under my breath.

"But we're down to—" Zian started to say.

"One last chance!" I interrupted as I waited for the Berserker to have his armor removed. "Trust me on this —okay, Z?"

One look at the musculature on my opponent and I wondered if I'd live long enough for my plan to work. His muscles seemed to have muscles, giving his frame the sort of build most people associate with an overdose of steroids. His face may have been human once, but there was nothing much left of that with the thinnest of lips, the filed teeth, and the glowing red eyes that lusted for blood. His skin was paler than you would expect, a very pale flesh tone that looked like it was two short steps from pure white. A number of scars ran down it, telling me that he hadn't always relied on the armor to keep him safe.

One of the Vikings ripped my shirt from my back while another handed the Berserker a vicious-looking dagger. What was left of the bastard's lips pulled back into a smile. "Now you die," he grunted.

My Navy training kicked in with a vengeance. I knew I was quicker and more agile than him. I would have to use that. Speed would be my best ally in this fight.

I made a feint at his chest that he fell for. By the time he realized that he'd thrust his knife arm out too far, I'd sliced the inside of his forearm with a quick swipe of my blade. That didn't seem to do anything except piss him off. He swung the knife at my throat. I just had time to duck under it before ramming my shoulder into his hips to take him down. I've run into softer concrete walls. Oh, and he didn't budge an inch.

I felt a couple of stabs sink into my left shoulder, thankfully not my knife arm. As I went down, I sank my own blade into his right calf and slid it all the way to his Achilles' heel. With a great bellow, the Berserker went down on one knee.

I was just getting my breath back when he staggered to his feet again and wrapped his arms around my chest. Before

I knew it, he had me upside down and then threw me across the stage like a rock from a catapult. I slid across the floor until one of the Vikings at the edge of the circle stopped me with a kick to my wounded shoulder. Somehow, I'd managed to hang onto my knife.

I got back to my feet as fast as I could, then moved to one side, placing myself out of range while I got my breath back. The Berserker came at me again. I noticed that he was moving a little slower with the leg I'd done impromptu surgery on. That gave me a slight edge, but he could more than make up for it with one blow if I got careless.

"Vale, we're down to two minutes!" Zian yelled into my earbud. "What in the name of the Styx are you waiting for?"

"The right moment," I whispered before making a lunge at my weakened opponent.

As I expected, he caught my arm but not before I had dropped the knife into my other hand. I buried the blade in his gut and then repeated the action Jack-the-Ripper style as many times as I could. I got six stabs in before he head-butted me backward, breaking my nose. I was seeing stars when I felt cold steel slice into my flesh again a couple of times in my upper chest. I felt him drive the second blow up to the hilt.

As my vision cleared, I got a too-close-for-comfort view of my attacker's face with that rictus smile on it. "Die," he gurgled, leaning in.

But he'd gotten a little too close. My teeth grabbed his wasted lower lip and bit down. He howled as I ripped the thin skin off his face and then drove my knife under his armpit. He, in turn, trapped my knife hand in his armpit and, with his other hand, ripped his own blade out of my chest. I bit back a scream as I used my free hand to grab his bull neck to deliver a head-butt of my own. My reasonably hard skull had to hit him four more times before he loosened his grip on my knife hand. I made it hurt coming out; the blade sliced all the way across the armpit.

He pushed me off him. One of the Viking spectators who were howling for their idol to finish me off took a second to push me back in his direction. My head connected with his arm way too hard as he clotheslined me, sending me back to the floor. I spread the force of the impact across my arms as I tucked in my head and slapped out the fall. Then I rolled over and did an ice pick number on the Berserker's right foot.

I had just pulled my second stab out when he used that foot to kick me like a soccer ball. But this time I was ready for it. I got my legs in position to stop myself before getting to the edge of the ring and lurched back to my feet.

"Vale, it's happening!" Kennedy yelled at me. "My pyramid's glowing!"

"Same here," Zian reported. "Ten seconds left!"

"Wait!" I snarled through the blood in my mouth.

"No!" the Berserker snarled back, his right leg all but useless now.

I was feeling fire from every one of the blows he'd managed to land on me. My chest wounds were throbbing and gushing out blood with every heartbeat. I was starting to feel faint from the blood loss. I shook my head and tried to spot Galatas.

She was just behind the Berserker, going back to her chanting while the rest of her people were distracted by the floor show. I could feel the power thrumming under my feet from the ley lines. Her pyramid was starting to glow too, the energies syncing up.

A bright blue beam flared from the pyramid, scorching two of the spectators surrounding me down to nothing in the space of a second. It made the rest of them back up, but the Berserker only had eyes for me as he made another stumbling charge in my direction.

Not sure that I'd even be conscious when I was done, I rolled past his right side and forced myself to get up again. The Berserker was already readying himself to have another go at me.

"Now!" I yelled as I launched myself at his weakened side and latched onto him. I used his momentum to spin him around and then executed a hip throw that sent him flying straight into the pyramid beam. He had just enough time to scream before the terrible force of the ley lines ripped his body into blue smithereens.

I collapsed to my knees on the floor. That superhuman effort had taken everything I had left. I watched the beam falter and wink out like a dying star as I struggled to stay conscious. I was dimly aware that the rest of the Berserker's fan club had made a run for the exits. But I had eyes only for Galatas and the now useless pyramid in front of her.

"A valiant effort, Mr. Vale," she said drily. "But far too late."

The white screen behind her darkened then turned into a swirl of necrotic energy that froze me to the bone marrow. A blind man could have seen the decay, chaos, and outright entropy that was spilling through that dark opening. The Underworld was stretching a clammy hand out to our world.

Somehow I found the strength to lever myself upright.

Some trick of muscle memory even allowed me to pick up the knife from where it was lying on the floor. I was half past dead, but damned if I wasn't going to go out without a fight— nothing like a little death to make you feel alive.

I could feel a wavering in the Underworld's energies, like an old-school TV with bad antenna reception. The final pyramid was holding everything together, but it was too much. The sheer strain of keeping an Underworld gate open was more than one charged-up pyramid could handle for long. However, when it came to anything and anyone from across the border, it didn't need long to do some serious damage ...

Galatas didn't seem to notice me approaching the gate. All her attention was focused on the shadowy figure that was walking toward her from the other side. From what I could tell, it was a man, or looked like one, walking with some sort of staff in his right hand.

The mayor opened her arms in welcome as the shrouded figure got closer and closer. The way she tilted her head back, I could imagine that she was smiling. I wondered if she still was when our mystery man reached forward to jab his staff right into her chest. Two points came out of her back ... a bident then. Just as quickly as she'd been stabbed, the bident was yanked back across the threshold. Galatas collapsed on the stage like a puppet whose strings had just been cut with a sword swipe.

Up against that kind of weapon, my little knife just wasn't going to cut it. I grabbed one of the candleholders and used my blade to knock the candle off it. Then I held it like a Japanese bo staff, dread in my heart over the real possibility that I had just met my match.

At that moment, the man on the other side of the gate did something I really didn't expect ... he sighed in exasperation. "What are you waiting for?" he demanded. "Destroy the pyramid!"

His response stopped me in surprise. But then I started hearing the noise made by the nasty things that the Underworld is full of growing louder behind the mysterious figure.

"Hurry!" he commanded, turning to face the incoming creatures. "I will not be able to hold them off forever."

I didn't need another invitation. I swung my candleholder at the pyramid with all my remaining might. It bounced off the stone without so much as chipping a single block.

"Dammit!" I whispered as I raised the holder up for another attempt. Before I could bring it back down, however, the pyramid cracked right on the spot where I'd struck it. The crack started to spider web, spreading to the rest of the pyramid as though it was an eggshell instead of solid stone. The structure crackled aloud as the stone began to disintegrate, and a blue glow started coming through the cracks.

I had just enough presence of mind left to step back before the whole thing exploded. The fragments fanned out like a pineapple grenade, catching my face and raised arms. The gate started to fade away as the energy that powered it was dispersed.

Through some trick of the cross-world lighting, I was able to get a glimpse of the face of the person Mayor Galatas had thought she wanted to see. I had never thought I would owe my life to the regal nightmare Lady McDeath had been visiting when I tried calling her at the start of the case. He gave me a stern but approving nod before he and the gate faded away to nothing.

That wasn't the only thing that had faded away. I felt my body pitch forward as my own batteries ran dry. I wasn't even concerned about doing more damage to myself as I saw the floor coming up to me.

29

A JOB WELL DONE

A pair of hands caught me before I could kiss the floor ... Kennedy.

"Goddamn!" she yelled at me as she laid me down and dug bandages out of her supply. "How the hell are you still alive?"

I would have answered with one of my wisecracks if I hadn't been so wasted. Zian came up and helped apply some iodine that woke me up in a hurry. After they had cleaned my wounds as best as they could, Kennedy covered them with bandages. They spent the next hour letting me recover my strength.

"The Vikings," I managed to gasp out at last. "They're ..."

"Not a problem anymore," Zian assured me. "The speed they were running from here, I wouldn't be surprised if they've already made it back to Valhalla."

Once they were sure I could travel, they found something to wrap me in, placed my gas mask on my head, and manhandled me to another exit Zian had found near his pyramid.

I stayed in my bed until the sun sank and came back up again, and then some. It was hunger that finally roused me up.

I found Lady McDeath waiting on the couch for me. She seemed to be the only person about. She was wearing widow's weeds, complete with a pillbox hat, a black veil, and arm-length gloves to complement the clingy black dress.

"I believe you dropped these," she said, holding up my Sig and my knife.

Once it was obvious that I wasn't going to say anything, she dropped both weapons on my coffee table.

"This matter was sloppily handled," she said.

I harrumphed as I limped to the kitchen. "You're welcome."

"Candice Kennedy now knows about our kind," she went on, rising from the couch. "And about Alterum Mundum."

"Well, given the fact that she was a major part in cleaning up you and your pals' mess, maybe you ought to cut her some slack," I suggested.

I found a slice of pizza on the counter and wolfed it down. "Besides," I continued, my mouth full of pizza, "it's not like we had much of a choice ... and we told her the bare minimum."

"Her help is the only reason why she is still alive," Lady McDeath said coolly, sidling up to me like a stray dog with a mean streak. "For her sake, I hope she will not try to dig deeper."

My insides clenched at that. Knowing Kennedy, it was a safe bet to assume she would ... I guessed I'd better ask Zian to keep an eye on her.

"If you're so unhappy with me," I snapped as I stomped back towards my bedroom, "maybe you should tell the Conclave to get a more discreet errand boy the next time things go bad."

I threw myself on the bed, feeling very hard done by.

Lady McDeath stood over me with a look of disapproval on her face. "You don't have the slightest idea how Alterum Mundum actually works, child. In the future, you would do well not to overstep your mandate."

"Hmm," I mumbled, closing my eyes.

Within seconds I was asleep. It was probably not the smartest thing I could have done in the presence of the embodiment of death on Earth, but after the last couple of days, I was past caring if I ever woke up again.

———

As it happened, I *did* manage to wake up the next day, aroused from slumber by the buzzing of my smartphone. Feeling twice as stiff as I had before, I managed to grab it from the nightstand and answer.

"Good morning, Mr. Vale," a familiar British-accented voice greeted me. "I trust that you slept well."

"I slept, Hermes," I replied. "It's kind of debatable whether I did it well."

"Ah, no matter," Hermes said. "I just wanted to congratulate you on the successful completion of your mission. The Conclave is quite pleased with the rather neat way you resolved this matter."

"Wasn't what I was told when I woke yesterday," I said.

"Ah, of course. Well, there were divergent opinions on your methods and level of discretion," Hermes admitted with mirth in his voice. "Still, the resolution of this situation is undeniable. We should be safe from a similar occurrence happening at this site for another three millennia ... perhaps ever again."

"How do you even know any of that?" I asked. "Don't tell me you've got a Conclave membership."

"Not quite so, no," Hermes said, and I swear I heard a smile in his voice. "Though what I do in my spare time, of course, is none of your business."

"One thing I didn't get," I admitted. "Why did Mayor Galatas want to destroy her own city? She fed me some mumbo-jumbo about the cosmic balance or something, but it wasn't clear."

"That point has also been debated," Hermes said. "But Zianyon may have found some sort of answer this morning, in the late mayor's family tree. Did you know she was descended from none other than Ma'at of Egypt?"

I groaned. Ma'at was the goddess of justice, balance, and the natural order in Ancient Egypt. That would explain Madam Mayor's weighing of the pros and cons of my existence upon our first meeting. I doubted that the line's founding mother would have felt too warmly about bringing the Underworld to Earth, however.

"So why didn't she conjure up some scarab beetles or something instead of calling He Who Rules Below?" I asked.

"Where did you hear that name?" Hermes asked in alarm.

"She told it to me right before she started prying open the gate," I said, my curiosity waking me up a little. "Mean something to you?"

"Perhaps," Hermes said. "If it is who I think it may be, that would explain much of her plan."

"Which was ...?"

"According to the data gleaned from her private journals," Hermes told me, "she saw Cold City as existing out of balance with its constant tearing down of older structures and building newer ones. She, therefore, concluded that the only way to break the cycle was to tear the city down."

"By opening a gate to the Underworld? That's like trying to fry a wasp nest by setting off a nuke."

"Agreed," Hermes said. "My time as a psychopomp of souls in conjunction with my Uncle Hades taught me that much. Still, it made sense in her deranged mind, and she seemed to think the ways of hekau she had knowledge of would be enough to contain the damage to the city limits."

"Which it wouldn't."

"No ... no, far from it."

"Speaking of your uncle," I resumed, as memories from last night came back to me, "he wouldn't be the type of guy to walk about with a long-staffed bident, would he?"

Hermes chuckled in lieu of an answer. "You've managed to avert a rather singular catastrophe, Mr. Vale. Let's keep it at that."

"I didn't do it alone. Zian was a key part of everything working out like it did. I'd thank him too."

"As much paternal pride as I take in your praise, I would

rather have had my son stay away, safe. I do have to ask yet again that you please try to avoid Zianyon's company in the future."

"Like I said before, Hermes," I told him, "I don't want to lie."

"Mmm ... well, in any case," he continued, "I believe the time has come to make my exit. You've another call that you'll want to take."

No sooner had he hung up than the phone started ringing once more. It was Kennedy.

"Morning, partner," I said into the phone.

"Morning?" Kennedy queried. "Try noon, hoss. You just now waking up?"

"Yeah," I admitted. "That fight took a lot out of me."

"Yeah," Kennedy said, a little quieter. "I was afraid it'd taken *everything* out of you." Then her voice brightened. "But I've got news. I broke the story on the mayor and her whole Orion Project to every major paper in town."

"Doesn't that kill the whole idea of an exclusive?"

"Not if you sell it to them first and don't tell your boss at the TV station until after," Kennedy told me. "Call me Lois Lane, would you ..."

"How's it being received?"

"Thanks to us sticking to the details we could prove," Kennedy said, "through the roof. Internet exclusives from the papers plus the story getting picked up by the Huffington Post, where it's trending on an international basis. 'Local Mayor loses it and blows up large chunks of her own town'— that's media gold."

"That can't sit well with your bosses at Headliner," I pointed out.

"Oh, if they could get away with it, they'd have fired me the second they saw the story," she said with more than a little glee. "But now they're in a bidding war on who gets me first. I've got a lot of job offers that I'll have to sort through by the end of the week."

"You're welcome," I said, getting up.

"Yeah, well, seems like you owe me as much as I owe you. Or need I remind you who spent a long time patching you up?"

"Fair's fair," I agreed.

"So the next time something big like this is going down, you'll put me in the loop?"

"Maybe," I said, remembering Lady McDeath's words.

We said goodbye to each other. I got up to give myself a very late breakfast, a shower, and a long-postponed shave.

———

The next day, I was feeling much better, especially knowing that Mrs. Thricin was safe. I'd sent her an email the day before telling her that I'd taken care of the problem. I admitted that I had no proof and would understand if she demanded a refund, but she needed to know that she could live her life again. The email I got back was poignant and to the point: "Thank you for everything, Mr. Vale. Expect another five hundred dollar check in a few days. PS Hope to see you at the grand reopening of the Cinema Leone."

I sipped at a cup of green tea while I looked over Kennedy's article. She had stuck to the research she and Zian had done at the offsite, detailing all of Mayor Galatas' crooked dealings with Arete and her ties to the now missing

Alonzo Vitorini, a known crime figure. The wolf killings, the De Sotos, and Fairwinds went unmentioned for obvious reasons.

Homeland Security had found Her Honor dead at the Cinema Leone before she could face justice. The death was ruled a homicide, but I doubted that anyone was going to do anything with it. I gave it three weeks before it slipped into the cold case pile.

In an update to Kennedy's original article, Arete was now finding itself the subject of numerous city, state, and federal prosecutions. All the surviving corporate officers and shareholders were grabbing their lawyers with one hand and their guts with the other. I saw a lot of instances of Let's Make A Deal in that company's future. In the meantime, all its assets were frozen pending a full investigation. Ditto the further destruction of the Cinema Leone, which had been granted national landmark status in the wake of the tragedy. An EPA cleanup was scheduled to make sure that it was safe for human occupation in the near future. Mrs. Thricin was quoted as saying that this was a grand opportunity to preserve an important piece of this city's heritage.

Before I could read more, my phone started giving me my unlisted number ringtone. I perked up at the prospect of a new client.

"Vale Investigations," I said in my best professional voice.

"Mr. Vale, please," a woman's voice on the other end said.

"Speaking."

"I was wondering ... is it possible we could meet? I would hate to discuss my problem over the phone."

"Of course," I assured her. "Do you know the Tombs diner?"

"Yes, I do," she replied. "Do you want me to meet you there?"

"I'll be in the back booth," I promised her. "Say, in an hour?"

She agreed, and we hung up. I got my shoes on and went out the door. The break was over—time for me to get back to earning my living.

NOTE FROM THE AUTHOR

Thanks for joining Bellamy Vale's team!

If you loved this book and have a moment to spare, I would really appreciate a short review where you bought it. Your help in spreading the word is gratefully appreciated.

Did you know there are more books in this series?

- Hostile Takeover #1
- Evil Embers #2
- Avenging Spirit #3 (coming 2020)
- Seasons Bleedings (Christmas Special)

All the books are available in ebook and print.

FURTHER READING

The Neve & Egan Cases Series.

Described by readers as 'a refreshingly unique mystery series'.

- Russian Dolls #1
- Ruby Heart #2
- Danse Macabre #3
- Blind Chess #4

All the books are available in ebook and print. There's also an ebook Box Set, with the complete series, at a bargain price.

ABOUT THE AUTHOR

Cristelle Comby was born and raised in the French-speaking area of Switzerland, on the shores of Lake Geneva, where she still resides.

She attributes to her origins her ever-peaceful nature and her undying love for chocolate. She has a passion for art, which also includes an interest in drawing and acting.

She is the author of the NEVE & EGAN CASES mystery series, which features an unlikely duo of private detectives in London: Ashford Egan, a blind History professor, and Alexandra Neve, one of his students.

Currently, she is hard at work on her Urban Fantasy series VALE INVESTIGATION which chronicles the exploits of Death's only envoy on Earth, PI Bellamy Vale, in the fictitious town of Cold City, USA.

The first novel in the series, *Hostile Takeover*, won the 2019 Independent Press Award in the Urban Fantasy category.

KEEP IN TOUCH

You can sign up for Cristelle Comby's newsletter, with give-aways and the latest releases. This will also allow you to download two exclusives stories you cannot get anywhere else: *Redemption Road* (VALE INVESTIGATION prequel novella) and *Personal Favour* (NEVE & EGAN CASES prequel novella).

www.cristelle-comby.com/freebooks

Printed in Great Britain
by Amazon

64647324R00203